Deadly
STUFF

JOYCE CATO

W🌐RLDWIDE®

TORONTO • NEW YORK • LONDON
AMSTERDAM • PARIS • SYDNEY • HAMBURG
STOCKHOLM • ATHENS • TOKYO • MILAN
MADRID • WARSAW • BUDAPEST • AUCKLAND

Recycling programs
for this product may
not exist in your area.

Deadly Stuff

A Worldwide Mystery/September 2015

First published by Robert Hale Limited

ISBN-13: 978-0-373-26960-0

Copyright © 2014 by Joyce Cato

Printed in U.S.A.

Deadly
STUFF

PROLOGUE

JENNY STARLING TURNED a corner in the seventeenth-century stone-lined corridor, and came face-to-face with a stuffed owl.

The owl, it has to be said, looked somewhat surprised. The travelling cook not so much. She did, however, draw her well-rounded, six-foot-tall form to a halt and contemplate the bird thoughtfully.

When she'd seen the advertisement in the *Oxford Times* for a cook/chef to work at St Bede's College during the summer months, catering to the conferences that the college hosted during the Long Vacation in order to replenish its ancient coffers, she'd applied instantly.

Naturally, with her references and experience, she'd sailed through the interview process, had been offered and had accepted the post. The college's resident cook had up and left for New Zealand for three months, in pursuit, so the local gossip had it, of a somewhat unreliable but well-heeled widow. This had left the bursar with a string of conferences booked in with no top-flight chef (as advertised in the glossy brochures) to offer them.

Jenny had been more than happy to get the gig. Not only did she get to live in for three months—free accommodation in this day and age was not to be sniffed at—but she also got to cook an extensive, if budget-controlled menu, for a large number of people daily, which was the Junoesque cook's idea of heaven. Added to all this bounty was the truly pleasant realization that she also had well-trained and willing staff to work under her. This, courtesy of the resident chef, who, so gossip also had it, was a bit of a tartar and expected first-class standards from his staff.

So it was that she found herself, this lovely July morning, exploring her way around St Bede's ancient buildings and quads, and contemplating whether she could possibly squeeze lobster bisque into her budget for sometime that week.

Now Jenny continued to eye the stuffed owl thoughtfully. It was, according to the small plaque on the plinth on which it was resting, an eagle owl. It was certainly huge and imperious looking, which Jenny supposed, was only your right, if you were an eagle owl.

When the cook had contemplated her first foray into academia cooking for a prestigious conference, she'd assumed it would be something suitably glamorous, as befits Oxford's status as one of the premiere universities of the world. A conference of neurosurgeons, perhaps, given the proximity of the world-famous John Radcliffe Hospital, which was a part of Oxford University's medical teaching programme. Or maybe something more artistic, like art restoration experts drawn to Oxford by the Ruskin, or perhaps some esoterically historical society intrigued by the university's ancient heritage.

What she'd had, was the Greater Ribble Valley & Jessop Taxidermy Society. This august body had come down for five days to give lectures and demonstrations, to talk shop, buy the latest gadgetry and goods, and generally do as all good conference-goers did—drink too much, gossip, and back-stab friends and colleagues whenever possible.

It was only Monday, the very first day of the conference and, even though they were still arriving in dribs and drabs, Jenny had overheard enough conversations to make her long dark hair stand on end.

She'd also seen several examples of the conference-goers' exhibits being bandied about, hence her *sang froid* in the face of unannounced stuffed owls.

'Oh, there she is. Sorry, I wondered where I'd left Bertha.' An apologetic voice had Jenny turn and smile at a harassed sixty-something with an overbite and a grey cardigan that looked as if it had been dinner every night for more than a couple of moths.

The old man retrieved the owl, beamed at Jenny, looked around vaguely and went off, probably trying to find his room. For her part, Jenny carried on towards her own bedroom, which was a pleasant, high-ceilinged room in one of the older buildings, and collected her laptop.

It was time to get down to planning tomorrow's menu. The willing helpers in the vast kitchens were already preparing the ingredients for today's fare, but she wanted to get a head start on her preparations for the rest of the conference. Although she had no doubts that she could keep within the budget set by the bursar, and still produce delicious, show-stopping meals, she wanted to make every day a gourmet experience—not just the opening night, and the finale, so to speak. And that took planning.

But Jenny was not the only one in St Bede's College on that fine summer day busily making painstaking preparations.

In another room, someone else was checking off things on their to-do list, and making careful preparations for tomorrow. But these didn't include anything as innocuous as checking out Oxford's covered market for the freshest vegetables, fish and meat, or a reminder to look up the best variation for a butter sauce on the internet.

And, if someone had been standing over their shoulder, and reading their notes, one or two items on the list would definitely have raised their eyebrows. Because what they'd be reading would be the blueprint for a perfect murder.

Or so someone supposed.

ONE

JENNY KNOCKED ON the door of the assistant bursar and waited. It was nearly two o'clock, and dinner was at seven, so she still had plenty of time to start to oversee the staff and check on their dinner preparations for the Great Jessies' (as she'd come to think of them) first night.

'Yes? Come on in!' The voice sounded somewhat harried, even through the thick oak door.

Jenny obliged and found herself in a typical St Bede's room. It was somehow gloomy, despite the large, high sash windows, mainly due she supposed, to all the wood-panelling and heavy, dark-brown furniture. Since the college had been going for over five centuries or so, she supposed that a fair number of the past alumni had left vast amounts of massive and now impracticable furniture and furnishings to their old alma mater, as well as their much more welcome books, collections and, of course by far the best of all, filthy lucre.

Jenny hadn't been talking to the man who'd hired her for above five minutes before she'd cottoned on to the fact that the college was perpetually seeking funding. Rich overseas students were courted with almost indecent fervour, whilst industrial and commercial institutions were cajoled, bullied, bribed and, Jenny wouldn't be at all surprised, blackmailed into offering scholarships, endowments and job opportunities for graduates. It was all, so the bursar had explained woefully, a far cry from medieval times, when the aristocracy were falling over themselves to enrol their prodigy at Oxford, and were willing to fill the coffers of the colleges in order to do so.

From this, Jenny had surmised that the bursar's own degree had been in history, and that his time was taken up almost solely with holding out his hat and begging for pennies.

So the fact that the taxidermy society currently in residence for their annual conference had several well-heeled members willing to pay the high fees had quickly explained much of what had hitherto surprised her.

Of course, the bursar, being one of the senior officers of the college, along with the principal, a titled industrial baron coasting through retirement, and the treasurer, an ex-government minister who was, frankly, slumming it, was far too important to deal with the running of the summer conference season. Hence she'd been told that for all her day-to-day decisions, it was to the assistant bursar that she needed to cosy up. And, indeed, the man who looked up at her now with a worried frown and badly bitten nails, looked in sore need of a little cosseting.

The nameplate on his door informed her that his name was Arthur McIntyre, BA, MA. He was, she guessed, somewhere in his early fifties, and was just in the process of losing his short dark hair. Perhaps to make up for it, he had grown a reasonably luxuriant moustache. At the moment his somewhat muddy, grey-brown eyes were eyeing her with both surprise and alarm.

As he got uncertainly to his feet, Jenny instantly

realized the problem. At perhaps five feet tall, or maybe just a bare inch over, she was still towering over him, and she instantly swept forward, beaming her best smile, quickly snatched out the chair in front of his desk and sat down, and held out her hand all at the same time.

'Hello, Dr McIntyre, I'm Jenny Starling. I'm catering to the conferences this summer. I thought I'd better just introduce myself and check in. Perhaps the bursar has mentioned me?'

A look of instant relief and comprehension swept over the little man's face and he shook her hand with a brief smile of his own and resumed his seat. 'Oh yes, of course. And I'm plain mister. Not a doctor.'

'Oh, sorry,' Jenny said. Although she knew from his nameplate that he didn't have a doctorate, practically everyone she'd met at the college so far, including the librarian, was a 'Doctor' something or other. And it didn't take a genius to guess that it must be pretty daunting—not to mention deflating to be one of the few common or garden Mr or Misses swanning around in these heady, refined waters.

And a little buttering up of your boss never hurt, especially on your first day.

'And yes, of course the bursar has spoken to me about you. I hope you're settling in all right. Is your room OK?' he added anxiously.

'Oh yes, fine thank you,' Jenny said, and meant it. It had a whopping four-poster bed, and armchairs built to last, as well as a wardrobe and set of drawers that took up most of one wall. And whilst big brown furniture might not be much in fashion nowadays, it was something that a woman of her size never sniffed at.

'Splendid, splendid. So, you've met and talked to

the regular kitchen staff then?' Arthur McIntyre said, somewhat nervously, Jenny thought.

'Oh yes. They've all been very friendly and helpful. I know the chef had his own way of doing things, and I have no intention of being the new broom sweeping all before me,' Jenny reassured him, perhaps somewhat less than totally truthfully this time.

In fact, when she'd met the kitchen staff, there'd been the usual mutual summing up on both sides that such occasions warranted. On their side, they were obviously anxious to know what sort of temperament she had and, more importantly, how easily she could be bamboozled. And she, for her part, had been keen to pick out the slackers from the professionals, and make sure that all the plum kitchen jobs were allocated fairly. And to show them who was boss, of course, in the nicest but firmest possible way. Since she'd never had any trouble in getting on with people and at the same time, getting exactly what she wanted, they'd very quickly settle down to an amicable way of rubbing along together.

As if sensing this, Arthur McIntyre seemed to relax a little. 'Ah, I'm glad things are running smoothly,' he said. No doubt it would have been part of his job to arbitrate had they not been.

Jenny smiled gently and somewhat thoughtfully. Something in the rather weary way he spoke, told her that here was a man not altogether happy in his job. And she could quite see that being even an assistant bursar for an Oxford college as big and old as St Bede's would be quite a responsibility. The Bursary Department was responsible for the daily running and upkeep of the college, which had to be a never-ending job. Not only did they have to deal with the maintenance of the buildings and grounds, but it also had to oversee all the cooking and cleaning that was done by the domestic staff, or 'scouts' as they were called for some unfathomable reason. And since the bursar himself seemed preoccupied with fundraising, it was easy to see on whose shoulders the weight of all this had landed.

'I thought you'd want to have my budget plans for the first conference as soon as possible,' Jenny said, and handed over a neatly printed list of menus and expenditure, which Arthur McIntyre accepted eagerly and began to peruse.

'Oh yes, thanks. It is, as I'm sure the bursar told you, most important that you don't exceed the budget that's been laid down.'

Jenny nodded. 'I think you'll find everything in order,' she said gently, but firmly. The little man shot her a quick, surprisingly shrewd look, and then he smiled somewhat bitterly. Jenny, a little alarmed, began to wonder if she'd come across as a bit more condescending than she'd meant to.

'I'm sorry, I hope I didn't sound rude,' she apologized at once. 'I just meant that I'm used to managing both food and money, and that you didn't need to worry.'

But Arthur McIntyre was already waving a hand in the air in that deprecatory way that was supposed to indicate nonchalance. 'No, no, it's not that. I don't doubt your ability at all, Miss Starling, just the opposite in fact. I was just thinking that it's typical of the bursar to be able to spot a gem so easily. You're clearly the perfect person for the job. I only wish I had the bursar's knack for omniscience.'

'Ah, one of those, is he?' Jenny thought with a knowing smile. But inside her heart was sinking just a little.

It was clear that the little deputy felt inadequate and probably disliked his boss intensely. Which was none of her business, of course, unless she found herself somehow in the middle of a domestic spat and pressed to choose a side.

Obviously a little more buttering up was called for. 'And please, call me Jenny. And you know, I can't stand those people who always seem to get everything right all the time. As my granny used to say, the sort who could fall in a rubbish heap and come up smelling of roses.'

Arthur McIntyre's muddy brown eyes began to twinkle and his narrow shoulders to relax just a little. 'Please, call me Art. Nearly everyone around here does, either to my face or behind my back.' He said it with just a shade too much bitterness for it to be comfortably funny, and Jenny smiled gently, deciding with her usual tact that a change of subject was in order.

'Will we be seeing you at dinner tonight, Art? I wasn't sure from the bursar whether or not many people from the college actually dined in hall when the conferences were on?'

'Oh no. Most of the dons scatter as soon as Trinity Term ends, and you won't see them again until Michaelmas. The principal, I believe, is in Kuala Lumpur trying to secure a research fellowship sponsorship from something big in coconuts. Or is it rubber?'

Jenny blinked. No doubt about it, they did things differently in Oxford.

'So you won't be dining with us?' she pressed. She liked to be sure of her numbers.

'Oh yes. I will. Well, most nights anyway. I'm not due to take my paltry three weeks until August. And there might be one or two others knocking about, of course. The Emeritus Professor in Classics is sure to be there. He's ninety-two and sharp as a tack, and probably hasn't left the college grounds for something like ten years or so. Come to think of it, he'll probably find the taxidermists fascinating. He'll be bending their ear on how Plato would have set about it. Or something along those lines.'

Jenny grinned. 'I look forward to meeting him. I hope he likes lobster bisque.'

LIKE ALL THE main dining rooms in Oxford colleges, the place where undergraduates and dons alike gathered to eat was known simply as 'hall'.

And the hall at St Bede's, Jenny thought, some four and a half hours later, was an amazing sight. Huge, with one length of near ceiling-to-floor windows stretching one length of it, it made you stop and stare. Beyond them, the college grounds, immaculately groomed and full of colour, provided an equally grandiose and formal setting.

Three massive chandeliers hung down from the ceiling at equal distances, spreading a scattered, crystal-reflected light onto a hardwearing, midnight-blue carpet. Long, wooden tables, so old, well polished and varnished, that they looked nearly black, spread out along 'high table' on the raised dais at one end where the dons would normally eat, and in two parallel rows down the length of the hall where the students usually munched. Matching padded, ornate chairs—over a hundred of them?—lined the tables. On the walls were vast portraits of past principals and distinguished old boys and, towards the end of the latter century, old girls.

Jenny knew that Somerville College, just down the road a bit, and formerly an all girl's college, could boast Margaret Thatcher and the mystery novelist Dorothy L Sayers amongst their alumni. St Bede's however, not only boasted ex-prime ministers and novelists, but one or two famous artists, several Nobel-prizewinners, masters of industry, a mad earl and a notorious womanizer, reprobate and friend of Keats.

Jenny paused and blinked at the name of the artist on one of the portraits. Surely that couldn't be an original, could it? It must be worth…. She gulped.

Whilst her mind was boggling at what it was worth, however, the professional part of her was also checking out the table settings, and finding no fault with the layout. Not that she had really expected to. The scouts here were all old hands at this game, and they only really needed Jenny to plot the menus, express her views on how they should be served, and generally keep out of their way as much as possible.

That didn't stop her from spending long, happy hours in the kitchen however, personally preparing and making certain dishes. It had been a bit of a juggling act to marry the careful budget with the logistics of preparing four courses for over a hundred sittings, and still produce interesting, appetizing food that both looked good on the plate, and challenged even the most jaded or conservative of palates.

But she was confident that she'd managed it, naturally.

And now, with the Great Jessies gradually arriving in their best bib and tuckers to start the conference off with a bang, so to speak, she could judge for herself whether or not she'd got the balance right.

The first arrivals began to mill around and check out the little place-names to find their spot on the long tables. Having staked their claims, they began to accept the glass of complimentary wine—first night only, and strictly one glass only—and chat. Jenny had thought that rather stingy, but the bursar had pointed out that the JCR or junior common room where the undergraduates usually hung out had a fully licensed bar and games room, and was the conference-goers socializing area for the duration. Unspoken was the tacit understanding that all the money they spent in the no-doubt over-priced bar went into the college's coffers, so free drinks were to be strictly limited.

Jenny could well imagine that the majority of their visitors would be heading straight there once the dinner was over in order to top up.

She smiled and nodded as several people greeted her and then checked her watch. Dinner started at seven, and she wanted to be here to see it begin. She was anxious to pick up comments on the starter.

'Hello, don't recognize you, do I? You must be college, right? Or are you a new member?'

Jenny turned to find a tall, skinny young man with sandy hair and attractive large hazel eyes looking at her.

He thrust out a large, competent-looking freckled hand. 'Ian Glendower. I'm trying to specialize in marine and freshwater presentation.' He grinned widely. 'In other words, if you catch a monster pike this big'—he spread his arms wide—'and for once, it wasn't the one that got away, and you want it stuffed and mounted complete with an antique or bespoke glass case, I'm your man.'

Jenny grinned. 'I don't fish myself, but if you've got a card, I'll recommend you to anyone I come across with a spare carp going handy.'

Ian grinned and reached into his inside jacket pocket

and produced a business card. 'Deal. And I'm not proud. It could be a minnow if that's all they can manage to hook. Times are hard for all of us these days. A pal of mine has recently taken to stuffing grey squirrels for a sad eccentric in Harrogate. He hunts the local parks for their corpses, apparently.'

Jenny shook her head sorrowfully. 'The bankers have a lot to apologize for,' she agreed solemnly. 'And yes, by the way, I'm college. I'm the cook, so please, if you have any comments on the food, direct them straight to me.'

'Right you are. Hello, gorgeous!' Jenny, correctly surmising that the sudden appellation wasn't directed at her, turned and saw a young girl standing behind her. A few inches shorter than herself, she had long, lush, brown hair and big bright-blue eyes. The eyes were definitely dazzlers, Jenny thought, and at the moment their lashes were batting at Ian.

'There you are. I thought I'd lost you,' the girl said, and glanced at Jenny with a swiftly assessing look. Since the newcomer was herself wearing a designer pants suit in a very becoming shade of copper, Jimmy Choo shoes and jewellery not to be sniffed at, Jenny quickly realized that the young girl was pricing her clothes, rather than checking out any serious competition for her man.

Jenny, in contrast, was wearing her second best, but strictly for work-use long black skirt, a faux-silk blouse in mint green, and a matching mint green, black and white short jacket. And all strictly Marks & Sparks.

Thus, was clearly not worth unsheathing her claws for.

'This is Pippa Foxton, my fiancée,' Ian Glendower introduced them.

'Not until we get a ring,' Pippa said, sharp and fast. It must have been her habitual come-back, because Ian grinned good-naturedly and took a sip from his glass of wine.

'Don't worry, I'm saving all my dosh for a sparkler the size of the Hope diamond. Well, the top left-hand corner of it, anyway,' he promised her rashly.

'Huh! Does the Hope diamond have a top left-hand corner?' Pippa shot back, and reaching out, snitched her beloved's strictly one free glass of wine and half-emptied it in a single, impressive swallow.

'Here, get your own,' Ian growled, with an even wider grin, but made no effort to retrieve his glass. Since Jenny suspected it was probably just cheap plonk anyway, she didn't really blame him.

'I'm not sure I qualify for a glass. Not being a—' Pippa leaned forward to whisper loud enough for any-one within earshot to still hear her—'proper member.'

Ian shook his head and rolled his eyes, but Jenny no-ticed that he still looked around quickly nevertheless. Seeing Jenny's curiously raised eyebrow, he shrugged. 'I sort of smuggled Pippa in under false pretences,' he admitted.

'She's not a taxidermist then?' Jenny asked, mak-ing sure her own voice didn't carry beyond her imme-diate circle.

'No way!' Pippa snorted. 'I'm a baker.'

Jenny, who had decided she probably didn't much like Pippa Foxton, found herself instantly questioning her judgement. 'A baker? Really? What, patisserie, bread?'

'Both. Traditional or new school, we do it all at Elite.'

'Elite?' Jenny asked. 'I don't think I know it.'

'We've just started up in Leeds. We're only a small bakery now, but we're growing fast. We're finding a niche market in speciality cakes—you know, divorce cakes with marzipan figurines on top with a woman or a bloke carrying a packed suitcase. Bankruptcy cakes, off-the-wall stuff. Our chief decorator has just got a commission to do a four-foot replica of a space shuttle for a rich kid who wants to be an astronaut when he grows up.'

'Ah,' Jenny said.

'It's what I'd like to get in to eventually, it's where the big money is, but at the moment I'm at the bottom of the ladder, baking the basic sponges and all the other run-of-the-mill stuff that we do.'

Her red-painted lips drooped into a pout and she quickly drained the glass.

'But if anyone asks, she's thinking of taking up taxi-dermy and joining the club,' Ian put in, giving Jenny a quick wink. 'Especially if Vicki Voight or that old windbag Maurice Raines asks.'

'Oh, Maurice is all right,' Pippa said airily. And held up her index finger and crooked it teasingly. 'I can easily wrap him around this.'

'Yes, I noticed,' Ian said flatly. 'You stay away from him, Pip. I mean it. He's got a bit of a reputation with women if you know what I mean, and he can be a nasty sod sometimes. Ask anyone. I might be wrong, but I think he and Vicki are having a bit of a spat right now. It's all heated and furtive whispers, and shooting each other looks that could kill.'

'Really? What's it all about?' Pippa asked avidly.

'Sorry,' Ian said, to Jenny this time. 'Club gossip. Vicki's our treasurer and social secretary—she set this

conference up, in fact. And Maurice is the club chairman. And a total windbag,' he added, this time to his
prospective fiancée. 'Honestly, Pip, I don't know how
you can bear to listen to him droning on,' he complained.

'You're the one droning on right now,' Pippa pointed
out wryly. 'Now be a sweetheart and get me some more
of this bloody awful wine, will you?'

You'll be lucky, Jenny thought, guessing that either
the bursar or Art McIntyre had drilled the scouts to give
out only one glass per member. Presumably they must
have a good memory for faces? 'Well, I need to circu-
late and see to the tables,' Jenny said. 'I'm the cook,'
she added, as Pippa gave her a somewhat startled look.

'Oh! Sorry, I thought you were a stuffer.'

Jenny blinked, quickly got the reference and smiled.
'No, I don't stuff dead things with cotton wool: I stuff
live people with good food!'

'We don't use cotton wool,' Ian said, and Pippa made
a theatrical grab for Jenny's arm.

'Quick, make a dash for it before he starts to tell
you all the gory details of what the stuffers *do* use!'
Ian laughed, Jenny smiled obligingly, disentangled her
arm, and left the pair to it.

She supposed they made an attractive enough couple, but something about both of them had rubbed
her slightly up the wrong way. Telling herself not to
be such a grouch, she checked the centre pieces and
couldn't find any stray fallen petals or out-of-kilter
white candles.

Good.

Her eyes did find those of a handsome man of around
thirty, however, who was standing just inside the entrance. He was over six feet, with dark hair and choco-

late brown eyes and she saw his gaze sweep across hers and start to move on, then widen slightly, and come back for a second look.

It was a circumstance that Jenny was used to. She knew she was a striking presence, being overly curvaceous by modern tastes, and that men found themselves unexpectedly attracted to her. She could, and sometimes did, take advantage of the confusion, if she felt like it.

Idly, she wondered if the handsome stranger was married or already taken, which would make him a strict no-no. Then her eyes noted the time on the clock, and all speculative thoughts of a predatory kind fled. It was fast approaching seven. She needed to get to the kitchens to see the starter being plated up.

She swept from the room, moving with a fast, lithe grace that left the tall, brown-eyed, brown-haired man watching her slightly slack-jawed.

IT WAS NEARLY ten before Jenny returned to hall. The first dinner had passed off without any catastrophes, and she arrived back along with the scouts serving the coffee and chocolate mints. Most people, she was pleased to note, were sitting back in their chairs, wearing that replete, satisfied expression that denoted a full and happy tummy.

People were beginning to congregate in groups as well, coffee cups now in hand, and she slowly made her way around, shamelessly earwigging for comments about the food. There were plenty of them, and all of them favourable.

Well, apart from one sad individual who clearly didn't know how Lyonnaise potatoes should be served. It made her shake her head sadly.

All in all, however, Jenny was pleased.

She helped herself to a spare cup of coffee which weren't rationed apparently, and found herself drawn to a loud, pontificating voice.

The owner was a man in his early fifties, Jenny guessed, with that previously lean and fit physique that was just going slightly to fat. Notwithstanding that, he was still a very handsome figure, with distinguished and lushly thick salt-and-pepper hair and a well-maintained goatee beard that actually suited his somewhat foxy-shaped face. His bright blue eyes were startlingly alert in a lightly bronzed face. Either he'd been abroad recently, Jenny mused, or he was one of those men who hit the tanning salons—or maybe the tanning lotion—regularly.

He had a captive audience comprised mostly of women, she noticed with a somewhat wry smile and, because he was obviously the kind who liked to hear himself talk, she couldn't help but listen to what he was saying.

'Of course Hutchings will always be one of the best. Started in 1860, by the great Victorian taxidermist, James Hutchings. His sons James, known as Fred, Walter and even his daughter Poppy followed in their famous papa's footsteps needless to say. They're famous for their foxes, of course, but also rare birds, shot in Cardiganshire.'

'Now I never knew that,' one brave soul ventured to interrupt the great man in his lecture.

'Oh yes. Their shop was on Bath Street, and later on Corporation Street.'

'Is this in York? Or Leeds?' a petite pretty-but-fading

blonde woman asked, frowning. 'I don't recognize the names. Or have they been renamed by now?'

The big man regarded the woman with a mixture of pity, contempt and sexual interest. It immediately set the hackles on Jenny's own back rising, but the blonde woman merely simpered and preened a bit under his admittedly dazzling blue gaze.

'Neither, my dear Marjorie. Hutchings were established in Aberystwyth.'

Most of the group tittered at their compatriot's lack of knowledge.

She turned a becoming shade of pink, and said off-handedly, 'Oh. Wales.'

'Don't worry, Marjorie,' her friend, a rotund redhead in an unfortunate spandex top, commiserated with her. 'Nobody knows more about Hutchings than Maurice here does. He's related to one of them you see.'

'As he will keep on saying,' Jenny heard someone mutter under their breath wearily, and turned away with a grin.

'Only distantly, alas, only distantly,' Maurice Raines demurred modestly. 'Of course, the thing that most people find fascinating about the Victorians is their obsession with the macabre, and Hutchings were no different. They were known for their stuffed oddities, such as a calf with two heads.'

Jenny, having heard more than enough, shuddered, and moved on. She finished her rapidly-cooling coffee and put it down at an empty table, and glanced at the plates. It pleased her enormously to see that practically every one of them was cleared. She hated to see food wasted, as a matter of principle. Especially food that she herself had cooked. It always smacked to her as less of evidence of people being on a diet, and more of an unspoken criticism of her culinary skills.

But the goat's-cheese blueberry and citron cheese-cake had obviously been a hit, since very little evidence of it remained.

'Oh no, he's not still going on about his famous ancestors, is he?' she heard a woman drawl to her companion over to her right. Jenny turned, her eyes softening slightly as they spotted the tall handsome man she'd noticed earlier, talking to a well-preserved, slightly dumpy woman with a mass of long honey-coloured hair, and carefully made-up greenish hazel eyes.

'Afraid so,' the man said. Then, spotting Jenny over his companion's shoulder, he smiled tentatively.

Jenny, taking up the invitation, moved closer.

'Hello. How was dinner?' she asked, getting straight to the point.

The blonde woman started a little, her gaze going up, and up, until it met Jenny's own, and a brief look of consternation crossed her face. Like a lot of small women, she seemed a little at a loss how to react to someone of Jenny's stature.

'Dinner was actually surprisingly good,' the woman said uncertainly. 'At these conferences, you come to expect fairly standard fare. You know, overcooked chicken and bland veggies. But for once, the hype in the brochures matched up to the reality.'

Jenny grinned. 'Music to my ears. I cooked it.' She held out her hand. 'Jenny Starling, I'm the cook for the summer here at St Bede's.'

'Oh! Right. Vicki Voight. I'm the treasurer of our little band of brothers, for my sins.' She smiled widely, but her eyes, Jenny noticed, looked genuinely strained.

Jenny shook hands. 'Pleased to meet you.'

'And this is James Raye.'

Jenny's hand took his and held it a moment longer. 'Pleased to meet you,' she said. And meant it. He wasn't wearing a wedding ring. Which, of course, didn't necessarily mean much nowadays, but was at least an auspicious start. As was the unmistakable look of interest in those pansy-brown eyes of his.

'Likewise. Very much so,' he said, somewhat clumsily. 'And the dinner, by the way, was superb. The scallops were a triumph.'

Jenny, who rather liked a bit of tongue-tied shyness in a good-looking man, smiled, her eyes sparkling. 'Most people scorn flattery. But I've nothing against it, personally.'

James Raye laughed. 'I'll remember that.'

Jenny felt rather than saw Vicki Voight stir impatiently beside her, and she wondered if they were a couple. If so, she needed to back off.

'Is your husband here, Mrs Voight?' she asked pleasantly.

'Geoff? Good grief, no. He wouldn't be seen dead at one of our conferences.'

'Good thing too,' James said. 'Or else one of this lot would have him stuffed and mounted before he knew what had hit him.'

Jenny chuckled, whilst Vicki gave him a playful swipe on his arm. 'Don't forget, you're one of this lot too,' she admonished.

'Don't remind me. How exactly did you persuade me to take up this hobby anyway?' James asked, giving Vicki an arch look.

'You were bored out of your mind, and at a loss

after the divorce. Don't try and deny it. You jumped at the chance to get out and about and meet new people.'

Jenny's ears pricked. Recently divorced, hmmm?

'That might be so, but I'm still not sure it's for me,' he said. 'So far, I haven't been exactly wowing my fellow taxidermists. My domestic cat was somewhat less than a triumph.'

Jenny blinked. OK. Best not go there.

'Oh, it takes practice. Years of it, if Maurice is to be believed,' Vicki reassured him. 'You should have seen my first efforts. But I swear that man thinks that he's the only one who can stuff a tiger.'

Jenny blinked again.

'One of the local wild-life parks is expecting one of their oldest tigers to die soon, and the science department of a university in Cumbria is making noises about buying it and preserving it as a teaching aid for conservation,' James explained, seeing her expression. 'If they keep being poached in the wild like they are, a dead stuffed tiger is probably the only one the next generation is ever likely to see,' he added grimly.

'James is a bit of an eco-warrior,' Vicki explained, a shade drily.

Jenny nodded. He probably knew her mother, then. She was probably out somewhere camped in a forest and saving some trees from a bypass. 'And will Maurice get the commission?' she asked curiously.

'Oh, the Greater Ribble has been approached, along with one or two other establishments. But we're by far the oldest and best society. We have no less than six members who own and run their own companies. We have the reputation, no doubt about it,' Vicki said confidently. 'And no, Maurice isn't the only one capable

of getting the commission. There are one or two others. Well, four at least, but Maurice, being Maurice, is
sure that he'll get it.'

Jenny, aware of James's speculative brown-eyed gaze
upon her, was just wondering herself how she was going
to gracefully cut herself and the luscious divorced hunk
free from Vicki's orbit, but before she could come up
with a strategy, Vicki suddenly came out with a pithy
and startling epithet.

'Speak of the bloody devil,' she added, and plastered
a patently false smile across her face. Jenny turned,
not at all surprised now to see Maurice Raines bearing
down upon them.

His eyes went straight to Jenny, his bright blue gaze
running over her with obvious interest.

Jenny sighed heavily. Just what she needed when trying to test the waters with James—an ageing Lothario
with ambitions above his station.

'Maurice,' Vicki said flatly. 'You know James?'

'No, can't say as I do,' Maurice said briskly. 'A new-
bie, aren't you?'

'Yes. I've been a member for just a couple of months.'

'Done much?'

'A cat. One or two fish. I'm currently working on a
corn snake.'

Maurice waved the corn snake away as irrelevant. He
turned to Jenny. 'Now you I'm sure I've never met. You
are, if I may say so, unforgettable.' He reached out to
take her hand and Jenny wouldn't have been surprised
if he'd attempted to kiss it.

He sounded as if he'd watched too many classic Hollywood romances. What was she supposed to do now?
Swoon at his feet? Jenny bit back a grin as she won-

dered what he'd do if she did. If he attempted to catch her, she'd squash him flat.

'Mr Raines, isn't it?' she said instead, firmly pumping his hand up and down and then releasing her own. 'Your fame goes before you,' she promised him archly.

Vicki snorted but wisely sipped her coffee and made no comment.

'Oh—all good I hope?' Maurice said with a laugh.

Jenny smiled and said nothing. Anyone could hope, after all.

'Down, boy,' Vicki said, with a false attempt at humour that had far too much bite in it to work. 'Jenny here isn't one of us. She's the lady responsible for the wonderful meal we all enjoyed tonight. She's the college cook.'

'Oh, for the summer conference season only,' Jenny corrected.

'Ah, I see. Well, you'll get no complaints from me, my dear,' Maurice said, smilingly showing off a set of very white and even teeth. Jenny would have bet her month's salary that they were all capped. 'I particularly liked the starter.'

Jenny smiled and inclined her head graciously.

'Vicki, I needed to see you about some rescheduling in the itinerary for tomorrow,' Maurice said, reaching out and peremptorily taking the treasurer firmly by the elbow. As he began leading her off, Jenny heard her already start complaining.

'Oh, come on, Maurice, I've already given you the prime mid-morning slot in the lecture hall....'

'Not a match made in heaven, those two,' James Raye said, somewhat uncomfortably, as the obviously hostile couple moved away.

'No, so I've already been told,' Jenny agreed. 'So,'—
she turned and smiled up at him—'what exactly made
you want to be a taxidermist of all things?'

It wasn't an idle question. A good-looking, recently
divorced man in his early thirties didn't need to resort
to such quite spectacularly desperate measures in order
to start socializing again, surely?

James laughed. 'I haven't got the faintest idea how it
happened,' he admitted. 'Vicki is a friend of my older
sister. I somehow found myself invited to dinner with
big sis, where I met Vicki. And from then on I seemed
to get drawn into the Greater Ribble lot by osmosis.'

Jenny smiled. Ah, that explained it. Easily led. And
obviously used to being handled by the women in his
life. Excellent. It meant that he'd already been thoroughly house-trained. As a prospective lover for a brief
summer flirtation, he was shaping up nicely.

'Have you seen the Fellows' garden by moonlight?'
she asked him. 'It's strictly private and off limits, but
I discovered an unlocked gate into the walled grounds
on my afternoon exploration.'

James laughed. 'Are you trying to get me into trouble?'

'Oh yes,' Jenny agreed, taking him gently by the
hand.

As THE TRAVELLING cook showed James Raye just how
lovely hollyhocks could be by the light of a silvery
moon, someone else, now circulating in the JCR and
drinking a fine malt whisky, went over their plans for
tomorrow in their head.

Timing was important of course. And, if the victim
arrived too early or too late, then a little improvization

might be called for. But the person planning murder was fairly confident that they wouldn't be seen. Or if they were, that nothing too compromising would be obvious to a casual glance from a passer-by.

But still. Best get an early night and lay off the booze. A clear head was essential.

The would-be killer smiled, bid several people good night, and retired to bed.

Once in their tall, high-ceilinged bedroom, the killer put the kettle on and then carefully retrieved the stolen bottle of medication from their suitcase. Carefully, the killer cleaned out a mug and wiped it dry, before pulling apart twenty capsules and emptying the powder into the mug. When the kettle was boiled, the killer then poured the boiling water over it, and dissolved the powder into liquid form.

From the research done, it was more than enough to kill a man.

Carefully, the killer set aside the water to cool, and began to undress before climbing into bed.

This individual contemplated their actions uneasily. The person concerned wasn't a monster, when all was said and done. Nobody in their right mind, after all, actually *wanted* to kill another human being. But the killer was being given no other choice. It wasn't, even, really their fault. They were being pushed into it by the malice of others. What was going to happen tomorrow was the result of other people's wrongdoing, as much as anything else.

And with that comforting thought, the individual turned over in the comfortable bed and, eventually, slept.

TWO

JENNY ROSE BRIGHT and early, smiling over her memories of the previous evening. James had looked as good in the moonlight as he had under the far more prosaic electric lights, and they had spent a pleasant hour in the gardens, strolling, chatting, and generally getting to know one another.

So far the signs looked good, but Jenny was picky about her men. Time would tell. Right now, she stretched and dressed and made her way down to the kitchens, although, in truth, breakfast could have been handled by the college's regular kitchen workers, since there was very little that needed overseeing by a professional cook.

As she stepped into the massive, white-tiled space, the unmistakable scent of toasting bread hit her nose and made her smile happily. Toast and frying onions were two scents that could be almost guaranteed to put most things right, in her opinion.

The scouts had already set up a selection of cereals, breakfast fruits and bread rolls on the side tables, to which the guests could help themselves. For those who preferred porridge, Jenny could see that a big pot was already simmering away, and was being attended by a competent-looking, grandmotherly woman, who wasn't about to let it stick on the bottom.

Excellent. Jenny beamed at her and got a happy beam back.

Then she walked across to the vast range of ovens, where two men and two women were at work grilling bacon, sausages and kidneys, and frying eggs.

Jenny nodded. 'Just what is it about the great traditional English breakfast that appeals so much, do you think?' she mused.

One of the women, a forty-something with tightly curled brown hair, smiled.

'Don't know,' she admitted, 'but nearly everyone orders it. I think it's something to do with being away from home. Calories and cholesterol don't count, so it seems, if you're away on holiday. Or in this case, at a conference. I reckon hardly anyone bothers with a cooked breakfast when they're at home, though.'

Jenny laughed and agreed, but nevertheless donned her apron to add her own speciality dish of the morning to the mix. She'd decided that it would be appreciated by the guests if St Bede's could offer them a slightly different option for those who were more adventurous; and so for the Great Jessies' first breakfast, she had created for their delectation, what she was calling her Oxford Herb Omelette.

When she'd been researching any famous food items connected with Oxford, she had, of course, come across the world famous marmalade, pots of which were on the tables upstairs in hall, naturally, but also something called the Oxford sausage, which was a very delicate mix of meat and herbs. Some recipes claimed it went back only a mere few hundred years, whilst others grandiosely claimed it had medieval origins, when meat products were regularly heavily spiced or herbed in order to try and disguise the taste of less-than-fresh meat.

Dismissing the interesting if off-putting history, Jenny had seen at once how the herbs used in the Oxford speciality sausage would lend themselves to an herb omelette, and had set about experimenting. Now she checked the chits, and saw that only six members had opted for it, as opposed to the full English, but she wasn't disappointed. As word spread about her specials she had no doubt that the demand for them would soon pick up.

Humming happily to herself she reached for the organic, locally sourced eggs, cracked them into a bowl and began to beat. She'd got a really good price for them by offering to buy the farmer's home-cured ham as well. She knew that if it was popular, then the regular chef was likely to continue using it, thus everyone won. As any wily cook knew, there were always crafty ways around a stringent budget. And herbs were dirt cheap as well.

So to speak.

As Jenny diced and gently crushed a variety of herbs in order to release their flavour, she felt calm, confident and happy. She had digs and a job set to last for the whole summer and, with luck, a new lover hovered on the horizon with which to share her evenings.

But, as it happens, that morning, she was not the only one taking stock of her life.

LAURA RAINES BRIEFLY took her eyes off the road to glance across and check out the lush, rolling green pastures of the Berkshire Downs. She smiled to herself, wondering what the green wellington set were doing this morning. Probably mucking out the horses and feeding the dogs and getting the kids off to school. Not necessarily in that order.

Although Laura herself had been born into a privileged, upper-middle-class background, she hadn't ever really bought into the whole *Country and Sporting Life* thing, and was more than happy to live in the swanky area of a large northern city. She liked the shops, theatres, restaurants and galleries, and she liked spending money. Most of it was her own, left to her by her dead papa. When he'd popped his clogs her mother, bless her, had promptly sold off most of his assets and had liberally dished out the proceeds to herself and her two children.

Now, as she headed south towards Hayling Island, and a discreet little hotel she knew, tucked away nicely out of sight and sound of anyone who might know her, she smiled happily.

Maurice was oblivious in Oxford, attending one of his awful conferences, which meant that she had five whole days before she had to get back to Harrogate and play the dutiful wife once more.

She met her steady, grey-eyed gaze in the driving mirror, and smiled grimly. Well, she wouldn't have to do *that* for much longer, at any rate. With the twins having reached their landmark eighteenth birthday only last month, they were both set to start university in September, Michael to Durham, and Thomas to St Andrews. And with her sons fledging the nest, it was time to turf out the real cuckoo as well. And not before time.

Laura slowed to approach a roundabout and glanced down longingly at her mobile phone. She frowned when her gaze met the unfamiliar blue-coloured casing.

Somewhere within the last few days, she'd mislaid her old phone, and had been forced to buy a quick replacement when a search in all the usual places had failed to bring it to light. No doubt she'd find it eventually, probably in the pocket of a seldom worn coat maybe, or a handbag. Even though she'd thought she'd checked in all of those places. Far more likely that the bloody thing would turn up somewhere really bizarre, like the back of the bloody fridge, or at the bottom of one of her boots. It was exasperating to lose it, when so much of her life was stored on it, but that was life for you.

She half-reached for the new phone, that she was still trying to learn how to use properly, and then shook her head. No, it was naughty to talk on the phone whilst driving. And wasn't it illegal too? She wasn't sure, but she thought that it probably was. Besides, when she talked to Simon she wanted to give him her whole attention and not have to worry about running into the back of a lorry.

Just thinking about Simon Jenks gave Laura a soft glow that was part physical and part emotional.

At forty-eight Laura had never thought of herself as the kind of woman to have an affair. She'd married Maurice straight out of university, and had fallen pregnant just at a time when she'd been seriously thinking of divorcing him. The twins' birth had scotched that idea, once and for all. She'd been brought up traditionally, and couldn't help but still think of herself in the same way. She'd been raised in the Tudor belt in a prosperous Sussex town, where she had attended a private girls' school, before just about scraping a place in Cheltenham Ladies College and going on to do a useless liberal arts BA at Reading. Afterwards, she wore all the right clothes, the latest perfume, and had found herself a decent job to pass the time and earn respectable brownie points whilst waiting to get married. Neither she nor her parents had ever expected anything else from her life.

Maurice had been her one act of defiance, since neither of her parents had particularly approved of him. Oh, he was personable and presentable enough, and had good manners, mixed well in society, and had brains enough not to embarrass anyone. But he had no money of his own, he spoke in a northern accent and he earned a living as a taxidermist, for pity's sake.

Her father, to his dying day, had told everyone at the golf club that his son-in-law was in the 'arts'.

Laura had to laugh softly to herself now.

Again, she glanced at her reflection, this time more anxiously, looking out for wrinkles and crow's feet, and wondering what had possessed her to waste her life and her youth on a man like Maurice.

Still, the quick check in the mirror assured her that she hadn't lost everything, not yet, anyway. Forty-eight was no age these days, she told herself stoutly and, if the worst did come to the worst, well, she could always have cosmetic surgery. Luckily she took after her mother, physically, and had a tall, lithe figure that would not easily run to fat, even with approaching middle age and the dreaded spread that was said to accompany it. Even then, as a last resort, there were such things as tummy tucks and liposuction to fall back on.

Her skin looked fairly clear, and her hair had always been that ash blonde shade that kept on looking good. And if it had a little more help from a bottle nowadays, well, who was to know but herself and her hairdresser?

No, she was not too old to learn new tricks. Clearly,

men still found her attractive anyway, even if Maurice had long since ceased to notice.

That thought brought her back, deliciously, to Simon, who was a whole decade younger than herself. Newly divorced and childless, he had come into her world like a shooting star, bringing life-changing chaos in his wake. Tall, dark and handsome, he was almost a walking cliché.

Until Simon, it had simply never occurred to Laura to be unfaithful. Although she hadn't actively loved her husband for years, she'd become in some strange way accustomed to him. Her lifestyle was comfortable, her boys were her darlings, and she managed to keep busy, being both a lady-who-lunched and one of those people who was constantly taking academic courses that appealed to her in order to keep her fairly good mind still active and challenged.

But Simon had changed everything. Suddenly, just like that, almost overnight or so it seemed, her life with her husband had become intolerable. His foibles no longer faintly entertained her, but actively grated. Her life felt sterile and emotionally barren. It was as if she'd suddenly had her eyes opened and the depth of the rut she was in had astonished and dismayed her. She began to see how much control she had lost of her life, and how much of it Maurice had suborned.

Not that it had taken her long to get the measure of her new husband. Right from the start of their married life, she'd quickly discovered that he liked chasing anything in a skirt. He also liked playing the big man, and he especially liked having a wife on his arm whose breeding and social status made him look so good to his cronies.

To begin with the infidelities had hurt and her ego had gradually shrunk. But, as time went on, she'd simply stopped caring. It had been then that she'd thought about divorce. Now, somehow, nearly twenty years had gone by without her noticing.

It had taken Simon coming into her life to prove once and for all just what a giant millstone Maurice was, and always had been, around her neck.

Well, she'd failed to rid herself of him once before, but there was nothing stopping her now. She smiled happily and turned on the radio, searching for a happy tune. She found a station playing hits from the sixties, and sang along to a half-forgotten tune about someone who was *truly sorry, Suzanne.*

As she continued to head for the south coast, an attractive, middle-aged woman, looking forward to spending time with her exciting new lover, she wondered what Simon was doing right that minute.

She hoped that he was making good time, for he was starting out a little later than herself and would be arriving in his own car. She giggled as the tune on the radio changed, and exhorted her now to *twist and shout*. With a bit of luck, she'd be doing both tonight, especially if Simon had followed all her instructions.

If he had, then later that night she would take him to her bed and show him some proper gratitude.

JENNY SUPPOSED IT might be considered a bit unorthodox to check out how things were progressing in hall when people were still dining, but she had to keep an eye on things, didn't she? And if there was a space going free at the table because one of the conference-goers was a late riser, or one of those poor unfortunate souls who couldn't face an early morning meal, well then! Why shouldn't she sit down at that empty place, and check out the quality of the food on offer for herself? It was part of her job to do a bit of quality control inspection, right?

So, when a scout approached her looking slightly puzzled, she ordered the full English and winked at her. Giggling, the young girl, clearly only there as a summer job, went to get her order, and Jenny turned a friendly face to the conference goer on her immediate right.

A stoop-shouldered older man, he was sipping orange juice and eyeing the toast rack thoughtfully.

'I see you've ordered the omelette. How is it?' she asked him cordially.

'Wonderful. Cooked, but still moist in the centre. And I can't quite pick out all the herbs. Basil, of course, rosemary, and I think a touch of thyme. And something else…'

'Sage?' she suggested.

'Could be.' The older man turned to her and smiled. 'You're not one of us. I know everyone in the society. Mind you, that's not saying much nowadays. I swear I've seen a couple of people already milling about that I don't know from Adam. I'd swear they weren't members of the Greater Ribbles at all, but still, I suppose Vicki and Maurice know their business.' Jenny smiled. So this sharp-eyed old man had already spotted both herself and Pippa Foxton as impostors, had he?

'Damn! Caught me out,' she said with a grin. 'Don't tell anyone, but I'm just cadging a free breakfast. No, actually, I'm the cook, and I'm just checking that everything's fine with the food and the service.'

'Ah, well then, let me assure you that it is. Dinner

was wonderful, and this omelette has a deft lightness of touch. And I'm also relieved to get your bona fides. For a minute there'—he leaned to one side and spoke through the side of his mouth in an exaggerated parody of someone trying to be discreet—'I thought you might have been one of Maurice's dreadful women.' His eyes twinkled before he nodded solemnly.

Jenny blinked. 'OK,' she said, elongating the word thoughtfully. 'Well, I'm pretty glad to be able to report that I'm not. Has many of them, does he? Dreadful women, that is?'

'Sorry, I'm an inveterate gossip.' The old man grinned into his orange juice. 'I'm Robert Llewellyn by the way.' He held out his hand in introduction and, as Jenny shook it gently, she couldn't help but notice both the liver spots on his skin, and the hard, bulging knuckles that spoke of arthritis.

'This is going to be my last year in the society, I think. I'm retiring. Obviously, I've lost any semblance of tact! Besides, my old hands aren't what they used to be, and you need to be nimble-fingered in this game,' he added sadly.

'I'm sorry to hear that,' Jenny said softly, and meant it.

'Oh, I had my time. Time was, everyone in the surrounding five counties came to me for badgers. Badgers were my speciality. Foxes too, of course, but I loved my badgers.'

Jenny nodded and smiled.

'Of course, Maurice didn't rate them. But then, nobody really cares what Maurice thinks. Except those who have to, poor sods.'

Jenny encouraged him to finish the omelette before

it got cold. That was the only thing about eggs—they cooled rapidly. Then she said casually, 'So who has to? Care about what Maurice thinks, I mean?' she asked. And then wondered why she was feeling so curious. After all, the doings of the Greater Ribble Valley & Jessop Taxidermy Society were hardly any of her business, were they?

Robert thought about it for a moment, however, and then sighed. 'Vicki, I suppose. She's treasurer, but Maurice is the real power behind the society. When he says "jump" she has to ask "how high?" Then I suppose there's people like the young up-and-comers. Ian, Francis, and one or two of the others, perhaps. Maurice always seems to get the commissions, and if he gets more than he can comfortably handle, or if he gets some that he considers beneath him, he sometimes doles a few of them out to his favourite acolytes and toadies, if they kiss his boots enough.'

'Ugh, that sounds revolting,' Jenny said.

'It is. But not as revolting as watching that man work his so-called charm on the ladies. I swear, I don't know what they see in him.'

Jenny shook her head in puzzlement. And wondered idly just who it was that Maurice had 'worked his charm on' that Robert Llewellyn had so objected to. Surely not his wife, not unless he'd either married a much younger woman, or Maurice had been into older women at some point. No, she mused, it was far more likely to have been his daughter, or a niece maybe.

But just then, her breakfast came, and Jenny turned her attention to it.

The sausages were crispy brown and done to perfection—not too greasy. The bacon, likewise was good quality and hadn't been pumped full of water, like so much of the stuff that they sold in supermarkets nowadays. The kidneys were a shade rare—she'd have to have a discreet and gentle word about that downstairs later. The tomatoes were grilled properly without being dry, and her egg, sunny-side up, had just enough runny yolk to be appealing.

All in all, not too bad.

She reached for the toast and tucked in happily. Beside her, Robert contemplated his orange juice and his knobbly hands and sighed.

JENNY HAD JUST eaten her second slice of toast, when the big man himself joined the table just a few places down from her own setting. She noticed that the younger man seated at the place to his immediate right, quickly drank up the last of his coffee and pushed away from the table and left, leaving half of his own meal untouched.

Maurice didn't seem to notice, but Jenny saw that the woman who was sitting on his left had watched the young man's departure with interest. She leaned across and began to talk with the chairman of the society with a bright smile lighting up her face.

Clearly, Jenny thought, Maurice was either loved or loathed. And since there was no one now sitting between them, she couldn't help but hear what they were saying.

'So, have you seen much of the city yet?' The woman, a fifty-something with attractive steel-grey hair cut in a bell-shape, had wide brown eyes and a gamine face. 'Last night I walked down to Christ Church and the meadows, but I didn't see any deer. Today, I'm hoping to get down to the Sheldonian and maybe even the Ashmolean Museum, time permitting of course. I wouldn't want to miss any of your lectures, naturally, Maurice.' She held out a silver-looking coffee pot and gave it a gentle shake.

'Coffee?'

'No thanks, I never touch the stuff,' Maurice said, wrinkling his nose fastidiously. 'There's a blend of tea I prefer, but I doubt that St Bede's would run to it, so I brought my own supply of tea bags and had a cup up in my room before I came down.'

'Oh yes, of course, I remember.' The woman poured herself a cup and then smiled at him eagerly. 'So, just what have you come up with to open the conference? You're giving the opening address, aren't you? I bet you've got something special up your sleeve.'

'Thank you, Maureen,' Maurice said. 'And yes, I have, but you'll just have to wait and see, like all the others. And to answer your first question, yes, I took a stroll last night to take in the sights. I also captured a few images on the old digital mobile phone. I wanted to get a nice cover shot of the dreaming spires and all that for the summer newsletter. That reminds me, have you seen Margery? She's supposed to be writing the next one, isn't she? I don't suppose it will even occur to her to get some atmospheric photographs of the place.'

'No, I don't suppose it would,' Maureen agreed rapidly. 'And I think it was so wise of you to insist on Oxford, when everyone else seemed so set on Edinburgh. I mean, Edinburgh's all right, and all that, but Oxford is lovely. And staying in a real Oxford college is so much nicer than putting up in some generic faceless hotel, isn't it?'

Maurice nodded and smiled, clearly pleased by the praise. 'Yes, I think so.'

'Much more classy,' Maureen agreed.

Jenny thought personally that she was rather piling it on, but then obviously Maurice Raines was the sort who lapped up praise and flattery, so perhaps she was right to over-egg it.

'How's your mother, by the way? I meant to ask before,' Maureen continued, clearly intent on building on her success with a touch of tenderness. 'She must be nearly ninety now, isn't she? I think it's so marvellous when you can keep your parents so long, don't you?'

Maurice, whom Jenny had noticed without surprise had also ordered the omelette, paused with a forkful of egg and herbs heading towards his lips. 'Well yes, when they've still got it all intact up here,' he said, putting down his fork in favour of tapping the side of his temple meaningfully. 'But poor Mother is starting to wander a bit now, I'm afraid, but it's her dicky ticker that's worrying us most at the moment.'

'Oh, I am sorry to hear that,' Maureen said at once. 'Is she still managing at home, or is she in the hospital? I'll have to send her some flowers.'

'No, we're keeping her at home for the moment. She has carers come in twice a day, but I suppose it's only a matter of time before even that becomes impossible. I've asked Laura to start looking into suitable care homes in the vicinity. That's the sort of thing that Laura's so good at.'

From the way Maureen's face promptly fell, Jenny surmised that Laura was probably Mrs Raines. Who was, presumably, absent.

'Oh yes, I'm sure she'll find somewhere nice,'

Maureen agreed, less than enthusiastically. 'So, like I said, we're all looking forward to your opening speech this morning, Maurice. Can't you give me a hint as to the highlights?' Maureen pushed back the sleeve of her long green blouse to check her watch. 'Only forty-five minutes to go. I won't tell anyone, I swear. It's to be in here, isn't it? Not in that JCR place?'

'Yes, it's in here. Once the last of us stragglers have finished eating, I dare say they'll be clearing the decks, ready for the day's activities. During the day as you know, hall is being used by the buyers and sellers. They'll be setting up their tables and stands here every day, which is where most of us will be congregating between our lectures and demonstrations, so it makes sense to start proceedings here. And because we're in a college, and we've got the choice of a number of lecture halls as well as other communal spaces to work in, we need a focal point. Something we wouldn't have been able to do in a bloody Edinburgh hotel right?'

'Oh, quite right,' Maureen fawned shamelessly. 'I think it's ever so clever of you to have thought of it, Maurice.'

Jenny, who'd begun to find the floorshow less entertaining, so much as slightly nauseating now, pushed aside her plate and rose.

As she did so, Maurice said, 'I don't suppose you've seen this journalist fellow who's supposed to be covering the event for the local press, have you?'

'No? Who's he?' Maureen asked avidly.

'Oh, just some freelance reporter I invited along to write up the highlights. If we can get a story in the papers here and back home, it'll give the society some good coverage and press.' And help boost your business too, no doubt, Jenny thought cynically. For she had no doubt that the reporter in question would have been well bribed to mention Maurice's taxidermy company very prominently in any and all articles.

But, as she made her way down to the kitchens to have a word about the proper way to grill kidneys, she knew that she'd be back at ten o'clock to hear Maurice's opening speech. For some reason, she wouldn't miss it for the world.

She was beginning to see the attraction of conferences. There was something about watching and listening to a group of people playing away from home that was fascinating to someone as interested in human nature as Jenny Starling.

Besides, what harm could it possibly do?

WHEN JENNY CLIMBED the stairs back to hall a short while later, she found Pippa Foxton and Ian Glendower entering just in front of her. Ian was dressed casually in jeans and a green-and-white check shirt, but Pippa, Jenny noted with a wry smile, was dressed in a pretty A-line skirt and what looked like a genuine raw-silk wraparound top in a matching shade. And, unless Jenny was much mistaken, she was walking like a professional cat-walk model on another pair of Jimmy Choo shoes in the very latest shade of lime green.

Blinking, she dragged her eyes away from the eye-catching footwear and glanced around. The hall was packed with people taking their places in the folding chairs that had been set out in rows, and facing high table, from behind which, presumably, Maurice was due to give his speech. Although some paperwork was already laid out on the middle table, there was as yet no sign of the great man himself.

Aware that she had no official status here, Jenny decided not to join the ranks of the true Great Jessies, and retired instead to a place at the back, up against the far wall. Here, most of the breakfast tables had been stacked. She leaned herself comfortably against a wall, and looked down at the edge of one of the folded tables and found herself looking at a chameleon. It wasn't very big, but it was a vivid emerald green, and its small claws showed stark and delicate against the pale wood.

Intrigued, despite herself, Jenny leaned down for a closer look. Although she wasn't a fan of reptiles, she could see the appeal in preserving such a specimen, for the skin was exquisite and she wondered which of the taxidermists had done the work on it. Although she was no expert, even she could tell it was fine work, for the animal looked perfect.

She reached down and very gently picked it up, placing it carefully in the palm of her hand and bringing it up to look at it in a better light. It had a tightly pointed green snout, a delicate flap of skin at the throat, and big, globular green eye-sockets, with a small, realistic-looking black eye right in the middle.

One beady eye suddenly moved to look down at her hand, whilst the other eye, independently, swivelled up to give her a questioning look.

'Oh, sorry,' Jenny said before she could stop herself. 'I thought you were stuffed.'

The chameleon turned both eyes to look accusingly down at her hand, and Jenny hastily lowered it back to the table. There, after an agonizingly long pause, it very slowly moved off her palm and back onto the wood.

Jenny glanced quickly around, but luckily nobody was paying her any attention. Instead, all eyes had turned to the entrance where Maurice Raines had appeared, wheeling in a large wooden crate on a trolley. He had about him the air of a showman, and there was a hush and a buzz as speculation filled the room.

Jenny looked back down at the chameleon.

The chameleon looked up at her. Jenny shrugged. 'Don't ask me, I've no idea what's in the crate.'

The chameleon contemplated the table thoughtfully. Just then, James Raye appeared at her side. 'Oh, good, you've found Norman.' He pressed a hand dramatically against his chest. 'I thought I'd lost him for good. I damn near had a heart attack. The thought of searching for him in a building this size was giving me palpitations.'

Jenny looked back at the chameleon.

Norman?

A chameleon called Norman?

Norman turned one eye to look at her, challenging her to comment. Jenny contemplated discretion and valour and all that sort of thing, and turned her attention back to James. 'I thought he was stuffed. Well, you can hardly blame me. He was so still—I mean, utterly motionless.'

James grinned. 'Lizards are like that. He's my niece's pet actually. Libby, that's my older sister, and her brood are off to Disneyland in Florida for a couple of weeks, and somehow I got custody of Norman. I couldn't leave him for five days back at my flat, and he's not the sort of pet you can really ask a friend or a neighbour to babysit, is he? Not like a fluffy kitten or a cute dog. So I had to bring him. Unfortunately, the small solarium—or do

I mean terrarium?—well anyway, the glass tank-cum-travelling-case thingy they put him in isn't as secure as his proper big tank back home, and he keeps giving me the slip.'

Jenny grinned. 'Now pause and take a deep, calming breath.'

James did so, and rolled his eyes, then looked down at the lizard, which seemed to be contemplating a small nail head that was protruding slightly from one of the tables. 'I swear that he should be called Houdini, rather than Norman, but that was Gracie's choice.'

'Gracie being your niece?'

'Right.'

Jenny glanced down at the chameleon, which froze in the act of slowly putting one clawed foot in front of the other. Aware that he was the focus of attention, both of his bulbous eyes looked up at them. If he could have spoken, clearly he would have asked them just what they thought they were staring at.

He was that sort of a lizard.

'I rather like Norman,' Jenny said.

The chameleon delicately put one foot down in front of the other.

'So do I, but I'd better get him back to his tank. I won't be a tick.' He carefully scooped up the reptile and headed quickly for the exit, casting a look to the front of the room as he did so.

Jenny saw that Maurice had now manoeuvred the crate into place, and had placed a large cloth over the front of it and was busily removing one side of the crate in order to facilitate a no-doubt spectacular 'show' at some point during his speech.

Which he now seemed ready to deliver.

Prepared to be entertained, Jenny settled her well-padded shoulder more comfortably against the wall, and waited to be amused.

SIMON JENKS SAW the motorway turn off sign for Oxford and indicated in plenty of time. He glanced nervously at the petrol tank though, and hoped that he'd have enough fuel to incorporate this detour on his trip down to Hayling Island without having to top up just yet. The cost of petrol nowadays was enough to bring him out in a cold sweat, but he knew that once he'd teamed up with Laura, he could persuade her to use his car during their little holiday, even though she would probably prefer to use her top-of-the-range BMW. Then, at the nearest petrol station, he could find his wallet low on cash, and she'd be quick to offer him the use of her credit card.

One of the many things that Simon liked about Laura was her generosity with plastic. Not that he was a total sponger, he thought hastily, but business was tight these days. The double, or was it treble-dip, recession was hitting him hard along with everyone else and besides, the little jaunt to the coast was all her idea, after all. It was only fair that she pay for the bulk of it.

He glanced at the large green plastic bag beside him on the passenger seat, which bore the logo of a prestigious store in Harrogate, and smiled. Besides, he'd already splashed out on what she'd asked him to bring—namely, one baby-doll nightie in a delicate shade of peach, a bottle of champers, and some Belgian chocolates, which she'd promised to make melt down in a most interesting way.

Simon glanced at his watch, a Rolex from his glory days before the divorce had stripped him clean, and saw that it was just gone quarter past ten. He hoped that he wouldn't be late. Laura's text message had been a bit cryptic, to say the least, but the actual instructions on where to go had been easy to follow.

Simon, as a freelance photographer, had been to most places in the UK and abroad too, in those heady and carefree days straight out of school when travel was cheap, and Oxford was no exception, but it had been years since he'd last visited the famous university city. If he remembered rightly, it had been to take a selection of photographs so that the makers of a 'Beautiful Britain Calendar' could select one for their March spot. It had been one of the colleges they'd chosen but not, he thought, St Bede's. Had it been the quads at Wadham College, or the famously friendly grey squirrels in the gardens at Worcester College?

Simon gave a mental shrug, and felt a pang of nostalgia for the days when the commissions had seemed to stream in. Just lately, though, they had been drying up. When money was tight, companies tended to cut the expensive little extras first. So lush brochures full of photographs had become a thing of the past. Since they were his bread-and-butter he'd recently been forced to try and break into the magazine market, which was already fiercely competitive.

To make matters worse, he'd come out badly in his divorce, he'd just celebrated his thirty-eighth birthday, and suddenly life had begun to look just a shade grim. At five feet ten, with dark-brown, nearly-black hair and large brown eyes, Simon had always known he was attractive to women. But somehow, here he was, facing middle-age, in a rented flat, a car coming up to ten years old, and a business that barely paid the bills.

No wonder he'd been feeling just a shade vulnerable and shaky when he'd met Laura Raines. She'd been dashing into a hotel restaurant to get out of the Yorkshire rain, and he'd just finished having lunch with the owner of a gallery that he'd been trying to persuade to show some of his artwork.

Simon took a long, slow breath and checked the progress of a large lorry hurtling up behind him. He moved over to let the juggernaut pass, and his thoughts turned once again to the new woman in his life.

Laura, it was clear, still thought of him as young. She looked at him and saw a good-looking man, a desirable man, a catch. She had soothed his ego without even trying, and taken away a good portion of his nervousness about the future, and for that, he was genuinely fond of her.

She truly didn't look her age, and Simon had been only too pleased to take up the invitation in her eyes on that day when they'd first met.

It hadn't taken him long to discover the lay of the land, of course. And an older woman with an expensive car, good clothes, and bling actually worth wearing was definitely worth getting to know. Her marriage had been an empty sham for years, and now that her boys were grown, she wanted out. The money was hers, he'd been relieved to learn, and Simon had no doubt that a rosy future awaited both of them.

He just had to play his cards right, that was all.

And that, he fully intended to do.

Simon Jenks eased his foot off the pedal, and approached a large roundabout that would take him towards the centre of the city. He glanced again at his watch.

No, he was all right. He still had plenty of time.

THREE

'AND THUS WE come to this fine specimen,' Maurice Raines said, with just a touch of bravura. He'd been speaking for only five minutes, and Jenny had to admit that he spoke well. He was both clear, and had an obviously genuine enthusiasm for his topic, and now, along with everyone else, she leaned forward just a little from her position propping up the wall as he whipped aside the cloth covering the large crate beside him.

There was an appreciative murmur among the crowd. Jenny found herself looking at a black, or very dark brown, medium-sized bear, with a white fur collar and bib. It stood on all fours, and seemed to be snarling at the audience.

'Those closest to it might be in the best position to guess the approximate age of this fine specimen.' Maurice smiled and then paused and nodded as someone close to high table called out that it was done sometime in the 1920s. 'Close, Phillip, 1931 to be exact.'

He went on to describe the taxidermist, a fairly well-known American practitioner of the art apparently, and within another five minutes he was obviously drawing his opening speech to a close, as he wished everyone a successful and interesting few days.

A couple in the back row applauded loudly, and Jenny was amused to overhear the husband say to the wife, 'That's got to be one of Maurice's shortest

speeches ever.' And his wife shot back, 'I know, that's
why it was so good!'

But Maurice wasn't quite finished yet. He held up
his hands for silence and got it instantly.

'If everyone who hasn't rented table space this year
could make their way straight to lectures or demos, it'll
give the ones who have tables to set up a chance to get
started. And for all of those, there's a free early lunch
provided for you in the JCR, and will be available from
eleven thirty to twelve thirty. I know you'll all want to
be ready and raring to go by two o'clock, when we have
our first free period. OK, that's all, folks.'

There was a general scramble as people obligingly
picked up their chairs, folded them and started stacking
them neatly around the walls. Jenny noticed that some
of the scouts who'd served breakfast suddenly appeared
to give a hand setting the tables back up. Several people began to lug in boxes and bags, and began setting
out their wares.

Some, she saw, were selling samples of their work,
and she paused to admire a scene wherein a barn owl
was about to snatch a vole from a tuft of grass. The famously silent feathers on the bird were exquisite, she
thought.

Others were setting out the tools of their trade and,
as these began to appear in artfully arranged displays,
Jenny couldn't resist wandering around, her mind sometimes boggling. She moved on from ranges of safety
glasses, where she was told by the vendor that the so-
lutions to clean and preserve hides could be dangerous
if they got into the eyes, and then paused, intrigued
by a stall that seemed to be selling nothing but plastic buckets, bowls and measuring cups. Here she was

told, again by the helpful vendor when he realized that she was attached to the college and a novice when it came to taxidermy, that they were all used in the process of tanning.

Another stall looked as if a needle-worker or someone in the needlecraft trade had wandered in by mistake, for she was selling needles, thread, glue, something called monofilament fishing line and even dental floss. Jenny didn't need to be told why someone would need these—obviously they were all used to sew up hide. Another stall was selling something called caulk, hot glue and superglue, needed, or so some of the signage said, for 'perfect mounting'.

She paused by a stall that wouldn't have looked out of place in a painter's studio, since it consisted mostly of oil painting kits, airbrushes, turps, linseed oil, and something called benzine hard oil finish, or white varnishing. Jenny had no idea what these might be used for and was still puzzling over it, when she felt someone come up and stand beside her.

'What the hell would you want all this stuff for?' an amused male voice demanded, and Jenny turned to see a young red-haired man with a camera slung around his neck, staring down at the wares on display. He was probably only just out of his teens, and had an extremely freckled face, with small, close-together blue eyes.

'No idea,' Jenny admitted wryly.

'Oh, you're not a taxidermist then?'

'No, just the cook.'

He grinned and made a show of putting away his notebook.

'No point in interviewing you then?' He gave a mock woebegone sigh.

'Not unless your readers are interested in how to create a perfect Oxford herb omelette,' Jenny agreed. 'You must be the reporter that Maurice Raines hired to cover the conference?'

'For my sins,' the young man said, thrusting out his hand.

'Charles Foster. Well, Charlie, really.'

'Pleased to meet you, Charlie,' Jenny said, taking his equally freckle-covered hand and shaking it firmly. 'Jenny Starling.'

Having covered that, they both gave the painting outfits another bemused look, and slowly wandered off to the next stall. Here Jenny felt her breath slowly hiss out as she surveyed a few of the more alarming-looking bottles that contained ominous labels such as arsenious acid and muriatic acid. Shellac, bicarb of soda, white glue and cotton batting didn't seem so dangerous, nor did the long-fibre hemp tow (whatever the hell that was), the fine flax tow and the sponges.

'Is arsenious acid something to do with arsenic?' Charlie Foster said, giving a low whistle through his teeth. 'I keep thinking I've wandered into one of those murder mystery weekends by mistake.'

Jenny, who'd had plenty of previous experience with murder, tried to shake off a nasty feeling of *déjà vu* and shrugged. 'Can't be. I mean, why would you need arsenic to stuff an animal?'

'Why would you need a paint kit?' Charlie grinned and shot back.

'It's for fish,' someone said helpfully as they hurried past carrying a large and heavy-looking cardboard box.

'Oh. That explains it, then,' Charlie said, and cocked a quizzical orange eyebrow at Jenny. 'Right?'

'Oh, definitely,' Jenny agreed. And then had a weird mental image of somebody painting a stuffed fish. Not painting a picture of a stuffed fish, but actually painting a stuffed fish.

'Is this place beginning to give you the creeps?' Charlie asked, nodding towards yet another table that seemed to sell nothing but knives, scissors, scalpels, and all things pointy and lethal looking. 'It says here that they're all fleshing tools,' he said, reading a little placard on the front of the table. 'Finest quality steel apparently,' and then gave a theatrical shudder. He wasn't tall, but he was incredibly thin and bony, and Jenny was instantly assailed by the urge to feed him up.

'I think it's time I headed back down to the kitchen. Have you eaten?' she asked.

'Huh?' Charlie said, hastily withdrawing his hand as his fingers had been about to pick up a particularly nasty hooked instrument that wouldn't have looked out of place in a Spanish Inquisition workshop. 'Have you seen the prices of some of these things? And yeah, I've had breakfast, thanks.'

Jenny supposed, gloomily, that it had been a bowl of cornflakes or, even worse, a pop tart, but didn't push it.

'So what do you think of our Maurice then?' he asked, following her slowly out of the room. 'Thinks a lot of himself, if you ask me.' At the doorway, they had to pause and wait to let two older men, who were carrying in a heavy box between them, to pass.

'You going down to have some of this free nosh in the JCR then?' one of the passing men asked his companion, and the other laughed.

'Too right I am. It's not like old Maurice to be so generous and offer free grub to us peasants. I reckon we're all going down just so that we can tell 'em back home that he put his hands in his pockets for once.'

'It was probably Vicki's idea. She's the treasurer, after all, so I suppose she gets to spend the budget how she likes.'

'Makes sense. I'll have to stand her a drink tonight. Oh, sorry love, did I catch you with that?' The man turned to Jenny who'd just stepped smartly back to avoid having her shins caught on one corner of the box.

'No, you're fine,' she said cheerfully, and glanced at her watch. It was still only a quarter to eleven. And since lunch wasn't provided for the conference-goers she had several hours to kill before she needed to get down to the kitchen to start overseeing the evening meal.

'I wonder who's catering to this lot in the JCR,' she said to Charlie with a suddenly worried frown. 'I'm pretty sure it's not supposed to be me.' At least, neither the bursar nor Art McIntyre had mentioned it, and surely they would have?

'Oh, it'll be bar snacks provided by the regular scouts, I expect,' Charlie said dismissively. 'I can't see Maurice letting anyone go overboard on the eats. You've met him, haven't you?' He tried to draw her out again with an engaging grin.

Jenny, realizing the young man was desperate to get something for his article, smiled wryly. 'Well, he's certainly a personality,' she admitted cautiously.

Charlie Foster grinned. 'Yeah, that's one word for him, all right.'

Jenny smiled. 'And I had the impression he likes to get his own way.'

'Same here.'

'He seems very popular with the ladies,' Jenny added deadpan.

Charlie rolled his eyes. 'Don't I know it. I've been asking around about our host, ever since I met him yesterday, and I get the distinct impression that he's a bit of a tom cat. Apparently, he was a bit of a lad when younger. I've had my ear bent by several people telling me what he was like in his younger days and how the ladies of his home town weren't safe. Mind you, I looked him up on the internet, and he was born and grew up in someplace called Wither Sedgewick, which is only a small market town up in the Yorkshire Dales somewhere, so I hardly think that qualifies him as a Don Juan.'

'I thought I heard someone say he lives in Harrogate nowadays,' Jenny said helpfully. 'So perhaps you need to dig for the dirt there.'

Charlie had the grace to blush. 'Sorry. But I can't seem to get enthusiastic about stuffed hedgehogs,' he said, nodding to a table and a case where the cute mammals were displayed in all their prickly glory.

'It's a tough job, but someone's got to do it,' Jenny said, in a fairly good Humphrey Bogart accent, and laid a comforting hand on the young man's shoulder.

'See, that's all the sympathy I get,' Charlie said, but rolled his eyes and followed her down the corridor. 'I'm going to find me a demonstration and take some photos, the more gruesome the better,' he threatened, waving his camera in the air. 'The editors love a bit of blood and gore.'

'That's the spirit,' Jenny said cheerfully and, waving the young man goodbye, headed back to her room.

In the back of her mind, however, lingered the image of a bottle of acid.

JENNY COULDN'T SETTLE. Her room was in an older part of the college and, since parts of it dated back to the time when Christopher Columbus was a boy, that was pretty damn old, but for once the lure of history being all around her failed to intrigue. She went to her diamond-shaped lead-paned windows and threw them open, looking down through fronds of pale-lilac wisteria at the ancient quad below. Mellow Cotswold stone and lawns so velvety green that they looked like the finest baize gazed back at her.

She saw a gardener dead-heading some shrubs and breathed in deeply of the sunny warm air. What she needed, she told herself firmly, was a walk around the grounds, perhaps even around the town. She grabbed her handbag, glanced at her watch, saw that it still wasn't quite noon, and wondered if she could find a decent place to grab a bite of lunch.

Her route out took her back past hall, and it was perhaps the unexpected silence of the place that made her stop beside the wide open entrance. Of course, everybody must be down in the JCR by now she realized, after she'd thought it through for a moment. She saw that most of the tables had been fully set up now, with only a few left that needed some finishing touches. She looked around, expecting to see at least someone standing guard, but the room felt oddly empty.

Weren't they worried about thieves? Jenny considered it for a moment. Presumably there were always scouts about. And also, presumably, the porter at the gatehouse didn't let anyone in who hadn't business being in the college in the first place.

But wasn't it open to the public?

She hesitated and then stepped further into the hall. 'Hello?' she called softly. But not even the resident college ghost—some emeritus fellow back in the 1880s who'd died in his rooms and remained undiscovered for two whole terms, apparently—bothered to reply.

She was just about to shrug and head back out, after all, it was not her gear that had been left lying around for any light-fingered passerby to snaffle, when a flash of blue caught her eye.

She turned, trying to place it, then realized that it was something on the floor that had caught her peripheral vision. Something colourful on the floor usually meant it wasn't supposed to be there. It was probably only a tablecloth or an exhibit that had fallen from one of the tables she supposed, but her natural instinct for tidiness simply couldn't leave it lying there like that to get dirty.

With a small sigh, she turned and walked further amongst the maze of tables, and then stopped abruptly.

She was looking down at a pair of shoes, with their shiny black soles pointing straight up at the ceiling. Rather fine, black leather shoes, to be exact. And above them, a pair of blue trousers.

Not a tablecloth then, Jenny thought inconsequentially.

Her next thought was that someone had been elected by the taxidermists to guard their stuff, after all. Her thought after that was that that someone had been caught lying down on the job.

Then she thought that she was being silly. Whoever

the shoes and trousers belonged to wasn't taking a nap, but was obviously on the floor doing something else. Picking up dropped stock perhaps. Or fixing an uneven table leg.

She abruptly realized that she'd been standing dead still in one place for a little while now, and that whoever it was on the floor hadn't moved much in that time—if at all. She also realized that she seemed to be breathing rather hard.

She took a step or two closer, and saw a white shirt and a matching blue jacket.

Who was the last person that she'd seen wearing such a suit? Jenny swallowed hard and took another step closer and then all she could see was scarlet. It seemed to coat the top of the white shirt with a glossy sheen, and was also pooled around arms and elbows, which were lying against the floor at a rather peculiar and downright uncomfortable-looking angle.

Maurice Raines had been wearing a blue suit during his speech, she thought.

Maurice Raines was now lying down in the middle of the tables, oozing scarlet all over the place. He looked distinctly untidy. She couldn't see his face very well, for his head was tilted back behind him on the hard wood floor.

He looks really uncomfortable lying like that, Jenny thought, and she couldn't imagine that the fastidious Maurice would be very pleased to be making such a mess either.

Jenny took another step closer and now she could see his face. His salt-and-pepper hair looked matted with rust. His bright blue eyes, so startling and attractive in life, looked a little like glass now, somehow clouded and dimmed, as they stared sightlessly along a length of floorboard. Jutting out of his neck at an obscene angle was something long and metallic. Scalpel-like.

'Oh,' Jenny said.

Well that explained a lot.

She looked down, saw that if she moved any further she would step in Maurice's blood and took a careful step back. And then another. And then another.

Beside Maurice, she noticed vaguely that a space on the table had been cleared, and that two cups of coffee had been set down there. They both had just the faintest whiff of steam coming from off the top of the dark-brown liquid. Neither cup looked as if they had been drunk from.

At the entrance to hall, Jenny Starling paused and took a long, deep breath, and told herself not to be an idiot. With fingers that felt curiously numb, she reached into her handbag and drew out her mobile. It seemed to take her a few seconds to remember how to use it, but then she pressed the number nine three times, and waited to be connected.

When a pleasant female voice asked her which emergency number she required, she asked for the police.

JENNY FOUND A chair out in the corridor and sat down. It felt a distinct relief to take her not inconsiderable weight off her feet, which were feeling curiously cold, and far removed from the rest of her.

She'd been told to wait, not to enter the room again or let anyone else enter the room, and that an officer would be with her shortly.

And all of that was fine by her.

So Jenny sat and waited. And thought.

This wasn't the first time she'd found a body—or been present when someone else had done so, if it came to that. Once, she'd catered a birthday party when someone had been poisoned, which had been a bit tricky, you had to admit. She'd also cooked on board a riverboat when someone else had been killed and dumped in her pantry, if you please. She'd even been snowed in at a remote farmhouse where a killer had been on the loose, when for the first time ever, she'd nearly burned the brussels. She'd even, for Pete's sake, helped out an aristocratic family when someone had had the bad manners to bump off the governess.

And now here she was, in that bastion of genteel aloofness, an Oxford college, and someone else lay dead a few feet away. There was no getting away from it— she seemed to have a knack for dead bodies. Well, for those and Yorkshire puddings and Dundee cake.

Which was something that any investigating officer called out to this particular crime scene was quickly going to cotton on to.

Gloomily, she wondered what the chances were that before the day was out, she'd have to telephone one of her parents to get her out of the jug and stand her bail. They had to be pretty fair, she supposed, which posed all the usual problems. Would she be able to even get in touch with her mother who was no doubt off somewhere inaccessible saving the planet? She couldn't see her dear mater wanting to climb down out of a tree house in some doomed forest simply in order to get her only offspring out of the pokey. Her father wasn't much of a better bet either: a celebrity chef, he was probably either in Hollywood cooking for a double-D bra-sized starlet, or maybe in Paris making some five-star hotelier's life miserable. Either way, getting on a jet and riding to the rescue was probably not going to be his number one priority.

She glanced up as she saw two uniformed policemen walking towards her. One of them was talking into a radio attached to his collar. Perhaps she should have called the bursar, or Art McIntyre for back up. Then she realized that the bursar would put the college first and foremost, and, if throwing her, Jenny Starling, to the wolves would save his establishment from embarrassment, he'd probably do it in a heartbeat, and with all the will in the world, Art would probably be about as useful in a crisis as a well-known odoriferous commodity in a colander.

Jenny watched them bleakly as they approached her, and then stopped by the entrance to ask her if she was the lady who'd reported a dead body.

Jenny briefly contemplated whether or not to admit to being a lady, then decided that now was probably not the time for semantics, and simply nodded curtly, and pointed into the hall with one finger. One of the uniformed men went inside whilst the other remained standing just in front of her.

Jenny wondered if he really thought she was going to make a run for it, and sighed gently. Her Junoesque curves weren't exactly built for speed, but even so, if she'd thought that her knees were in any shape to take the strain, she might have given serious thought to giving it a go. As it was, she was still feeling distinctly shaky and so decided to stay put.

She took a long, deep breath as the uniformed officer came out and gave his companion a speaking look. Without looking at Jenny, he bent his head to talk into the radio again, no doubt confirming that this wasn't a crank call and asking for back-up and a SOCO team.

Here we go again, Jenny thought grimly.

DETECTIVE TREVOR GOLDER indicated left at the Martyr's Memorial and said, 'Bloody Chief Inspector Morse.'

Beside him, Sergeant Peter Trent bit back a grin.

When their boss had called them in to tell them that they had a suspicious death at St Bede's College, and that the case was theirs, Peter Trent had known that they'd be in for it. Whilst Inspector Morse, that wonderful creation of an Oxford don, had been popular for so many years with the public in general, DI Golder was known not to be a fan. Inevitably, once word got around down at the station that he'd got a live one— or rather, exactly the opposite—in an Oxford college, prime Morse country if ever there was any, then every lowly constable up to the know-it-alls who ran traffic would soon be taking the Michael.

Sergeant Trent could hear them now: and just how long would it be before the comedians started calling him Lewis?

Not that he minded being thought of as Morse's loyal sidekick, now that he'd been given his own TV series!

'The first snotty-nosed little sod who mentions Morse around me is going to find himself working in Records for a month,' Trevor Golder muttered darkly, as he drew the car to a halt on double yellow lines on the Woodstock Road.

'Better park over there in the pub car-park, guv,' Peter Trent said, helpfully pointing.

Trevor grunted but did as he was advised. He wouldn't put it past those twits in Traffic to have him towed; that seemed to be their level of humour in Traffic these days.

The two men crossed the busy main road and stepped into the hallowed portals of St Bede's. There, the porter took their names and directed them to hall. No doubt, by now, the word was spreading, and Trevor wondered what officious college bigwig he'd have to placate before he could start to do his job properly.

The porter watched them go thoughtfully.

Trevor, despite being the senior man in rank, was nearly a decade and a half younger than Peter Trent, who was now in his early fifties, and could have retired the previous year had he wanted to. Whereas Trent was white-haired, with a neatly trimmed white beard and pronounced crow's feet at the corner of twinkling brown eyes, Golder was heavier, taller and had thinning light-brown hair. The porter continued to watch the two police officers disappear into one of the main residential blocks, then was immediately on the telephone to the bursar.

He knew better than to telephone the principal's office.

Everyone knew that the principal was hardly ever in college. In the Orient, yes. On the golf-course, yes. In a country cottage belonging to a former disgraced politician, yes. In college? No.

'So what do we know so far?' Trevor asked, as they made their way to the crime scene, more out of habit than because he hadn't been paying due attention to his superior officer's brief initial instructions.

'A woman caller from the college logged a triple nine at eleven fifty-eight. Responding uniforms confirm a deceased male in suspicious circumstances. SOCO is already on site,' Trent confirmed crisply.

Trevor sighed as they stepped into a large hall, redolent with the scent of history and academic achievement.

'Bloody Morse,' he said morosely.

THE TWO MEN walked up a wide wooden staircase, past paintings depicting prior smug or aloof academics, and found themselves in a long landing. A stuffed owl in an alcove stared out at them as they passed and half-way down, Trevor saw a young constable in uniform straighten up a little at the sight of him.

He was standing next to a striking-looking woman who was sitting, straight-backed, in a chair pressed against the wall. He glanced at her curiously as he stepped by her and into the hall, where white-suited technicians were already at work.

What he saw was a tall, large-boned, beautiful, dark-haired woman with the loveliest eyes he'd seen in a long time. And she gave him an enigmatic look back that made his toenails curl.

Trevor made no move to go further into the room until he was spotted by one of the SOCO team, who pointed down at some temporary wooden partitions and beckoned to him that it was all right to come closer. As they did so, Trevor was surprised to notice that a large, stuffed, black bear was standing in pride of place on a slightly elevated platform that housed high table. Beside it, was a porter's trolley, and an empty case.

Dragging his eyes from it, Trevor and Peter Trent moved in for their first view of the victim.

'One Mr Maurice Raines,' the pathologist, who was kneeling beside the body, looked up at them and held out a black wallet, now neatly encased in an evidence bag. 'Aged between forty-five and fifty-five, I'd say. A little overweight, but relatively fit, for all that. No signs of defensive wounds that I can see, and I don't see why the cause of death shouldn't be the obvious one.'

Both police officers looked at the metal implement still embedded in the body's neck.

'Bloody hell,' Peter Trent muttered graphically.

'Bloody hell is right,' the pathologist agreed cheerfully. He was a smallish, compact man in his early thirties, who'd worked for a long time in the A&E departments when he'd been earning his stripes, and had the confidence of a man who'd seen it all. Or thought he had. 'As you can see, he bled out. I'd say it was odds on that he died from either shock or exsanguination. If he was lucky, his heart would have given out fairly quickly and it would have been lights out before he really knew what was happening.'

Peter Trent swallowed hard and looked away.

'OK. We won't get in your way,' Trevor said, turning around and nodding curtly at his sergeant to follow him. He was a great believer in letting the professional technical staff get on with the how, when and whats, whilst he concentrated on the who and the why.

'Constable,'—he nodded at the young man in uniform and then glanced curiously at the striking woman who was still waiting patiently in the chair—'I take it this is the young lady who called us?'

'Yes, sir. A Miss Jennifer Starling. She was hired by the bursar of the college a few days ago to cater to the summer conference season here.' The constable, a bright lad who was anxious to get on, clearly hadn't wasted his few moments alone with the principal witness so far.

Trevor nodded gravely. 'Ah,' he said. So she was not a college regular then. That could prove very helpful indeed. He was already anticipating that the college would quickly close ranks against him once it realized the severity of the situation. Unless he missed his guess, their main priority would be in keeping the publicity to a minimum whilst interrupting their moneymaking enterprises as little as possible. The fact that a man lay dead would probably only be construed as unfortunate. He could almost see some gown-wearing, bespectacled college bigwig saying as much even now.

'Did you know the victim, Miss Starling?' Trevor asked quietly.

'Not really. That is, I knew who he was. He was the driving force behind the current conference that we're hosting right now. Or at least, that is how I'm sure that he saw himself,' she corrected herself quickly. Remembering some of the less than reverential comments she'd heard others making about him, she doubted that the late Mr Raines's opinion of himself was shared by everyone.

'Which is?'

'I think they're called the Greater Ribble Valley & Jessop Taxidermy Society,' Jenny said. 'I just tend to think of them as the Great Jessies.'

Peter Trent grinned over his notebook.

'Right,' Trevor said, blinking slightly.

Jenny glanced at him curiously as she was sure she'd heard him mutter something under his breath about bloody Morse but she must have got that wrong.

'You found the body just before noon? Did you call us right away?' Trevor asked next.

'Yes. I was just leaving to have a walk around town. I won't be needed in the kitchens for a few hours, and wanted to stretch my legs. When I was passing hall, I looked in, well, mainly because I was curious to find it empty, and then saw Mr Raines lying on the floor. I realized he was, well, dead and called you right away. I didn't step in any of the blood: I didn't touch the body in any way, I didn't see anyone else leaving the hall or going down the corridor in front of me, and I didn't hear anyone talking or any footsteps. I noticed nothing in particular when I was in there.'

She paused and waited.

Trevor Golder stared at her hard for a few seconds, and then nodded slowly. 'OK. That was a very concise and pertinent statement. Thank you. You said you didn't really know Mr Raines? Had you in fact met him or talked to him?'

'Briefly. I checked up on them after dinner last night, just to get some feedback on their enjoyment of their first meal in college. I spoke to Mr Raines briefly, along with Vicki Voight, who's the society's treasurer and one or two other members. A Mr Ian Glendower, and his girlfriend, Pippa Foxton. I should tell you that I was also present in hall this morning when Mr Raines gave his opening address, and later spoke to the journalist whom the conference hired to cover their event, a Mr Charles Foster. Also, at breakfast, I spoke to one of the older members, I think his name was Robert Llewellyn. Oh, and a newer member of the society called Mr James Raye.'

Peter Trent listed the names with silent admiration.

If only all witnesses could be this clear-thinking and methodical, his life would be a lot easier.

Trevor's eyes narrowed as the college cook continued speaking. He could see that she was pale, and her hands were clasped still and tight in her lap, both signs of shock, he was sure. Yet she was keeping a remarkably clear head. It was almost as if she'd done all this before. The moment he got back to the station, he'd be sure to have a computer search made on Miss Jennifer Starling as a matter of priority. Not that he thought her a serious contender. Whoever had killed Mr Maurice Raines must have bloodstains on their clothes and probably hands as well.

Of course, the college cook could have killed him, gone back to her room, washed and changed and then called it in. Being the first person to find the body always kept anyone at the top of the suspect list, in Trevor's opinion.

'Do you know of any reason why anyone would want to kill Mr Raines?' He asked the stock question without any real hope of anything useful coming of it. So, when the witness was curiously silent, he found his interest peaking.

Jenny hesitated uneasily. 'Not of my own knowledge,' she said eventually.

Trevor glanced at Trent, who raised one white eyebrow. 'That's a rather carefully worded statement, Miss Starling,' Trevor said at last. 'Do you think you could be a bit more forthcoming?'

'Like I said, Inspector, I mingled a little with these people. Like people anywhere, they're fascinated with and by themselves, and they…gossip.'

'Nothing wrong with gossip, not in my line of work,

anyway,' Trevor said cheerfully. 'Please feel free to pass it on,' he encouraged.

Jenny sighed, not for one minute fooled by his hearty and friendly demeanour. Still, he was being canny, and that was a good thing. All in all, she rather liked her policemen to be wily. It made her feel safer.

'I had the impression from several people, that Mr Raines was a bit of a ladies' man,' she said carefully. 'I also sensed that things were a little…cool, perhaps, between Mr Raines and the treasurer, Mrs Voight. And I think Mr Glendower might not have appreciated the attention Mr Raines had been paying to his girlfriend.'

And as if mentioning her name had somehow summoned her up, Pippa Foxton's attractive form suddenly appeared at the far end of the hallway and began to walk towards them. She slowed as she took in the uniform of the younger police constable, and her pretty face sharpened with curiosity. 'Hello? Something wrong?' she asked uncertainly. 'Don't say we've had a robbery! Oh good grief, don't tell me someone has made off with Emily's damned hedgehogs! We'll never hear the end of it.'

She laughed uncertainly, and glanced from Trevor to Peter. She was wearing very tight-fitting jeans and a white silk top that clung to every curve she had. Both Jenny and Pippa noticed both men noticing.

'This is Miss Foxton,' Jenny said neutrally, but with a wry twist to her lips. She was rather curious as to which of the two men the little minx would vamp first.

'Oh, call me Pippa,' the young girl said automatically and smiled winsomely.

'Detective Inspector Golder, this is Sergeant Trent,' Trevor said.

'So, what is going on?' Pippa asked sharply.

Now that's what I call a good question, Jenny thought grimly.

'Can you tell me your movements of this morning, Miss Foxton?' Trevor Golder said, ignoring her demand but covering it with a friendly smile.

Pippa took a long, deep breath, which strained the tiny white buttons on her blouse in a most spectacular manner. Both men had to drag their eyes away from the threatening-to-pop little pearl buttons and the older man even seemed to blush, just a little. Jenny thought that was rather sweet.

'Well, we had breakfast, of course,' Pippa began, but before she could go on was swiftly interrupted.

'We?' Golder prompted gently.

'Me and Ian. My fiancé. Well, sort of fiancé. Maybe not. Anyway, we had breakfast, right here in hall.' She indicated the room beyond, her bright blue eyes darting here and there as she caught sight of the white-suited SOCO figures moving about. Luckily, the corpse was out of sight on the floor amid the sea of tables. 'That must have been around half past eight to nine o'clockish, I suppose. Then we sort of all milled around, whilst we waited for Maurice to officially open the conference.' Pippa shrugged. 'That was it, really.'

'You knew Maurice Raines well?' Trevor asked.

Pippa, if she realized the implication behind the police officer's use of the past tense, didn't show it.

'Oh, Maurice is a sweetheart. Well, sort of. He's a bit of an old goat too, if you know what I mean, but you can't really take him seriously, somehow. Ian couldn't stand him,' she said off-handedly.

Jenny winced inwardly, but said nothing. Was the

girl really so genuinely unconcerned and blissfully unaware, or did she have some reason for dropping her boyfriend in the brown stuff?

'Oh?' Trevor said sharply.

'He thinks Maurice is a bit of joke, really. Well, he doesn't like the way Maurice flirts with me, but like I tell Ian, he's just being old-fashioned. Men like Maurice would consider it rude not to flirt with a young girl, if you see what I mean? But Ian doesn't like it. And of course, Maurice is a bigwig in the society and Ian is all bent out of shape because he thinks they should be backing younger blood. Oh, it's all very medieval, I can tell you. Anyone would think stuffing dead things was on a par with painting the bloody Mona Lisa, if you listen to some of them,' she finished disgustedly.

Then, as if aware that her petulance probably wasn't making a favourable impression, she suddenly grinned and tossed back a long tress of glossy brown hair.

Trevor nodded, trying not to watch the flight path of the tress. 'I'm a little confused. You don't speak like a member of the society: are you not a conference goer yourself?'

'Well, yes and no. I mean, I'm here at the conference, but I'm not strictly speaking a member.'

'You're not a taxidermist yourself?' Peter Trent clarified for his notes.

Pippa Foxton gave a theatrical shudder that moved parts of her body in a way that had both men carefully averting their glances. 'Oh good grief no! I'm a baker. I came down to be with Ian, that's all. A bit of a cheap holiday really, if we're being honest. I get to see Oxford, and Ian gets to schmooze with the others, and everyone's happy.'

'And this is OK with the others?' Trevor asked. 'You not being a taxidermist, I mean?'

'Oh, they don't know. Well, perhaps some of them guessed, but they don't care.'

'Did Maurice know?' Trevor asked sharply.

Pippa giggled. 'He was beginning to suspect. Ian said I was thinking of joining the society, and this conference was a way of me making up my mind. But really, Maurice wouldn't have come over all chairman-of-the-board about it. He liked me,' she added, with such supreme insouciance that Jenny actually had to grit her teeth.

'Right,' Trevor said deadpan. 'So, back to this morning. You had breakfast, you listened to the opening speeches, and then what?'

'Oh, I went with Ian to his first lecture. He was giving it, that is, not listening to it. He had agreed to give a talk to the very newest and wannabe members, a sort of beginner's guide, sort of thing. He'd been muttering about it all week long, about how that sort of thing was a bit of a sop and how he should have been giving a more prestigious talk. You know how men are. I stopped listening after his first grumbles. But I went along to sit and take notes and cheer him on so to speak. Mind you, it got so mind-numbingly boring after a while that I slipped out early. I was just coming back here to have a look around the tables when I bumped into you. And here we are.'

Jenny slowly digested Pippa's story. She watched Inspector Golder and Sergeant Trent do the same. She wasn't at all surprised by Trevor Golder's next question.

'Did Mr Glendower blame Mr Raines for being given such a low-priority task?'

Pippa blinked. 'I don't know. He might have. Mind you, Maurice wasn't giving the best lecture either, I do know that, because I heard Vicki saying that for once he'd given that to…oh, someone else. I forget his name. Vicki will be able to tell you. And I know Ian was surprised by that, because apparently Maurice always snaffles the plum jobs for himself.'

But not this time, Jenny found herself thinking. And wondering why. It was not like a man with the personality of Maurice Raines to do himself out of a treat.

'Let's go back to the opening speeches for a moment,' Trevor said. 'Maurice Raines gave this, right?'

'Oh yes. He had some big black stuffed bear that he seemed really chuffed about,' Pippa said cheerfully. 'He went on a bit about how it represented all that was good about taxidermy, and then told everyone setting up tables that there was a free lunch down in the JCR and that was it. Things sort of broke up, and everyone went off to do their own thing.'

'JCR?'

'Stands for the junior common room, Inspector,' Jenny explained.

'So it's a sort of club room,' Trevor nodded. 'I see. Sergeant, you'd better find this place and start taking down names. Find out who was the last to leave hall this morning. Was anyone talking to Mr Raines, you know the sort of thing. Take some uniforms with you.'

'Guv.' He left, beckoning the two younger constables to come with him.

'All right, Miss Foxton, did you speak to Mr Raines after his speech?' Trevor turned once more to his witness. He hadn't missed the fact that Miss Starling was still present and listening to everything with quiet intelligence, but for now he was content to let things be. The college cook was beginning to interest him. He suspected that she possessed a fine intelligence, and if only he could figure out how, he was sure that he could get it to work to his advantage.

'Oh no. Ian wanted to get going and get set up,' Pippa's cheerful voice dragged his thoughts back to the interview in hand. 'For all he was grumbling about it, I could tell he was eager to show off to all the newbies.'

Trevor smiled. 'Do you know of anyone who might have any reason to want to hurt Mr Raines?'

Pippa laughed. 'Well, probably only Mrs Raines.'

Jenny sighed heavily.

'Do you know Mrs Raines?' Trevor asked sharply.

'Good grief no. I just meant, well, Maurice being like he was. I imagine anyone married to him could cheerfully want to strangle him from time to time.'

Trevor nodded. Pippa put her hands on her hips. 'Look, are you going to tell me what this is all about now? Why all these questions?'

Jenny glanced across curiously at Trevor Golder. Was he going to tell her, and take the opportunity to gauge her reaction? Or was he going to keep her in the dark?

'I'm afraid there's been a fatality, Miss Foxton. Mr Raines is dead,' Trevor Golder said quietly.

Pippa stared at him for a long, silent moment, and then nodded. 'Oh. Right. I thought it had to be bad. Whatever it was.' She waved a vague hand at hall where the search for evidence went on.

And then, after a thoughtful pause, she said simply, 'Poor old Maurice.'

FOUR

DR JULIUS GLOVER-SMYTHE, Bursar of St Bede's College, Oxford, had never much liked his name. At the elite public school that he'd attended, he'd inevitably been called Julie and mocked accordingly by the rugby contingent whilst the reds had mocked the snobbish corruption of the honest, proletarian 'Smith.'

Thus ridiculed by the jocks, and ostracized by the politicals, he'd turned all his energies to actually studying, which had amazed both his teachers and his parents alike, who'd expected nothing from him but the modest success needed to go into one of the less enervating professions.

But, after gaining a place at Oxbridge, and a rather undistinguished second class degree, Julius had decided he liked Oxford well enough and might as well stay. He had taken his time and been canny about it, had picked his spot well and had steadily worked his way up the hierarchy, until gaining the heights of his present post. It was a non-teaching job, which suited him just fine, since he wasn't particularly fond of students. He also liked being an administrator and was good it, but most of all, he enjoyed wangling money out of people.

Now, as he listened to the porter, who knew everything and had long since been Julius's eyes and ears in the college, he sighed heavily. He'd been looking forward to a quiet, lucrative summer, and this news was extremely unwelcome.

'All right, Franks, you'd better send in Mr McIntyre,' he said tersely, when the porter had finished.

The porter nodded solemnly and withdrew. Julius thought for a moment, and then rang a friend in the Press.

The friend in the Press, Michael Jaeger, was quickly able to bring him up to speed on the life and career of one Inspector Trevor Golder. Married, with three teen-age daughters, he was born locally, joined the Force at eighteen, and had steadily risen to his current rank during a respectable but unimaginative career. And, whilst the friend was sympathetic to his old pal's troubles, he was also tediously insistent on getting the scoop.

Julius, aware of the need to manage the publicity at all costs, was more than willing to meet him halfway, and gave him a very careful version of the little he knew so far. 'But, Michael, please keep it all low-key, will you? Stress that it was a member of the conference, and not anyone on staff, who's deceased. And whatever else you do, make it as clear as a pikestaff that there's not a student involved. If you can hint that the culprit is almost certainly to be found within the other conference members, that would be marvellous.'

'I'll do what I can, Julius, but you know how nervous the powers-that-be are nowadays. Forget the libel laws, they're all still wetting their pants over the phone hacking scandal. Everyone's being very careful what they print nowadays.'

Julius sighed. 'Try not to mention the college by name too often.'

'Some hope,' came the dry response.

'I know, I know. The principal is going to have a cow,' Julius said, which for some reason sent his friend off into fits of laughter. 'It's all right for you, but you're not the one who's going to have to deal with him. When he finds out, that is.' Julius suddenly brightened. 'Which, with a bit of luck, might not be for some time yet.'

'He's not in Oxford then?' Michael said, then answered his own question almost immediately. 'No, of course he's not. It's the Long Vacation. He's probably abroad somewhere, right?'

Julius sighed. 'I hope so,' he said with feeling. He hardly knew where the principal was during term time, let alone out of term. 'But even he'll read the papers eventually, or some busybody will see it as their business to inform the old duffer that we've got a murder inquiry on our hands.'

'Sorry, old bean,' came the cheerful response. 'Not much I can do to help you there. But why don't you ask your new cook to keep an eye on things?'

Julius, a tall, good-looking man in his mid-forties, held the phone away from his ear for a moment and frowned. Was he finally losing it? 'Sorry, Michael, I could have sworn you just said that I should get the cook to look into it,' he repeated.

On the other end of the line, he could sense his old friend's impish sense of glee and he sighed wearily. 'Now is not the time to play silly buggers, Michael. For heaven's sake, this is serious.'

'I know it is, old bean, hold your horses and all that,' the friend in the Press said, relenting a little. There had been a time when he had rather fancied Julius Glover-Smythe. Himself, and half the old public school, of course. 'I'm not being funny, actually. A little bird told me the other day that you'd hired Jennifer Starling to cook for the conference season. Is that right?'

Julius pulled his mind back to the Amazonian woman he'd hired, and then nodded. 'Yes, that's right. Her name is Starling. Why? What's wrong with her?' he demanded in sudden, sharp alarm. 'She had excellent references, I checked.'

His friend chuckled. 'I have no doubt she does. And she cooks like an angel as well, or so I've heard. But that's not what she's famous for. Well, not in our circles anyway.'

'Oh?' Julius said stiffly. 'Don't tell me I've got something else to worry about besides some fool of a taxidermist getting himself bumped off on college premises. Oh Lord, she's not some sort of Madame Whiplash is she?'

'No such luck, duckie! And was the stiff really a taxidermist? I love it!' Michael said, suddenly distracted. 'Can't you just see all the tabloid puns? Dead Stuffed. I mean, it's a headline-writer's dream.'

Julius shuddered. 'Michael, please! I'm glad you're enjoying this, but I'm the one in charge here, and the buck stops with me. And everyone knows that I'm really the one running St Bede's, and with most of my staff away for the summer, I'm just left with that fool Arthur McIntyre to help me sort things out.'

'OK, OK, keep your hair on, old son. I'm just saying, having your Jenny Starling on hand is a stroke of luck. You always were a jammy sod, Julius,' the friend said enviously, no doubt remembering past misdemeanours which had left Julius untouched. Then, when there continued to be an ominous, if not downright Arctic silence from the other end of the line, he reluctantly concluded that he'd had his fun for the day. 'Look, Jenny Starling is well known in some circles as a bit of a sleuth.'

'A sleuth?' Julius repeated, his voice for once rising an octave.

'Yes. You know, an amateur solver of crimes. Really, old son, you need to get yourself a better dictionary,' Michael said sardonically. 'Anyway, apparently, she's helped the police catch killers on numerous occasions. Not that either she or the police force involved will admit to it of course: They keep it very much to themselves, and the lady herself has never given an interview. But still, we in the Press get to hear about such things, and a number of my colleagues on rival rags have reported on her. She's quite the Miss Marple it seems.'

'How very Agatha Christie,' Julius said drily.

'No, I mean it, Julius. If I were you, I'd get her on side and ask her to be your eyes and ears. You won't regret it. Trust me.'

Julius sighed. Just how much *did* he trust Michael? Not much, if truth be told. He rather thought Michael had always fancied him, but the rotund, beer-drinking, piggy-eyed, fourth son of a baronet had never been his type. But, Julius had to admit, he knew his stuff, and his job as a high-prestige reporter for one of the better papers, proved it.

'Really? I must say, I find that rather surprising.' He thought back to his interview with the cook, then added thoughtfully. 'Having said that, however, she is a rather impressive individual.'

'Yes, I've heard that too,' Michael said drolly. 'Do

you think you could get her to let me have an exclusive interview?'

Julius Glover-Smythe said something very unprintable and hung up. A moment later, there came a knock at the door, and he called out irritably, 'Come in.'

He sighed as Art McIntyre came nervously into the room. He looked apologetic, but then he nearly always did. He reminded Julius of a dog that expected to be kicked, and so, perversely, that's what he always felt like doing. Unfortunately, it had been Julius's predecessor who had hired him, and now Julius was stuck with him. The man would have been perfectly acceptable as a secretary or clerk, but he simply didn't have the gumption or the brains to help manage such a large and stately enterprise as St Bede's.

Unfortunately, for now, Julius had no other choice but to work around him.

Julius hid another heavy sigh, and said flatly, 'Ah, Art. Come in and sit down. We seem to have something of a situation and I'm going to need your help.'

Art nodded solemnly, then went pale as the bursar filled him in on that morning's events.

'So, what can you tell me about these people?' the bursar concluded sharply. He hadn't mentioned his friend's suggestion about the cook, and didn't intend to. He wasn't sure yet what he intended to do with Michael's unexpected suggestion that she be his intermediary, but instinct told him that the less people who knew about her, the better.

'They're perfectly normal clients, Bursar,' Art said, and quickly racked his brains for all that he knew. 'They paid in advance of course, and we did all the preliminary checks. Their society has been going for over a hundred and fifty years. Their speciality is a little, well, unorthodox perhaps for most people's tastes, but there were no red flags at all that I could see.'

'Their cheque cleared all right?'

'Oh yes, Bursar.'

'And you've observed nothing…odd about them?'

'Well, I haven't really seen much of them, Bursar. They only started arriving yesterday.'

'Hmm. And they're really taxidermists, are they?' Julius said, as if wishing he could suddenly turn them into something less outlandish. Like naturalists, or flat-earth believers.

'Yes, Bursar, I'm afraid so,' Art said miserably. He opened his mouth to point out that it was the bursar himself who had the final say on allocating the conference openings, and must thus have deemed the taxidermists to be of a calibre suitable to the college's requirements of its conference clientele. But then, mercifully, he had a sudden, instinctive flash of self-preservation that made him concede that now would probably not be a diplomatic time to say so.

'All right. Well, get yourself up to hall and talk to the chap in charge there. That's an Inspector Trevor Golder, apparently. Tell him that I want that body out of the college as soon as possible. And gather the scouts together and warn them not to talk to the Press. Anyone giving an interview can expect to lose their job.'

'Yes, Bursar,' Art said miserably. He wasn't sure that was legal, was it? Trust the jurisprudence dons to be gadding about all over the globe just when he could do with consulting them.

'You dealt with this man Raines,' Julius said sharply. 'How did he seem to you?'

'Actually, I dealt more with Mrs Voight, the society's treasurer, Bursar. And that was primarily by email.'

'Hmm. All right, Arthur,' Julius said, clearly dissatisfied. 'Let me know how things progress. Oh, and when you get the chance, tell the new cook that I'd like to see her as soon as possible.'

Art blinked, but nodded and left quickly. Outside, in the ancient corridor, he began to sweat, despite the cool thickness of the walls.

Maurice Raines. He'd known that the man was trouble the moment he'd set eyes on him. Luckily, however, he couldn't have made good on his threat to talk to the bursar, or else the interview he'd just had with Julius would have gone very differently indeed.

Art fumbled in his trouser pocket for a handkerchief, and quickly wiped his face. At least, with the man dead, his dangerous tongue would be still as well. Unless he'd made some sort of written notes. With a quick furtive look around, Art scurried over to the residential block where he knew Maurice Raines had been allocated a room.

Unfortunately, the murder victim's room had already been sealed by blue-and-white police tape, and Art suspected that there were probably already police officers inside making a search.

Art had never missed an episode of Morse, so it didn't come as a total surprise. Shoulders slumped, the little man set about doing the bursar's bidding.

SIMON JENKS SAW the first sign for a turn off to Hayling Island and indicated in plenty of time. His hands were still shaking, and he'd already had to pull over onto the side of the road once in order to be sick. Now his stomach still roiled, but since he'd already lost his breakfast, he fought back the desire to dry-heave and took long, slow breaths instead.

Only one thought, so far, had been rattling around in his panic-stricken mind. *He had to get to the hotel and ask Laura just what the hell was going on.*

But now he began to wonder. Should he just get directions for the nearest police station and go straight there and tell them everything?

Simon nibbled nervously on his bottom lip. Would they believe his story? It seemed so thin and lame, even to his own ears.

And what if it had all been some giant mistake? Or a gag, maybe?

But even as his heart leapt in sudden hope, he knew he was just fooling himself. He was in deep, deep trouble, and for the first time in his life, he wasn't sure of the best way to get himself out of it.

He'd always known that in this life you had to take care of number one. Nobody else was ever going to do it for you, were they? But what was the best way of doing that now?

Laura had to hold the key. She was the one responsible for this somehow. She had to be.

But why had she done this to him? He could have sworn the woman was truly in love with him. Beautiful still, wealthy and desperately middle-aged and longing for one last chance of a great romance, she was everything he'd wanted and needed at this point in his life.

And he'd been making her happy, he was sure of that.

This just didn't make sense, he thought with a growing sense of frustration now. None of it made sense. And until he had a better idea of what was going on, he had to put off going to the police. The more he knew, the better a position he would be in to get out of this whole mess.

It might even still be possible, after all, to save something from the wreckage. If Laura had a plan in mind, or answers that made sense.

Into his mind flitted the image of the Oxford college. Beautiful stonework, leafy green gardens. But then....

He shook his head, and the images, away. That way lay panic and desperation. He had to keep a clear head. He had to think.

And if he had to toss Laura to the wolves in order to save his own skin, then of course, that's what he'd do.

Up ahead, the signpost told him that he was only ten miles from his destination. He began to pray that Laura would have an explanation. That somehow, despite how things looked, there was a way out for him.

It had been a long time since Simon Jenks had prayed that hard.

PETER TRENT HAD found the JCR easily on the ground floor of one of the larger residential buildings. It looked like a cross between something like a boating or sports club, a town pub, and an old-fashioned gentlemen's reading room.

The room itself was large, and stuffed with odd bits of furniture that the college probably didn't want elsewhere. There was a long, fully functioning bar along the back wall, and a vast fireplace that looked as if it would be worth a fortune in a reclamation yard, on the facing wall. In between were three pairs of French windows leading out to a croquet lawn. Solid wooden tables with buttoned leather armchairs were scattered around the room, with one wall dedicated to bookcases and their various tomes.

At the moment however, it was full of people standing about with plates of party food and holding pints of beer, and all agog at the news that Peter and his two young colleagues had brought. So far the consensus between the police officers was that the majority of people seemed to be either amazed or uneasily excited, rather than shocked. And nobody seemed to be feeling a particular sense of sorrow or loss.

'So, you were there when Mr Raines unveiled the stuffed bear,' Peter said. It was his fifth quick interview of that lunchtime, and he was getting more or less the same answers from everybody.

'That's right. He had it in a crate. Impressive specimen.' The interviewee, a woman in her late sixties, nibbled a rather soggy-looking salmon canapé.

'And when was the last time you saw Mr Raines, madam?'

'Oh, about half past eleven or so. I'd finished setting up my table, and he chivvied me and George about not missing the free lunch down here. George, that's my husband, made some joke about there being no such thing as a free lunch and we came away.'

Peter nodded. A few of his other interviewees had said much the same thing. He'd have to check with the two uniforms, but he was beginning to get the impression that the victim himself had been intent on having the hall to himself for some reason or other.

Like Jenny Starling, he too had noticed that there had been two cups of coffee on the table next to the body. He was beginning to think that maybe Maurice Raines had been meeting someone, and wanted to have a little privacy whilst he did so. He'd have to put his theory to Trevor when he had a minute.

He thanked the sixty-something, who was now tucking in to a little sausage roll, and wandered over to one of the uniforms. A few quick words confirmed his thoughts, he told them to carry on, and then went back upstairs to find his guv'nor.

Trevor Golder was still in the corridor outside the entrance to hall, but now there was a little, balding man with him. Over the top of the newcomer's head, he saw Trevor catch sight of his approach, and raised a querying eyebrow. Was he to approach, or give his boss some time alone with the new witness?

'Ah, Sergeant,' Trevor said, beckoning him over, 'this is Mr McIntyre, the assistant bursar. Mr McIntyre, Sergeant Trent.'

'Sir,' Trent said politely.

'Mr McIntyre was just wondering when the body was going to be removed,' Trevor said, deadpan, 'and I was just explaining to him that it'll probably be a few hours yet. Our forensics people have to give us the go-ahead first, Mr McIntyre.'

'Yes, I see,' Art responded unhappily, and looked again at Jenny Starling. He'd been surprised to see the new cook sitting down in the inspector's company, and he was mindful of Julius's edict. 'Miss Starling, Dr Glover-Smythe would like to see you as soon as possible.'

'Miss Starling will be along shortly,' Trevor said, with a gentle smile. 'But since we have you here, Mr McIntyre, what can you tell us about the deceased?'

'Mr Raines? Nothing,' Art squeaked in surprise. 'I mean, we had correspondence with the society, naturally, but I talked mostly over the telephone with Mrs Voight.'

'But you'd met Mr Raines?' Trevor pressed.

Art's pulse rate rocketed. 'Oh, only in passing. To say hello to. I saw him last night, after dinner, I think. But only to say hello to.'

Trevor smiled briefly. The little man was almost jumping with nerves. But was that due to anything in particular, or was he just naturally a little manic?

Jenny was wondering much the same thing, although having been interviewed by him, was more inclined to think that it was more a crisis of nerves than anything else. But then, as she knew only too well, in a situation like this, who could ever really say?

Certainly, she could think of no reason why the assistant bursar of St Bede's would want to kill a relative stranger. Surely, the inspector would be looking for the killer primarily amongst the society members themselves? Didn't statistics prove that most people were killed either by their family members, friends or personal acquaintances?

Trevor, who was also wondering why Art should be so nervous, nodded at Peter Trent. 'If you could just give my sergeant your particulars, Mr McIntyre, we won't keep you. Or you either, Miss Starling. I dare say you'll be wanting to go and see Dr Glover-Smythe.' And made a mental note to find out just who he was when he was at home.

Jenny, who had no real desire to find out what it was the bursar wanted, smiled stiffly, and rose to her feet. Her height, at something close on to six feet, took Trevor by surprise, but he was careful not to show it.

'If you don't mind, madam, I have a WPC standing

by. It would be very helpful if you wouldn't mind going back to your room and changing your clothes first. We need them for forensic evidence. To rule you out of the investigation, that is.' He said it politely, as a request, but they both knew it was no such thing.

'Of course,' Jenny said, without rancour. They probably want to check for blood spatter, she thought. Whoever had stuck a fleshing tool into Maurice Raines's neck must have got blood on them, surely?

'Then you can go about your normal business, I think,' Trevor said congenially.

'Thank you, Inspector,' Jenny said, somewhat drily, smiled briefly at the still perspiring Art, and then joined the WPC who was waiting for her at the end of the corridor.

Trevor watched her go, listened as his sergeant took down his notes from Art McIntyre, then shook hands with him and watched him leave also.

The little man looked very happy to be going.

'Bit jumpy, the little bald chap, isn't he?' Peter noted neutrally.

'Yes. What did you learn from the group in the JCR?'

Succinctly, but leaving out nothing relevant, Peter Trent filled him in on what he'd been told, and what he surmised.

'The coffee cups? Yes, I noticed those too. Forensics have taken a sample for testing, naturally. But from what I could see, they hadn't been drunk from. With a bit of luck though, we might get some worthwhile fingerprint evidence from them. You think the vic had arranged to meet someone there?'

Peter Trent nodded. 'According to a fair number of the stallholders, it was Raines himself who made sure that they were all out and gone, by the very latest at around about twenty to twelve. Why would he do that unless he was expecting someone?'

'Hmm. And whoever he arranged to meet killed him.'

'Could be.'

'Make sure and ask the scouts if any of them served the victim with the coffee. I rather think, though, that Maurice Raines, or perhaps his killer, made the stuff themselves in the little kitchenette just off there.' He nodded to a door opposite. 'I've asked forensics to check it out when they're finished at the main crime scene.'

'OK, guv. You have something in particular you want to do?'

Trevor nodded. 'Perhaps. I'm going back to the station for a half an hour or so. I want to run a trace on our very helpful first-finder. There's something about her attitude that's niggling away at me.'

The sergeant nodded knowingly. The people who discovered bodies were always very closely looked at, in any investigation. Often the killer took the chance on reporting the dead body, because they thought that it would account for any forensic evidence they might have left behind. 'Her clothes didn't looked stained to me, guv,' Peter said thoughtfully.

'No. And her shoes were clean as well. But I asked the WPC to make a thorough search of her room after she's changed. Though I doubt, if she is the killer, that our Miss Starling would have been stupid enough to leave her bloodstained clothing in her room for us to find. But it has to be done. We'll also need to get search warrants for the public areas of the college. I'd like to get a warrant to search each and every conference

attendee's room as well, but I doubt we'd find a judge
to go along with that.'

Peter nodded gloomily. 'So what do you want me to
do next, guv?'

'Call in some more manpower. I want to know where
every member of the Society of Stuffers were between
eleven-thirty, when we have plenty of witnesses who
saw our vic alive and well, and twelve noon, by which
time we know he's dead.'

'Guv,' Peter sighed. 'That's a lot of timelines.'

'Yes it is, Sergeant, so you'd better get cracking,'
Trevor said, with little sympathy, but a wide grin.

IAN GLENDOWER LOOKED up from the table where his
class were busy practising his preferred treatment for
moleskins, and glanced at the clock. He was surprised
to see that it was nearly one o'clock, and time for the
lunch break.

He looked around and scowled when he failed to
find Pippa's lovely face gazing back at him from anywhere in the room.

He'd been allocated, in the same building as hall, a
large, pleasant room for his first lesson/lecture, which
was clearly used as a residential room for a student
in term time. But it had a usefully large square table,
with plenty of light coming in from the sash windows,
and so had been just right to accommodate both himself and the half-a-dozen or so newbies who'd signed
up for his lecture.

At first he'd grumbled about it, but, in fact, it had
turned out to be quite a satisfying experience, with none
of the pupils ever having handled the exquisite mole
pelts before. He'd started off by giving a quick lecture

on the use of moleskin in fashion—not strictly in a taxi-dermist's remit that, but it proved that he was a Renais-sance man—before demonstrating how best to go about preserving such a luxurious hide before mounting it on a plaster cast of a mole.

There had been a time whilst he was demonstrating how best to get a perfect finish during the mounting process, when everyone had been gathered around in a tight, rapt circle, making him feel a bit like a magician demonstrating his powers. And he was sure that one of the two girls in the group rather fancied him, not that he was interested of course.

All of which meant that the time had simply flown by and Pippa, damn her, had taken advantage of his ab-sorption to sneak off. Perhaps she was pouting because he hadn't been paying much attention to her, he mused. She could be remarkably jealous and petty sometimes. But he didn't really mind that, since it only proved that she was much more needy than most people thought. Strangers saw only her big baby blue eyes, her long, luscious hair and gorgeous figure, and assumed that she was confident and hard-bitten. It made him feel protective of her to know differently.

He dismissed the class, who actually seemed reluc-tant to leave, which soothed his somewhat battered ego a little more, and smilingly promised them that the af-ternoon's session, when they actually got to make a tab-leau with the pelts, would be even better.

Once they'd gone, he left the makeshift classroom quickly and walked back to his own room. He was so sure that it would be empty, and that Pippa would be absent for the rest of the day just to teach him a lesson, that when he burst in and Pippa looked up at him from the bed, he stopped dead on the threshold. He stared at her blankly for a moment, then slowly walked in and shut the door behind him.

Pippa looked up from the magazine she'd been reading, her face blank and innocent. 'Well, finally,' she said. 'I thought you'd *never* finish. Listen, Ian, you're never gonna believe what's happened.' She sat up, cross-legged on the bed, and irritably swept off a long lock of hair from her cheek.

Ian opened his mouth to ask her where she'd been, when Pippa carried on, 'Maurice Raines is dead. Someone's actually *killed* him. Can you believe it? There are coppers swarming all over hall.'

Ian, aware that he was still standing there with his mouth open like a gaping fish, snapped his jaws shut and then frowned. 'Are you having me on?'

'No, honest.'

'Maurice is dead?'

Her beautiful, large blue eyes watched him carefully. 'Ian, you haven't done anything daft, have you?' she asked, sliding to the side of the bed now and standing up in one lithe sinuous movement. She nonchalantly ran her hand along the top of the bedside table, as if checking for dust, but he could see her watching him from beneath her lowered lashes.

Ian stared at her. 'No! What do you mean?'

Pippa laughed, a shade uncertainly, he thought, and made a show of dusting off her hands. 'Oh, you know.' She shrugged one shoulder prettily. 'You know how you are sometimes.'

His face hardened. 'No. Just how am I?' he challenged.

Pippa sighed. 'Well, all intense. Like you are now, in

fact,' she pointed out, putting her hands on her hips. 'My mum always says to be careful of you, 'cause you're so thin-skinned, and you know she's right. You always do seem to feel things more than anybody else. I mean, the things that other people just shrug off, you seem to take to heart and brood on. You must know that's true. You get het up about things that are like water off a duck's back to the rest of us. Come on, Ian, you know you do,' she cajoled, laughing lightly.

But he could feel the weight of her gaze, measuring him, and he felt suddenly vulnerable.

Ian flushed. 'I can't let things pass me by, that's all. Not if it's something I care about. I think people are too damned apathetic half the time, and that's just not me.'

'Exactly,' Pippa said, walking slowly towards him. 'That's just what I'm talking about. And you didn't like Maurice, did you? And with this tiger-stuffing thing coming up, you were getting really hot under the collar when you thought he was hinting that he wouldn't let you near it.'

Ian went pale as he suddenly realized just what she was getting at. 'Just what the hell are you saying, Pip?' he asked gruffly.

'Well, someone killed Maurice, didn't they? You know you can tell me, Ian. If—'

Ian Glendower began to laugh. He couldn't help it. He reached for her, pulled her into his arms and kissed her soundly. Pippa's nails dug slightly into his shoulders and she felt a little stiff in his arms. When he pulled back his head to look down into her beautiful face, he laughed again and then shook his head in exaggerated bemusement.

'You really are a silly little twit sometimes, Pip,'

he murmured with tender exasperation. 'How could I have killed Maurice? I went straight from hall, where he was alive and well, and then met my class, where I've been ever since; in front of six or so impeccable witnesses who can swear that I never left the room! How on earth could I have bumped off the horrible little man? With the aid of telekinesis, or some sort of voodoo magic maybe?'

Pippa's face cleared, and she giggled in that delightful way she had that always made Ian feel like giggling right along with her. 'Right—'course you were!' She gave herself a playful head-slap. 'And I was there too, so you've got seven witnesses. We're all of us OK, even your students, because we've all got alibis!'

'Exactly,' Ian said, his eyes glittering just slightly. 'So, now we've got all that sorted, what say we do something much more interesting?'

He nudged her back suggestively towards the bed, and this time, when Pippa's arms came around his shoulders, it was in order to hug him tightly and again she gave a little giggle.

VICKI VOIGHT, SITTING in a viewing room with five others, glanced through the darkened gloom to check her watch. Surely it must be lunchtime by now?

They were watching the lecture screen, where a scene depicting the skinning of a baby seal in full white winter coat was being shown in graphic detail. The team of taxidermists involved had been hired to produce a tableau for a winter show in a mid-west American museum, and clearly knew their stuff.

Vicki wondered, cynically, what the chances were that their society would ever be asked to do such a large and interesting tableau, and decided that, Maurice's tigers aside, the likelihood had to be very slim.

Still, she'd certainly never seen such a marine animal being worked on before and, although she'd found it informative, the novelty was rapidly wearing off. Besides, she was hungry. A friend who knew Oxford had given her the names of a few good places for lunch, and she was looking forward to trying them out. Preferably with a man, if she could find one.

Although she was married, the spark had long since gone, and her husband back at home had probably decided that while the cat was away the mice would play, so why shouldn't she do the same?

Surely she could find some suitable male in a city the size of Oxford, who was interested in a quick dalliance, with no holds barred? After all, wasn't that the philanderer's dream come true?

Finally, the film came to an end and the owner of it thanked them for watching. Vicki, along with the others, made a charge for the door only to find two uniformed constables waiting for them. It soon became clear that they wanted name, rank and serial number, plus a brief statement as to their movements from 11.30 to 12 noon and Vicki, as treasurer, quickly took the lead.

'What's this all about, Constable,' she asked loudly of the one who looked marginally older than his companion.

'Just routine, madam,' he said mildly.

Vicki snorted. 'Don't give us that. We'll find out eventually anyway,' she pointed out realistically, and caught the eye of several society members, who nodded encouragement. 'Has there been a theft?' she asked sharply.

This set off a murmur of worry amongst the others,

who all began to agitate to be allowed back to their rooms to check on their belongings. They became so restive, in fact, that the PC was obliged to impose a little authority.

'I'm sorry, but we need to take down your names and addresses. I'm afraid there's been a fatality.'

The word brought an abrupt silence to the little throng.

'Who's dead?' Vicki was annoyed to find that her voice was wavering, and coughed, and tried again, this time with some authority in her tone. 'Is it someone from our society, or from the college?'

'I really do need to get statements from you all as to your whereabouts from eleven thirty until twelve.' The constable tried again to avoid answering.

'Well that's easy, we were all here,' Vicki quickly spoke for everyone. 'After Maurice's opening speech, those of us who had elected to watch the seal tableau came straight here. The film was due to start at eleven, and we were all in our seats by then, and it's only just ended, as you can see for yourselves.'

'I see. And it's like a sort of mini-cinema in there, is it?' the constable, who was nobody's mug, asked blandly, peering over her shoulder at the now shut door.

'Yes. There's about seating for twenty, and a cinema screen. Go ahead and check it out for yourself,' Vicki offered, although she had no doubt that they would be doing that anyway.

'And the lights were dimmed for the duration of the showing?' the canny constable asked again.

'Yes, that's right,' Vicki said, perplexed for a moment about what could possibly be the significance of that, before she caught on. 'But the entrance is situated in the front of the room, and if anyone had left, the light from outside flooding through the opening would have been clearly visible to the rest of us, Constable, I assure you. None of us sneaked out at any time.'

'Perhaps to use the loo?'

'I don't think so,' Vicki said thoughtfully, casting a quick look around. Five heads shook in negative and she nodded. 'No, we've all got remarkably well-behaved bladders, apparently.'

Somebody at the back giggled nervously.

The young man sighed, then brightened. 'But there must be a fire exit though, probably a door at the back. Fire regulations state they must be kept unlocked.'

Vicki nodded. 'I would imagine so. But if it's like most fire exit doors that I know, it'll be heavy and noisy and hard to push open, and I doubt very much that anyone could have sneaked out without us all hearing.'

The constable nodded, but silently vowed to check it out for himself once he'd got all their details. Just to be sure.

When they'd all given their names, addresses, daytime landline numbers and mobile phone numbers, they were allowed to leave. The others, discussing it avidly amongst themselves, went off in a group towards the gatehouse, and the exit onto Woodstock Road, and thence to town, but Vicki, her rumbling tummy forgotten, headed straight for hall. She needed to see just what was going on, and what the damage might be.

But she wasn't, at that point, particularly worried. She knew she had no reason to be.

The constables immediately checked out the viewing room for themselves, of course, but even the elder of the two had to admit that the fire door *was* heavy and noisy, and creaked loudly when it was pushed open. Furthermore, no matter how many times he tried to open the door, either quick and fast, or slow and sneaky, it always made a racket.

But perhaps the noise of the film had been loud enough to cover it? Should he ask for it to be run again, so that he could hear for himself, or would Inspector Golder think it a waste of time? On the other hand, he might give him credit for showing some initiative. This was his first murder case, and he wanted to get noticed and make a good impression on the top brass. That was the way to promotion, after all. Trouble was, it was hard to tell which way the DI would jump. Perhaps he'd be better off mentioning it to Sergeant Trent. He seemed like a decent bloke who'd give credit where it was due.

'Funny, she never pushed to know who was dead,' his mate said, interrupting his line of thought. His companion had only been on the job for a few months, and was inclined to be still a bit wet behind the ears. 'She seemed the autocratic sort to me. I've got an aunt just like her. I was expecting her to give you a much harder time over it,' he admitted.

The older one was about to slap him down, but then, grudgingly, realized that he had a point. 'Yeah, she didn't really seem all that curious, did she?' he said thoughtfully.

FIVE

'AND, OF COURSE, it's just our luck that's there no CCTV worth having,' Peter Trent said. It was nearly six o'clock that evening, and the assistant bursar had loaned the police the use of a lecture room for their operations. A full-scale murder inquiry was underway, a press liaison officer had been seconded to deal with the media, and the room was full with busy people setting up computers and extra phone lines, and—most importantly of all—a coffee post. Some hero had managed to get several coffee percolators and a can of good grade coffee beans from the kitchen. The sergeant knew that the big and oddly beautiful cook had been behind that, but he let the constable who'd come back with the booty get all the credit.

They'd been in contact with their counterparts in Yorkshire, and had been informed that although Maurice Raines's children had been found and informed by a family liaison officer, Mrs Raines was absent from the family home. It was a glitch that Trevor could have done without, but his colleagues up north had done their homework, and had reported that the neighbours weren't particularly surprised or worried by her absence. As one old biddy had put it, once the husband was away, the wife liked to play.

Which was an intriguing bit of information, and one he had sent two members of his team to follow up. It was just a pity that the helpful neighbours were unable to point them in any specific direction.

Laura Raines, it seemed, was a lady who knew the value of discretion.

'No CCTV at all?' Trevor said now, taking a sip of coffee from his mug.

'Only on the outer perimeters of the college,' Peter Trent confirmed. 'Which makes sense, when you think about it. They're interested in trouble from the outside, rather than within.'

'That's typical of a bloody college,' Trevor said grimly, draining his mug and slamming it down on the desk top. Even though he'd put in much longer days than this, and then some, he was feeling oddly tired. Perhaps it was because he was already beginning to sense that this was going to be a dog of a case. 'Were we dealing with your average Joe attacked and murdered on the streets, chances are we'd have it all on film—or if not the actual crime, some valuable peripheral evidence showing us the faces of potential witnesses maybe. But die in the hallowed halls of an Oxford college, and no way does anything useful get recorded. I blame bloody Morse.'

He said this last with a wry twist of his lips, just to show that he wasn't really serious, and Peter shrugged. He knew when he was needed to play devil's advocate and did so now.

'You can't really blame them for not having any cameras inside though, guv, can you?' he pointed out reasonably. 'I mean, students and fellows alike live here, not just work here. And nobody wants to know that Big Brother is watching if you slip out in the middle of the night to go to the loo. Or worse, tiptoe along the corridors to somebody else's door, that you shouldn't be tiptoeing along to. If you see what I mean.'

Trevor did. Only too well. He sighed. 'It's not just that. It's…' At that moment, there was a momentary hiatus in the room, that sudden dimming of conversation and cessation of movement that only happened when something has attracted attention, and Trevor turned to look as Jennifer Starling paused in the doorway.

At nearly six feet tall, with her longish almost black hair and that unfashionable but undeniably eye-catching hourglass figure that she possessed, he was not surprised that her presence hadn't gone unnoticed.

With another sigh, he rose from his chair and nodded to his sergeant to follow him. He approached the Junoesque cook with a gimlet-eyed smile. 'Ah, Miss Starling, thank you for coming.'

Jenny smiled back briefly. When summoned by the police, she didn't really see that anybody had any other option but to obey, but she appreciated his manners nonetheless.

'Not at all, Inspector Golder. I'm only too glad to do anything to help. But,' she glanced at her watch meaningfully, 'dinner is at seven-thirty and as it is the main meal of the day, I really need to be in the kitchens. I'm serving trout and apricot in aspic that can't be left unsupervised for long, or it won't set properly.'

'I don't intend to keep you long. We just need to get a few things straight.' He led her to a small side-room, which was obviously used as a makeshift kitchenette for the lecture room. Peter Trent found a small cupboard to lean up against, whilst his boss put his back to a small, chipped, white porcelain sink. Jenny stood in the centre of the room between them, feeling a bit like the filling in a sandwich.

Since she had no intention of turning her head to look at first one of them and then the other, like a demented spectator at a tennis match, she fixed her gaze firmly on the inspector and waited. She suspected that he'd chosen this arrangement precisely to wage some sort of psychological warfare, and she was in no mood to play silly buggers. Even if he did suspect her of murder, she had a fig and nut salad to prepare.

'I've been doing some digging on you, Miss Starling,' Trevor said, and watched as her shoulders, previously straight and attractively set, slumped just a little. A look of annoyance and consternation was quickly followed by one of resignation. She held out a weary hand and waved it vaguely in his direction.

'Let me stop you right there, Inspector,' she said. 'In spite of what you may have been told, I don't and never have intended to interfere with a police investigation. I don't consider myself a Father Brown, or a Lovejoy, or any other type of amateur sleuth you care to name. I just want to cook.'

'I'm pleased to hear it, Miss Starling,' Trevor said smoothly, feeling for the first time that this might not be as bad as he'd first thought. When he'd filled in Peter Trent on just who their cook was, they'd both been filled with misgivings. Nearly all of the top brass had heard Jennifer Starling's name mentioned in the recent past. She'd been mixed up in several murder cases before, but had always been on the side of the angels. Well, at least, as much as could be expected under the circumstances. Nobody in the police service liked members of the public getting involved in what was not their business, but at least she'd never tried to publicize her involvement, or gain from it financially.

And, having spent the best part of over an hour talking to the coppers on the previous cases where she'd been involved, he was willing to give her the grudging benefit of the doubt. His fellow senior investigating officers' reports on her had been mixed, of course, just as you'd expect when talking to a lot of different people with different personalities and their own axes to grind. And, although a few had been less than impressed and somewhat scathing in their assessment of her, even they had had to admit that she'd had her uses. Others had openly admitted to their admiration for her intelligence. But all had been of the opinion that she was, overall, more of a use than a hindrance.

When he'd relayed all of this to his sergeant, a man whose experience and common sense he valued, they'd discussed it at length, and had finally agreed to play things by ear. This initial interview with the hot potato that was Jenny Starling, was the opening gambit in what he hoped wouldn't be a long drawn out process.

So far, anyway, he liked what he was hearing, and to be fair, all of the officers he'd talked to about her had admitted that she had been reluctant, but helpful, in the pursuit of their inquiries. They'd all expressed the same belief that in talking to people and nosing out the lie of the land around her, she was exceptional. As one of them had put it, 'what people won't say to a copper, they'll say to her. And if she thinks it's relevant, she'll pass it on to us.'

Trevor had caught the significant part of that sentence at once. And if Miss Starling didn't think it was relevant, she'd keep it to herself, he'd mentally added.

Still, all in all, Trevor was feeling optimistic. 'All right, Miss Starling, let's not beat about the bush. You have form...that is, you have experience at this sort of thing—'

'Not by choice, that's for sure,' Jenny muttered mutinously. She'd just finished talking to the bursar, and was feeling resentful. Why did she have to get mixed up in all this? She was not the police, and she wouldn't blame Inspector Golder for reading her the riot act if she started putting her nose in. Besides, she'd only been employed at St Bede's for a matter of days and it was only a summer-long job anyway. What loyalty did she really owe them?

On the other hand, someone had murdered Maurice Raines, and that was just not on, no matter how you looked at it.

'The bursar's asked me to keep an eye on things,' she admitted stiffly, and looked up in time to see a flash of anger cross the inspector's face. 'I know,' she agreed glumly, 'that's just how I felt too. But—' She shrugged helplessly—'If I don't keep him in the loop, you'll have to. Or worse, he'll bully poor old Art McIntyre into doing it.'

At the thought of the little assistant bursar constantly appearing at his shoulder, with his fussy, ineffectual little ways, Trevor gave a mental shudder. No, it was by far better to have Jenny Starling in that role. At least he could be reasonably sure how far he could trust her. There'd be no leaks to the Press, and if some of the suspects confided in her, or she picked up the odd bit of gossip, what harm could it do? Besides, Trevor was canny enough to know that his chances of solving the case had to be better with her on his side, than pitched against him.

'OK, fine. But let's get some ground rules straight,' Trevor Golder said, catching his sergeant's eye to see what he was making of this. Slowly, Peter Trent gave a nod of unspoken agreement.

'First of all, anything you learn or discover, and I mean *anything*,' Golder stressed sternly, 'you bring straight to me. I don't care if you think it's relevant or important, I want to know about it.'

'Agreed,' Jenny said. 'I've never kept anything back from the police, and I don't intend to.' Then she thought back for a moment, and gave a mental wince. Well, perhaps she'd been tight-lipped about certain things, but only things that weren't the police's business, and had no bearing on the crime. She certainly didn't intend to become Golder's spy, mindlessly reporting back on everything she might learn. Had she been the superstitious sort, she would have crossed her fingers at that point, but since she wasn't, she simply met Detective Inspector Golder's gimlet gaze and smiled sweetly.

'Secondly, I want your word you won't discuss anything about the case with anyone else. And I'm not just talking about to reporters, but to anyone else either. Not your friends, and not your family. You keep it firmly zipped,' he added, patting his own lips in order to reinforce his point.

'Oh, that goes without saying,' Jenny said instantly. It was truly fine by her: she'd always been able to keep confidences and secrets, and preferred to keep things to herself anyway. Besides, who was she going to tell? Then she thought of the sexy and still unclaimed James Raye and felt a brief stab of regret that she wouldn't be able to be as open and honest with him as she preferred to be with her men.

Then she gave a mental shrug. Ah well, you couldn't have everything in life, after all.

'All right. Finally, I want to know what your thoughts and theories are, as and when you're thinking them,' Trevor said, mindful that more than one or two of his predecessors had mentioned Jenny Starling's annoying habit of quick thinking, which was not always shared with them.

Jenny blinked, surprised by the last request. 'OK,' she said carefully, drawing out the two letters uncertainly. 'But won't that be a bit distracting? I mean, I'm a messy thinker; my mind tends to come up with and discard all sorts of theories. If you really want me to tell you everything, you'll probably be begging me to shut up before the day's out.'

'Just give me the highlights,' Golder said sardonically.

Jenny shrugged. 'Fine, but if you want me to theorize, you're going to have to keep me informed to some extent. You know what they say—data in, data out.'

Golder smiled grimly. 'Sure. I'll tell you what I feel comfortable letting you know.'

Jenny suddenly grinned. She couldn't help it. 'Which won't be a whole lot, will it, Inspector?'

Golder grinned back, then slowly subsided against the sink. He hadn't realized until then, just how tense he'd been. 'Not that there's much to tell you at the moment. I was just discussing our lack of evidence with Pete, here, when you came in.'

'Oh?' Jenny said, glancing at the sergeant then back to his superior.

'We've got no CCTV, and the preliminary inter-view reports seem to be suggesting that everyone has an alibi,' Golder said flatly.

Jenny blinked. Whatever she'd been expecting him to say, it certainly hadn't been that. 'What. *Everyone?*'

Golder smiled wearily. 'Well, it's early days yet, I admit. And we haven't got around to questioning all the college staff, that's a job for tomorrow. But as for the conference-goers themselves, yes. You see, the thing is, the timing. We know Maurice Raines had to have been killed between eleven-forty, when he was the last one left alone in hall, and a few minutes to twelve, when you found him. Usually, having such a short time-frame for a murder helps us enormously.'

Jenny could well see how it might. 'Right. But?'

'But in this case, it rules practically everyone from the Great Jessies right out of it. Those who had been in hall all went down to the JCR for the early free lunch. So out they go. They all have multiple witnesses to their whereabouts. The rest all scattered to lectures, film presentations, demonstrations or what-have-you. And all of those involved group activities. Not one of them went off on their own. So you see—'

'Yes,' Jenny said flatly. 'The Great Jessies all have impeccable alibis. Or rather, to be more accurate, I should say that they all alibi each other.' Suddenly she gave a little cry.

'What? You've figured out a way to break the ali-bis?' Trevor asked, startled and wide-eyed.

'What?' Jenny asked, baffled. She had, in fact, just caught sight of her watch. 'No, of course I haven't. I've just realized my paté should have been in the fridge ten minutes ago!'

And with that, she dashed off.

'Oh yeah,' Trevor said, meeting Peter Trent's astounded look. 'They all warned me about that too.'

'What, guv?'

'Miss Starling's first priority is always food, apparently.'

THE NEXT MORNING, Jenny was back in hall for breakfast. The forensics team had still been at work there last night, leaving the college staff to put on dinner as best as they could in the JCR. It hadn't been an ideal arrangement, what with mismatched tables and chairs and less than piping hot food, but the conference-goers had got into the spirit of the makeshift nature of it, in the true Dunkirk spirit.

The SOCOs must have worked through the night to clear the hall for business as usual now she mused, and wondered if the bursar had been bending someone's ear on the need to get back to normality as quickly as possible. She wouldn't put it past Glover-Smythe to have friends in high places. Either way, it was a relief to have the place back in use. Luckily, all traces of the tragedy that had occurred there had now vanished.

She smiled at the scout standing in the doorway who took her order, a tall, motherly-looking woman who seemed to regard Jenny rather too closely for a few seconds. Jenny hesitated, wondering if she wanted a word about something, but when the other woman simply nodded and turned away, she glanced around the large room and saw Golder and Trent seated at a table for four near the back wall, nearest the toilets. No doubt they'd taken the worst table to be both as polite and as unobtrusive as possible. She wondered if the imperious bursar would ever get to know about such scruples, let alone appreciate them, and somehow doubted it.

In a fit of proletariat solidarity she went to join them, noticing that as she did so, the scout who'd taken her order watched her go all the way.

'Inspector. Sergeant.' She indicated the warm sunny weather outside the sash windows. 'What another lovely day it is,' she greeted them warmly. She was always happy to have more people to feed. 'I hope you like the breakfast here. My speciality today is the porridge—it's made the traditional Scottish way, cooked slowly overnight with mainly water, then cream added in the final stages, but I've added a sort of muesli-like undertone with sultanas and raisins soaked in sherry overnight. You have to try it and tell me what you think.'

Trevor, who hadn't eaten porridge since he was a kid, and had vague memories of a glue-like, grey-tinged substance, smiled rather less than enthusiastically. 'Sorry,' he said mendaciously, 'I've already ordered the full English.'

'Me too,' Peter Trent added hastily.

Jenny, who knew all about men and their ways, smiled sweetly and said that it was no bother, she'd ask a scout to bring them the porridge first. And proceeded to do just that. She had no doubts at all that they'd thank her for it later.

'So, what's new?' she asked brightly, returning to the table and reaching for the coffee pot.

Golder, resigned to the porridge, sighed heavily. 'Not much. The victim's laptop is currently with our computer nerd, who found a few encoded or encrypted files on it, and is currently trying to break in or find the password, or whatever it is that they do with them,' he said, proving himself to be something of a technophobe. 'And we found the victim's mobile phone in his pocket so we've been tracing all his previous calls and text messages. Nothing stands out so far—it's mostly business-related, and the few personal calls were all benign.'

'So no traces of him having an affair or being blackmailed then,' she said matter-of factly.

'No,' Trevor said drily, not sure whether to be amused or shocked by her *savoir-faire*. 'Not so far anyway.'

'I've heard several people mention that he was a bit of a ladies' man,' Jenny said gently.

'Yes, we're getting that vibe too,' Trevor agreed. 'But so far nobody's willing to come out and name names or to point any fingers at their fellow conferencees. Or perhaps he's just been careful not to, er, fish in waters too close to home as it were, and had wisely decided not to look for his extra-marital activities within the Great Jessies.'

'Either that, or he and any of his amours have been very discreet,' Jenny said with a twinkling smile that made Peter Trent hide a quick grin.

Trevor pretended not to notice. Let his sergeant fall for the cook's charm if he so chose. He himself, was going to keep to a strictly professional stance with the lady.

'One thing of note, perhaps,' he continued smoothly, 'we haven't yet been able to trace his wife. Apparently, she's gone off on a little jaunt of her own, whilst her husband was away.'

Jenny caught on at once. 'Oh. They had that sort of a marriage, did they? Let me guess—the kids are grown and out of the nest, and Mrs Raines finally got fed up with Maurice's little peccadilloes and decided that what was good for the goose, etc.'

'Isn't human nature a wonderful thing?' Trevor agreed drily.

As Jenny helped herself to a second cup of coffee, the motherly-looking scout returned with three steaming bowls of porridge. She placed them down gently, her eyes carefully averted, and left.

Jenny watched her go, thoughtfully.

The two men stared down at their bowls and at the glutinous-looking, off-white mess within, then with almost identical long-suffering sighs picked up their spoons and took a taste.

Jenny, who'd come straight from the kitchens, and already knew just how it tasted, watched them with twitching lips. Peter Trent caught her eye first and saluted her with the spoon and promptly tucked in. The inspector made no comment or gesture, but was the first of the three of them to polish off his portion, Jenny noticed, with approval.

Once the porridge was dispatched with all proper reverence, Jenny glanced around the room. Not surprisingly perhaps, their table was the centre of attention, although most of the conference-goers were acting as if they didn't exist.

She could well imagine that the gossip mill was going at full tilt, with everyone having their favourite pet theories, and she was going to make it her business today to talk to as many of them as possible and see which way the consensus was leaning.

'So, I take it the conference is going to go ahead? They're not cancelling it?' she asked, and Trevor nodded quickly.

'Oh yes. I forgot to tell you. I had a word with Mrs Voight yesterday, and told her that I would prefer it if everyone stayed in college for the next few days anyway, and since that was the case, she said that she didn't see why the conference shouldn't go ahead. She's going to make the announcement about it after breakfast, I think.'

'No doubt she'll say something along the lines that that would be what Maurice Raines would have wanted, I should think,' Peter added. 'It's what they usually say in circumstances like this.'

'Whereas, what Maurice Raines would really have wanted and expected was for the world to come to an end and for everyone to weep buckets over him, and not possibly be able to go on,' Jenny said drolly.

'That's how he struck you?' Trevor said, and nodded. 'Yes, that generally seems to be what we were picking up on yesterday. Oh, a lot of them admired him as a taxidermist, apparently. And he had his fans, usually amongst the women. One or two even admitted he was good for the society, but nobody really *liked* him. I doubt that anyone was feeling so cut up about it that they wanted to pack up their bags and go home.'

Jenny sighed. 'Sad, isn't it. Still, you don't get murdered because you're not liked, do you?'

'Not in my experience, no,' Trevor said flatly.

'And whoever did it, presuming it was a Great Jessie,' Jenny mused, 'wouldn't want to stand out from the crowd by kicking up a fuss and demanding that the conference stop, or that they should be free to go home.'

'Nothing so obvious,' Trevor agreed glumly. 'I got the feeling that most of them were either curious or excited about what's happened. One or two seemed a little scared or squirrelly,' he admitted, 'but on questioning them a bit further, it seems that they were more worried that there might be a murdering maniac in their midst. Someone who had it in for taxidermists apparently, and that they might be next on the list, rather than out of any fear of being accused of doing the crime.'

'So, I take it you've come across no real motives yet then?' she asked diffidently. 'I mean, apart from any possible love/sexual jealousy angle, which, let's face it, has hardly been proven yet. The victim's womanizing reputation might just be all idle gossip, or even something that Maurice Raines himself was careful to cultivate.'

But before the policeman could reply, their plates were removed, and the full English was set down in front of them. After that, they all tucked in and conversation waned. Neither police officer was used to being fed like this on the job, and both were more than happy to make the most of it. Eventually however, over toast and orange juice, they got back to business.

'Has it occurred to you just how lucky the killer was to find Maurice alone in the hall? And how lucky they were again, not to be seen or caught?' Jenny mused. 'I mean, why not kill him in his room, late at night, when you could be sure that he was alone and when you could sneak about under cover of darkness without being seen?'

Trevor nodded. 'Yes. We have a theory about that though. According to Mrs Voight, Maurice Raines did several things yesterday that were, shall we say, not really in character.'

'You mean arranging a free meal for all the vendors?' Jenny said. 'Yes, I already know about that.'

'Of course you do,' Trevor said flatly. 'But he also failed to take one of the prime lecture spots for himself. Normally, the first lectures of the conference are the most sought after, apparently, and lecturing at them is where most of the kudos lies. Always before, Maurice's lecture was the most popular of the lot. He may well not have been particularly liked, but everybody admits that he was a top man in his field, and he liked to demonstrate it to all and sundry.'

Jenny's gaze sharpened. 'But not this time?'

'No. This time he gave his spot to someone else.'

Jenny slowly put down her cup. 'So, he arranges for the hall to be empty of the vendors, and that he himself should have his agenda free and clear. He was meeting someone, wasn't he?'

Golder nodded. Well, he'd been warned that this cook was quick. And sharp. And she was clearly going to live up to expectations.

'But who?' Jenny said. 'If, as you say, all the Great Jessies were at lectures and things, who was he planning on meeting? You have checked that everyone was where they said they were, right?'

'Yes, and it's being double-checked right now,' Trevor said sharply, biting back a comment primarily involving grannies and sucking eggs, and nodding instead at the constables who were moving around the room, stopping at every table to have a quick word.

'It has to be a woman, don't you think?' Peter Trent said cautiously. 'I mean, given his rep, and how careful he was to arrange the free time.'

'But not with a Great Jessie apparently,' Jenny said. 'Could it be someone in college? Someone working here? I know from listening to the gossip, that it was

Maurice Raines himself who specifically chose St Bede's,' she said. 'I think a lot of them wanted to go to Edinburgh or somewhere this year.'

'So you're saying that he wanted to be here, specifically here, I mean,' Peter Trent tapped the table, 'for a reason?'

'Could be,' Jenny said cautiously. 'You need to find out if he had any previous contact with the college, or with Oxford maybe. Perhaps he'd just found himself a woman who lived locally, and only needed to be generally geographically close,' Jenny pointed out. 'I mean, the college is open to the public after all. She could just walk in. But then again, if that was the case, surely they'd meet up in his room?'

'Perhaps they intended to,' Trevor said. 'They could have planned to go on to his place from hall. If the woman came in from outside, and didn't know St Bede's well, it might be easier for her to find the hall than one specific room in one of the residential houses. This place is a bit of a maze.'

'Did you find any Oxford numbers on his mobile?' Jenny asked.

'No. Only the college number itself. He phoned Art McIntyre's number several times for instance. But that's not surprising, given that he was fixing it up to have his conference here, and that McIntyre is in charge of accommodation and all the arrangements.'

'Right,' Jenny agreed absently. And noticed, once again, that the motherly-looking scout kept shooting curious glances at her as she served at a table nearby. Jenny wondered what it was she wanted, and how important it might be, but she knew better than to try and find that out whilst she had the police in tow.

She reached for the jug of orange juice and thoughtfully poured herself another glass.

AS JENNY SIPPED her orange juice, in a converted Victorian house just off Keble Road, with a pleasant view of Keble College itself, Art McIntyre watched his wife spooning out scrambled eggs from the saucepan onto a dish and sighed.

It was a generously proportioned and spacious flat, and therefore correspondingly expensive, with three bedrooms, a kitchen-diner and large windows throughout, and was mortgaged, of course, up to the hilt. Nor was the nice flat his only expense: his two children seemed to demand and gobble up an ever-increasing amount of cash. Luke, his 10-year-old son, was currently into fencing, and the lessons and equipment needed weren't cheap. And his lovely little Hermione, although only six, was going to be the next great British ballerina, and if Art thought a fencing master was expensive, it was nothing to the fees charged by Madame Nostrova and her dancing academy.

'Do you want two or one?' Barbara, his wife of the last fifteen years, held up the toast freshly burnt from the toaster, and Art smiled weakly. 'Just the one, I think,' he said, ruefully patting his rotund tummy. 'Must try and cut back a bit,' he said, making Hermione giggle.

But the truth was, he didn't have much of an appetite nowadays. Why did life have to be so bloody difficult all the time?

'OK, one it is,' Barbara said cheerfully, and slapped on some butter. Art watched her with a mixture of fondness and exasperation. Barbara was one of those pleasingly plump, pretty women who seemed to find life a breeze. She coped with motherhood as a matter of course, ran the home and her husband with equally benign efficiency and also worked as an assistant librarian at the public library. The income helped out the family finances enormously, but Art also knew that she enjoyed dealing with the public, which was something that had always been beyond him. She coped with life as if it were nothing, whereas Art had always found life to be one long challenging struggle.

It was not that he didn't have brains. He did. He'd trained as an accountant, and he actually liked hard, painstaking work, but somehow, that never seemed to be enough.

Take his job at St Bede's, for instance. He'd been doing it for nearly seven years, and knew it inside and out. And yet, Maurice Raines, even over the telephone, and from a distance of, what, nearly a hundred miles away or more, had managed to make him feel like an incompetent fool. And in person, he was even worse. He'd made Art feel like…well, like strangling him.

He blinked as Barbara put a plate of scrambled egg on toast down in front of him. She then told Hermione that if she didn't stop playing with her cereal—which was fortified with iron—and eat it she'd never grow up to have strong, dancer's legs, and reached for her mobile phone to check something on one of the apps. She barely broke stride to do it either, her husband noticed fondly. Multi-tasking, Art mused. Wasn't that what women were supposed to do so well?

He felt a momentary sense of panic as he wondered what he'd ever do without her. Then he reassured himself that he'd never have to. His Babs would never leave them. She was as solid as a rock.

He watched her frown over something on her mobile, then jumped a little as she called through the open door to tell Luke, still dawdling in his bedroom, that he was going to be late for school if he didn't get a move on. She then moved back to the stove to absent-mindedly make her own breakfast.

Art smiled. Good old Babs. He wondered what a woman with long, curly, blonde hair, dimpled cheeks, and a cuddly figure saw in someone like him. And he felt the usual trickle of unease slide up his spine. What if she found someone else? Once or twice, he'd caught her going out of the house in a little more make-up than she usually used, and smelling of perfume, which she rarely wore. What if she was seeing another man?

Art winced as indigestion stirred in his stomach, and he pushed his plate away with a grimace. He really had to stop thinking the worst all the time. His old mum had always been the same—she wasn't happy if she wasn't worrying about something. No wonder he was worried he might be getting ulcers.

Over by the stove, his wife continued to frown down into her mobile phone.

In St Bede's, Trevor Golder pushed back his chair from the table, and his sergeant took the hint and did likewise. 'Right, we've got a lot to get through.' Trevor reached for his notebook, where he'd made copious lists. One of which was to start chasing up forensics for results.

His lips twitched a little as he wondered what the lovely woman sitting opposite him would say if she knew that he'd prioritized her results first. But after learning who she was and of her reputation, and guessing that he'd have to deal with her in the case one way or another, he'd wanted to be sure. Needless to say, the test results on her clothes had came back negative for blood spatter, and that no trace of a connection between her and their victim had been found. Which meant that, for now, he was ruling her out for the killing of Maurice Raines.

If told, she ought to be relieved, but somehow he wasn't sure that she'd appreciate the preferential treatment. Still, he needed to be sure, and now it meant that she was yet another suspect off the list. Mind you, the inspector thought grimly, it looked as though, if the preliminary results were anything to go by, they'd be wiping absolutely everybody else off the suspect list as well!

He hid a sigh, and made a mental note to get on to forensics first thing. He had a feeling that this case might turn out to rely heavily on the hard, physical evidence.

'Miss Starling, I expect I'll be seeing you later?' he said mildly.

Jenny sighed. 'I expect so.' She really wanted to get back to her kitchen and start planning the evening dinner, but she knew she had to see someone first.

Trevor nodded briskly. Peter Trent winked at her, and the two of them left. When it was quite clear that they'd gone, she turned slowly in her chair and scanned the room. Sure enough, the motherly-looking scout was already approaching her table.

Jenny smiled up at her as she arrived, hoping to put her at her ease. 'Hello, sit down for a few minutes. I bet you've been rushed off your feet! I'm Jenny Starling.'

'Thanks,' the older woman said, sitting down and looking around at the now fast emptying room. 'But the worst is over now. You're the cook, right? The one the bursar said we should speak to, before we take anything to the police?'

Jenny hid a wince, and hoped that that particular instruction of Glover-Smythe's never got to the inspector's ears.

She sighed. 'Yes, that's me,' she admitted. 'Problem?'

'Not with me,' the older woman said quickly. 'But my daughter Debbie works here as a scout too. Just does the early morning shift, before going on to her regular job, like, at Debenham's. She's on the perfume counter now, and doing ever so well, she is. But she's got a mortgage, and her husband was laid off a couple of months ago, so they need the extra money until her Brian gets another job.'

Jenny waited until she paused for breath, and then slipped in quickly, 'And Debbie saw something that has something to do with, er, what happened yesterday?'

'Oh no. Not the murder,' the older woman said quickly.

'Well, not really. Well, maybe, but maybe not.'

'OK, glad we got that cleared up,' Jenny said with a laugh. Her companion had the grace to laugh as well.

'Sorry. It's just that when Debbie told me, I didn't know what to do for the best. I think you'd better come and speak to her yourself, but you'll have to be quick, mind. She needs to get off to work in twenty minutes.'

Jenny, wisely, made no promises. 'Where is she?'

'In the serving room.'

Jenny knew that the serving room was just off hall,

which had a whole range of dumb waiters connected to the main kitchens directly below. 'OK, let's go and hear what Debbie has to say,' Jenny said brightly. She was curious, but frankly, didn't hold out much hope that it would amount to much.

LAURA RAINES STARED out at the restless grey-cum-blue sea and knew just how it felt. The beach at Hayling Island was almost deserted, and she wasn't particularly surprised. Not only was it early in the season yet for most holidaymakers, but the ground here was one of those hard-on-the-ankles, pebbly shorelines that was fit for neither sunbathing or building sandcastles.

She had spent one of the worst and most sleepless nights of her life, and, like the vast, moving body of water, she felt as if both her mind and her body was incapable of staying still.

She simply didn't know what to do.

She and Simon had talked themselves almost hoarse yesterday, going over and over everything, time and time again, going through permutation after permutation, and still they hadn't come to any solid conclusions on what they should do now.

Not surprisingly, given the enormity of what they now faced, they had both been too keyed up to do anything other than toss and turn beside each other in bed all night long. And this morning, unable to eat anything, Simon had taken himself off ostensibly to buy a paper for any news that they might have printed about her dead husband. In reality, she suspected that he simply wanted to get away from her. Which hurt her far more than she knew was good for her.

She simply couldn't lose Simon—no matter what.

She sighed and walked awkwardly over the pebbles, wondering what would look the least suspicious. Go to the police, or wait for them to come to her? So far, there had been nothing on the television news about Maurice's death, but perhaps it was too early for that. And if there was nothing reported in the papers, especially if they didn't give out the name of the dead man, then they simply couldn't go to the police, could they? How could they explain knowing that he was dead?

She'd told no-one, not even the kids, where she was going, nor did they have her new mobile number. Her nearest neighbours probably knew that she and Maurice were both absent, but they, presumably, were still in ignorance about what had happened as well. Ostensibly, she had no way of knowing that she was now a widow, so to come forward, would be as good as a confession.

No, as agonizing as it was on her nerves, she had no other choice but to wait for the police to find and question her. The thing was, what did she say then? How much did she admit to?

Laura Raines felt like shouting at the sea in her rage. How could she decide that, without knowing what was going on?

Deep inside, the poisonous worm that had been growing inside her for the last twenty-four hours or so, wriggled nauseatingly again. Had Simon told her everything? What if…?

No. She couldn't start playing that game. She'd drive herself insane. She shook her head at herself, cursing herself for being a stupid, lonely, pathetic middle-aged woman. But even as she walked across the treacherous shoreline, she knew that she wasn't grieving for Maurice, or even worrying about her own skin; she was thinking only that she couldn't lose Simon. Whatever happened. Now that she had love again, she'd do anything to hold onto it.

Hadn't she risked everything already?

On the beach at Hayling Island, Laura Raines suddenly gave a harsh, ironical shout of laughter. What did it really matter now if she risked so much more?

In St Bede's, Jenny Starling made her way to the incident room. She tapped on the outer door, waited until it was opened by a constable, and introduced herself.

'I'd like a word or two with Inspector Golder. It's important,' she added.

She saw the constable look at the woman beside her, dressed in the neat brown pinafore-uniform of all the St Bede's scouts, and he nodded. 'Come on in. He's over there.' He pointed to one of the desks by the window.

Jenny, who already knew where Trevor and his sergeant had set up shop, nodded and walked over.

It was Peter Trent who saw them first, and he tapped his superior on the arm to warn him. Trevor Golder turned around and watched them curiously.

Jenny smiled across reassuringly at Debbie. 'That's him. See, he's a perfectly nice man. Don't worry, he won't bite. Just tell him what you saw, just like you told it to me, and then answer all his questions. Don't be too keen, think it through first, to make sure you get it right. And if you don't know something, don't try and elaborate, or make things up, or tell him what you think it is he wants to hear, just say that you don't know.'

The scout nodded, but somewhat dubiously. 'OK. You will stay, though, won't you?' she pleaded. And it was this appeal that Trevor first heard as they neared his desk. It made him sigh, but he reached out and nabbed another chair for the cook. Peter rose and offered his own chair to Debbie.

'Ah, Inspector. This is Mrs Debbie Dawkins,' Jenny introduced brightly. 'She's a scout here. She was working yesterday morning. Apparently she's one of the ones you haven't got around to questioning yet,' Jenny said.

Her tone rose at the end, making it a question, but in fact she knew from listening to Debbie's story that yesterday she'd worked at the college until noon since it was her half-day at Debenhams when she only did the afternoon and evening slot. And that she had indeed left before being questioned by the police.

'Right.' Trevor smiled at them both. 'Please, take a seat.' Jenny took a chair and pulled it back a little, giving them at least the semblance of privacy. Both the policemen appreciated her tact.

'Debbie has something to tell you that I think you'll find interesting,' Jenny said, and then shut up, leaving them to it.

Trevor turned to the newcomer, trying to hide his excitement, but his eyes sharpened in anticipation. 'Oh?'

SIX

DEBBIE DAWKINS SMILED uncertainly at the inspector. 'I'm sorry I haven't come to see you before now, but yesterday I'd already left when, well, everything kicked off. Of course, Mum phoned and told me what had happened when I got in from work at the shop, but last night I was so busy with the kids and getting dinner and everything that I didn't really give it that much thought.'

Debbie was a small, rounded woman, with dark hair, eyes and complexion, the latter of which blushed a little now as she contemplated that last lie. For of course she'd thought about nothing else all night, once her mother had told her that one of the conference people had been 'done in', as she put it. Like most people, she'd thought that serious crime was something you read about in the papers, or watched on TV. Most of all, it was something that happened to other people. So to be so close to it had, obviously, occupied her mind almost to the exclusion of everything else.

And, just like almost everyone else who'd been in college that day must have done, she'd gone over every minute of her time there. By the time she'd finished analysing everything that she could remember, it hadn't taken her long to realize that she just might have seen something of importance.

Now, as she sat before the two policemen, she shifted uncomfortably in her seat. She was guiltily aware that, by rights, she should have been on the phone to them right away. But the thought of having police come to the house in the evening, much to their neighbours' crowing entertainment, had been more than she'd felt able to deal with after another long and tiring day. Likewise, the prospect of going down to the station to make a statement had seemed beyond her. All she'd wanted was a hot mug of chocolate and to get off to bed, especially since she had to be up bright and early the next day.

'When I saw Mum this morning, and she told me more about it, where it happened and all that, I realized I needed to speak to you. Mum told me I should see the new cook first'—here she flicked a glance at Jenny, who winced and tried to look nonchalant—'and so I did, and she told me I needed to see you right away, and here we are,' she finished brightly.

Trevor Golder nodded. He shot Jenny a brief, glimmering look that told her that he and she would be having a conversation shortly about how exactly she'd become an intermediary between the police and the scouts, but for now he concentrated on his witness.

He nodded to Peter Trent, who quickly got the formalities over, jotting down her full name, address, phone number, and employment details at the college.

'Now, what time did you arrive for work yesterday morning?' Trevor took over the interview seamlessly, starting off, as he usually did with voluble and nervous witnesses, with something simple and unthreatening.

'Oh, usual time, just gone six. I went straight to the kitchens to help prepare the breakfasts, and then started on the housework in the communal areas in my station for an hour or so. Then I went up to hall to help wait on tables when it was time to serve.'

Trevor nodded. 'And did you notice the deceased at all?' he asked curiously.

Debbie's rounded face flushed again. 'Mum said he was the puffed-up one who was so full of himself?' she asked tentatively. 'Sort of oldish, but still kind of good-looking, in a way? That's him, right?'

Trevor smiled slightly. 'That sounds like Mr Raines, yes,' he said, but handed over an enlarged photograph of him that had been taken from his driver's licence.

Debbie took it and nodded. 'Yes, that's the chap. Then I sort of knew who he was. I'd seen him around, like, but I never served him or nothing. He wasn't my table.'

'Right. So you never spoke to him?'

'Don't think so.'

'So, what was it you wanted to tell us?' Debbie shot a quick, nervous glance at Jenny, who gave a slight nod of encouragement, and the scout took a long, deep breath.

'Well, see, it was like this. Yesterday I worked through to just before twelve. Normally I'm away by eight-thirty, like, 'cause I have to be at my day job at Debenham's by nine. But yesterday's my half day at the shop, so I didn't need to be in until one. So I stayed on to clear up after breakfast, and help out two of the others with their cleaning area. They've got the JCR on their patch, and the big entrance hall, so they always need extra staff, see? The black and white tiled floor in there gets dirty something chronic for a start, what with everyone walking through it. In the winter it's worse, mind, very muddy it is, but in the summer like now, it's more dusty.'

Debbie took a deep breath, and then blushed again. 'Sorry, you don't want to hear this. But it does explain why I was hoovering the carpets on the main staircase when I saw him.'

Both policemen sat up a little straighter at this. 'Wait a minute. Let me get the geography right in my mind,' Trevor said. 'You were on the main staircase, leading up to the first floor, where hall is situated?'

'Right,' Debbie confirmed, with an encouraging smile. 'It's not easy to get your bearings in a maze like this, is it? It took me ages to work out where all the nooks and crannies were when I first started work here, I can tell you.'

Trevor smiled a brief acknowledgement. 'And you were hoovering. What time was this?'

'Ah, now there you have me,' Debbie said uncertainly. 'It was getting on late, like, because I only had the staircase to do, and then I knew I could get off. So it must have been somewhere between a quarter to twelve and five to. I know, because when I went out through the car park, I glanced at my watch, and it was just going on for ten past twelve, and I'd had to take the hoover back and change out of the old pinny and brush my hair and whatnot.'

Trevor nodded, well pleased with the answer. The time frame was looking good.

'All right, and what did you see? Be careful now, take your time.' He leaned forward a little on his seat, his tone becoming avuncular. 'You were hoovering. And then…?'

'Something made me look up,' Debbie said, a shade nervously, now that she was getting to the meat of it. 'I was not quite at the top of the stairs, so I was sort of peering over the top, at floor level. I think it must have been a shadow moving that caught my eye. You know

how when, something just out of sight moves unexpectedly, it gives you a little bit of a start? My husband says
that's something to do with animal instincts, you know,
from when we lived in caves, and were hunted by sabre
tooth tigers and things.'

Trevor nodded impatiently. 'And what did you see?'
he demanded.

'A man come out of hall,' Debbie said promptly, and,
for once, succinctly.

Peter Trent's pencil, which had been scribbling over
his notebook, now paused expectantly.

'Who was it?' Trevor asked calmly.

'Oh, I don't know,' Debbie said at once.

Trevor nodded patiently. 'Not someone who worked
in the college then?'

'Oh no. I know all of them by sight if nothing else,'
Debbie confirmed.

'Was it one of the conference people, do you think?'
Trevor asked cautiously, well aware that the college was
open to the public, and therefore, conceivably, could
have been anyone as yet unidentified.

'Could have been,' Debbie said cautiously.

'But you didn't recognize him as someone you'd seen
before?'

'No. But then, well, they've only just come, haven't
they? This latest lot, I mean, they've only been here a
day. Usually you get to know them after a few days,
maybe even learn a few names and find out some
stuff—which ones like their bacon crispy, and which
ones are on the pull, and the nice ones, and some who
give a tip. Then, more often than not, just when you've
got used to them, they're gone and the next lot come in.
This current lot have only been here a day, like I said,

so I haven't really started recognizing who's who yet. Maybe this bloke I saw is at the conference, but I just haven't come across him yet.' Debbie paused, seeming to give a mental check over what she'd said, then nodded. 'See?'

Trevor did, and sighed. He'd have to arrange it so that she got a good look at all the male conference-goers and see if she could pick him out. But for some reason, he didn't hold out much hope that she would.

'OK. What can you tell me about this man. Was he tall?'

'Ish,' Debbie said, unhelpfully. 'I mean, he's not as short as Art, say, but not quite as tall as me husband, who's about six feet.'

Peter Trent wrote five feet seven to five feet ten in his notebook and waited.

'What colour was his hair?' Trevor asked. 'You're doing really well,' he added, encouragingly.

'Dark, not black, but really dark brown. I think his eyes were dark brown too, although he was coming out of hall, as I said, and was a fair bit away. But I could see his eyes, like, I mean, people with pale eyes, they sort of fade into the face in the distance, don't they? So I think the fact that I could see his eyes, meant they'd be darker, rather than paler. See?'

Trevor did. 'You say he came out of hall. Which way did he go? Did he come past you, down the main staircase for instance?'

'Oh no. I'd have got a good look at him if he had, wouldn't I? No, he went off the other way.'

Trevor nodded gloomily. He would. The policeman had been trying to work out for himself the layout of the college, but as Debbie herself had said, it wasn't easy.

Bits of building seemed to have been added on here and there, higgledy-piggledy, for over 500 years, which led to some very confusing layouts.

'There's a narrower staircase at the other end of the corridor,' Debbie obliged blithely. 'It leads down to a side entrance that lets you out just opposite the Fellows' garden. From there, you can cut straight across the lawns to the library, although the groundsmen don't half tell you off if they catch you at it, since you're supposed to use the gravel paths, or down to the bottom, and out into Walton Street. There's a gate in the wall that lets you out without having to go all the way out the front and past the lodge.'

'Of course it does,' Trevor said flatly. Which meant that the porters who manned the main lodge might never have seen this mystery man either coming or going.

'What was he wearing, miss,' Peter Trent put in gently. 'Was he in a suit, like, all nice and formal, or something tatty?'

'Oh no. Not a suit. But not tatty, either. I think he was wearing dark jeans and a white T-shirt. Bare arms; it was hot yesterday, like today. He had quite hairy arms, I think.'

Trevor Golder suddenly tensed. 'A white T-shirt? Was it a plain one, or did it have a pattern on it, could you tell? Something in red, perhaps?'

Jenny Starling looked up quickly. Thinking back to all the blood that had been shed in hall, she'd already long-since realized that the killer must have been considerably bloodstained after killing Maurice, and she appreciated the clever way the inspector had phrased the question. He didn't want to upset the witness by explaining about the gore and asking her if she'd seen bloodstains on the man she'd seen, and he'd also avoided the trap of leading her in her answers. No doubt, it would be something the lawyers would appreciate too, once it came to trial.

'Oh no, it was pure white,' Debbie said with confidence, unaware that it was not the answer the policeman had been hoping for. 'He walked past one of the windows on the way out, see, and it was bright white in the sunlight.'

Trevor sighed. Still, the man had been wearing dark jeans. Perhaps those had caught the worst of the blood spatter? And the witness had admitted that the man was quite a distance away.

'How old would you say he was?' he asked next.

'Oh, not old. In his mid-thirties I'd say. And quite buff. I mean, he was fit, like. I got the impression he was good-looking,' Debbie added helplessly, again with another blush.

'Clean-shaven, could you tell?' Trevor asked next.

'Oh yes. No beard, not even stubble, and no 'tache, either. I don't like men with face fuzz,' Debbie admitted, then blushed again. 'Not that that matters, naturally. I was just saying,' she mumbled, suddenly studying her kneecaps.

'Did he say anything?' Trevor asked without much hope.

'What, to me, you mean?' Debbie asked, looking up again and clearly startled. 'Course he didn't, he didn't even see me, did he? I would have been just a head peeking up above the stairs to him, anyway, even if he'd looked my way. Besides, he went in the opposite direction, didn't he? I told you.'

Trevor held up a placatory hand. 'Yes, I know. I'm

not accusing you of lying, Mrs Dawkins, or trying to trip you up. But I was just thinking that nowadays, we all seem to have a mobile phone attached to one ear, and I thought he might have been using it, and talking to someone on that. Or maybe he'd met someone in the corridor going away from you and said "good morning" or something like that.'

'Oh no. None of that,' Debbie said. 'He just went off, quickly like.'

'Quickly?' Trevor pounced. That was new.

'Yeah. Walking fast, but not actually running.'

'How did he seem to you?' Trevor asked, more cautiously now. 'Did he look like he was in shock, or panicking maybe?'

'I dunno,' Debbie said, frowning and clearly thinking about it. 'I got the impression he looked pale, and maybe a bit shaky. He walked quick, like I said, but sort of jerky too. Like he wasn't sure his legs were gonna hold him up. A bit like my husband after one pint too many, know what I mean?'

Trevor did.

Jenny coughed gently.

Everyone looked at her, and Jenny cast Trevor Golder an apologetic smile, and said softly, 'You said he had a short-sleeved T-shirt on, Debbie, did you notice anything on his arms?'

The little round scout blinked. 'His arms. Like what? A tattoo, do you mean? Nah, I wouldn't have seen anything like that, he was too far away. And his skin didn't look bruised or nothing, you know, like tattoos can look from far away. I mean, they mainly look blue or black, don't they, from a distance, even if they ain't. But both his forearms just looked normal. Pale.'

Jenny nodded, and caught Trevor's eye. In other words, they probably weren't covered in blood either. But whoever had stabbed Maurice Raines in the neck must have been holding the fleshing tool in their hand, and it was impossible that he or she hadn't got at the very least their hand and forearm stained with blood. Since there weren't any washing facilities in hall, if the man Debbie saw had been the killer, then he must have had some means of wiping his arms down, or else....

Trevor, who hadn't missed the significance of the witness's answer either, sighed gently.

'Do you think you'd recognize the man if you saw him again, Mrs Dawkins?' Trevor asked. 'Think carefully now,' he cautioned.

Debbie sighed and frowned and then shrugged. 'I dunno, do I? I mean, how can I say? I was down close to the ground, being three or four stairs down, like I was, so I was sort of looking along the floor at him at a funny angle. And he was a fair bit away, but on the other hand, I got a good look at him in the sunlight. I might,' she said cautiously, 'but unless I do see him again, how can I tell?' she pointed out reasonably. 'Look, I've got to get off to work now. My manager won't like me being late, even if it is to help out you lot. Can I go now?'

Trevor smiled charmingly. 'If, after work, you were to sit down with a police sketch artist, do you think you could come up with a likeness of this man that you saw?'

Debbie Dawkins looked doubtful. 'Well, I could give it a go,' she said at last.

TREVOR TOLD PETER TRENT to make sure that all the conference-goers who fitted her description were dining in hall that night, and then to pick up the witness from her home and make sure she got a good look at them all. If that produced no joy, than he was to baby-sit her through the e-fit process.

Jenny, her job done, managed to murmur something and slip away from their makeshift office before the inspector could remember that he had a bone to pick with her about her role as intermediary for the college staff.

She'd just stepped outside, intent on finding out where James Raye was, and asking him to join her later on for lunch, when she heard her name being called.

She looked along the side of the pleasant, rose-brick building that she'd just exited, and saw a young man hurrying towards her. His mop of red-hair and excited, freckled face, were instantly recognizable.

'Hello, Charlie.' She greeted the young reporter with a careful but polite smile. She was not happy talking to members of the Press, even if they were as young and inexperienced as this one: she was savvy enough to know that the fact that he was barely a stringer for the local papers meant nothing. Just because he was small fry, didn't mean that he didn't have big ambitions, and he would be less than human if he didn't see being in on a story as big as this as his shot at career advancement. He'd be desperate to make his mark, and Jenny Starling had no intention of becoming anybody's 'source in the know'.

'I was hoping to catch you again,' Charlie Foster said with a grin. 'The plods won't let me in to the buildings. They've even stopped the rest of the media mob from coming into the grounds by closing the place to the public. They only let me in because I've got the paperwork from the taxidermy society inviting me to do the article on them.'

And how long would it be before Inspector Golder insisted that Vicki Voight rescind her permission for that, Jenny wondered, and smiled to herself? 'And, of course, you're going to restrict your interviews solely to the topic of how best to set about stuffing a peacock, right?'

The youngster grinned. 'Right! So, word has it that you found the body. Care to comment?' he asked eagerly, trying to check surreptitiously that the small tape recorder he had running in his top shirt pocket was working.

Jenny, who had really good hearing, could tell from the minute whirling sound it was making, that it was.

'On how to stuff a peacock?' she asked guilelessly. 'I haven't a clue. But if you want to see a really good example of the taxidermy art for your readers' delectation, there's a stuffed bear still in hall that's a prime example. Oh, sorry, you can't go inside, can you?' she said sweetly.

'Oh, come on, give us a break,' Charlie whined. 'If you tell me something, I'll tell you something. Something interesting,' he wheedled.

'About the murder?' she asked sharply.

'Even better—about your boss. I've been talking to the cleaners here, and I've come across a nice little bit of gossip. Come on, doesn't everyone need a little bit of dirt on their boss?' he winked.

Jenny sighed. 'I can't imagine Glover-Smythe having a speck of dirt on him,' Jenny said flatly.

Charlie Foster blinked. 'What? Who? I'm talking

about your boss, you know, the little nervous guy. Fat, bald.'

'Art McIntyre?' Jenny said. 'What about him?'

'Well, according to the cleaners here, he's a bit of an office joke. They all run rings round him. And they say that this Maurice Raines guy was having a right go at him about something the night the Yorkshire lot arrived. Called him incompetent, and all sorts. He wasn't happy about the way he'd allocated the rooms for a start, and that he'd ignored something really serious and important about the ventilation needed in one of the lecture rooms, or something along those lines.'

Jenny, who didn't want to start wondering about why an exhibition of taxidermy might need a specific amount of ventilation, said quickly, 'I hardly think that constitutes gossip, Charlie. You run a big place like this, you're bound to get customers with a gripe about something. So what?'

'Ah, but it's not just that, is it?' Charlie said, looking around and then leaning closer to her and lowering his voice dramatically. 'According to the cleaners, Raines threatened to take his complaints to the bloke's boss—the bursar himself. Again, according to the cleaners, it's common knowledge that the bursar is just itching to come up with a good reason to sack him.'

'They're called scouts, not cleaners,' Jenny said absently. And wondered. Was Art McIntyre's job as vulnerable as Charlie's 'sources' were making out? Or were they just indulging in some malicious gossip? Or even stringing the youngster along? She could imagine some of the middle-aged, world-weary comedians around here spinning the eager young pup a line, just for the entertainment value alone.

On the other hand, there might be something in it. As a motive for murder it was weak, but then, as she well knew, worse crimes had been committed for less.

Jenny sighed. 'You'd better come with me,' she said.

'What? Where?' Charlie asked, as she turned and headed back to the door.

'To see Inspector Golder. What, don't you want the opportunity to speak to the officer in charge?' Jenny smiled, as the young man suddenly paled.

Instantly, he straightened his shoulders and the glint of battle came into his eyes.

'Of course I do.'

'Well, come on then.' Jenny led the way back to the incident room. As she pushed open the door and held it open for the youngster to precede her, she saw Peter Trent look up and, from the way his eyes narrowed warningly, she knew that the sergeant was well aware of Charlie's profession.

As she walked towards their desk at the back, she saw Trent lean down and say something urgently to his boss, who reared up and shot them a blistering look. Consequently, even before she'd reached his desk, she got her two-pennies-worth in first.

'Inspector Golder, this is Charlie Foster, a reporter for the local papers. He has information that might help your investigation,' she added firmly. Then as she reached the inspector, whispered a warning about the tape recorder in the young man's pocket.

'Is that right now?' Golder said, both in response to her warning, and to her news. 'So, what can you tell us, Mr Foster?' he asked blithely.

It was then that Charlie showed his youth and inexperience, by telling the inspector what he'd heard without first trying to use it to barter for a few usable quotes. It was, in fact, a testimony to Golder's tact and skill that when Foster left, he was feeling as if he'd done rather well out of it, although the inspector had, in fact, let slip not a single thing that the rest of the media pack didn't already know.

Back in the incident room, Trevor, Trent and Jenny were discussing the young reporter's information. Trent had just picked up something from the floor and was looking at it with interest.

'You know these people better than I do,' the inspector said to the cook. 'Does it sound likely to you?'

Jenny smiled ruefully. 'I know them better than you do by about twenty-four hours,' she pointed out with some exasperation. Then she sighed. 'I did get the feeling that the bursar is the big Indian chief around here though,' she conceded. 'And I have to say, when Art interviewed me, I wasn't exactly quaking in my boots. He's a nice man, but I got the impression that he was, if not exactly in over his head here, then at least not really happy in his work. But then, he's one of those people with a nervous disposition anyway, so having someone like Glover-Smythe undermining you at every turn….'

She trailed off and shrugged helplessly.

'Right then, we'd better get him in and have a word then,' Trevor said. 'See what this argument was about and see how serious it was, if nothing else. If McIntyre's job is looking as dicy as they say, and if Raines did threaten to go over his head to his boss, then things might have turned nasty.'

'Right, guv, I'll go get him,' Trent said. And it was then, when Jenny turned to look at him, that she realized just what it was that the sergeant was handling.

Seeing her notice, the older man smiled and held out his hand. 'I've been coming across these things all over the place,' he said, holding out the exhibit for their inspection. 'It must be the conference-goers forgetting about them and leaving them lying about. It was a stuffed mouse this morning. Sitting on a table out near the JCR. Gave me a start, I thought the damned thing was real at first, but it was a white one. Some old dear with a blue rinse and glasses like Dame Edna came rushing in, looking for it. Apparently small mammals are her thing,' Trent mused indulgently.

'I know what you mean,' Trevor said. 'I came across a stuffed red squirrel on one of the window ledges not so long ago. For a split second I thought the poor blighter had somehow got inside and was trapped.' Trevor looked down at the offering in his sergeant's hand. 'That's the first reptile I've seen though. Apparently, they're hard to do because their skin is so fragile, or so some old duffer was telling me just after breakfast.'

Jenny looked down at the familiar, small green chameleon sitting on the sergeant's palm. Norman swivelled around one conical eye to look at her questioningly.

'Er, Sergeant....' Jenny said.

WHEN SHE GOT back from delivering the escape artist known as Norman to one very relieved James Raye, Art McIntyre was already in the incident room. That he'd only just arrived, Jenny could tell, from the way he was arranging himself carefully on the seat.

'Ah, is there something I can help you with?' Art was saying. If he noticed Jenny's silent approach and continuing presence, he pretended to ignore it.

'If you could just clear up one or two points for me, sir,' Trevor said amiably. 'Is it true that you had an argument with Mr Raines on the night that the taxidermy society first arrived in college?'

Art McIntyre froze in his place for a second; then his shoulders slumped just a little in defeat. 'Dear me, word does get around here, doesn't it?' he said mildly, but Jenny, and no doubt the others also, could clearly hear the underlining tinge of bitterness in his tone. 'Yes, there was a minor disagreement,' he agreed flatly.

'About, sir?' Trevor prompted gently.

'Mr Raines wasn't happy to have so many of the society staying in one residential house—over half of them in one building, in fact. He had requested that they be more widely scattered throughout the college campus. He said something about not wanting them to form cliques, and that it made for a better dynamic.' Art shrugged. 'It all sounded like psychobabble gobblede-gook to me.' Art sighed. 'But it's just easier for the scouts to clean rooms if college guests aren't scattered far and wide. But Mr Raines wouldn't see reason, but I didn't take it personally. It was nothing, believe me,' Art tried to reassure them, looking from one policeman to the other and smiling ingratiatingly. 'You should hear some of the non-consequential things some of our conference-goers complain about.' He gave a short, pitifully unconvincing laugh.

Jenny's eyes narrowed in sudden thought. Now just why would Maurice Raines want his people to be scattered about here and yon? Unless it was because he wanted to make sure that they weren't all congregated under his feet, of course. The inspector's theory that maybe he was conducting an affair during the conference, and wanted room and privacy in order to do so, was looking more and more likely.

Unless…. Jenny frowned and began to think. Hard.

'And that was all, was it, sir?' Trevor carried on the interview smoothly, letting the scepticism show in his voice. 'There was nothing else?'

'Oh, I don't know. He made some comment about one of the windows in the lecture room being stiff, I think,' Art said vaguely.

Trevor nodded. That might be interpreted as inadequate ventilation, he supposed, with some amusement. 'And did Mr Raines threaten to take his complaint to the bursar himself?' Trevor persisted, again in that mild, amiable way that was so clever at luring the unwary into a sense of false security.

Art flushed. But whether in remembered anger, or because he was embarrassed by the question, it was hard for either policeman to tell. 'Oh, they all do that, Inspector,' Art said, waving a hand dismissively in the air. 'I never take it seriously. The bursar knows what clients can be like. I wasn't in the least worried. I'm sure Mr Glover-Smythe would have backed me to the hilt, if it had ever come to it,' Art lied magnificently. And if it hadn't been for the fact that he was sweating uncomfortably, and looking rather like a disconcerted bullfrog, his feigned nonchalance might have been even halfway believable.

Trevor decided to let that show of bravura go, and nodded instead. Now might not be the best moment to push it. 'All right, sir,' he agreed with a small smile. 'Just for the record, you were in your office all morning yesterday, isn't that what you said?'

Art instantly went pale with fright. 'Yes,' he said

feebly. He'd never before had to account for his whereabouts at the time of a murder, and the experience was
making him feel distinctly faint. He wondered, with a
hint of hysteria, if he was going to be sick, and swallowed convulsively.

The inspector didn't seem to notice his sudden dis-
comfort. 'All right, sir, that's all for now. My sergeant
will walk you back to your office. Thank you for your
time.' To Trent he quickly whispered some instructions
into his ear, and watched the pair depart.

Then he turned to his companion. 'So, what do you
think?' he asked. Then, receiving no reply, looked over
at the impressive cook. Today she was wearing a long,
red, crushed-velvet skirt and a red, blue and green flow-
ered blouse over a white background. With her thick,
dark hair and lovely blue eyes, curvaceous figure and
pale complexion she was a sight to raise any man's spir-
its. James Raye, Trevor Golder couldn't help thinking,
was a lucky man to have attracted her attention.

But, right now, his thoughts weren't on the vaga-
ries of romance. 'Miss Starling!" he said again, slightly
louder. That the woman was deep in thought was obvious, and with this particular woman, he wanted to know
exactly what she was thinking.

Jenny started. 'Hmm? What? Sorry, Inspector, I was
miles away.'

'Yes, so I could see. So spill it, then. What's on your
mind?' he demanded shortly.

'Stuffed bears,' Jenny said promptly, nonplussing
him totally.

'Huh?'

'I was just wondering why a man as vain and as
full of himself as Maurice Raines,' Jenny explained

patiently, 'did all the shifting and hauling of that stuffed bear himself, on the morning that he gave his opening speech.'

'Oh,' Trevor said. But for the life of him, couldn't see the relevance.

But Jenny was barely paying attention. Because now her mind had gone on to something else that was worrying her. Something to do with the two full cups of coffee on the table that had been beside Maurice's dead body. Something about that hadn't ever made much sense and she should have known at once what it was. Now that she had remembered something that she'd overheard at breakfast that first morning, those cups of coffee could only make sense in one particular way. But could it really be true? Wasn't she taking two and two and making twenty-two, instead of four?

And yet…. How else could it have been?

Trevor, seeing that he was going to get no sense out of her, turned back reluctantly to his paperwork, whilst Jenny, with all thoughts of James Raye and the prospect of a pleasant lunch all but forgotten, continued to sit and think.

Over and over again she went over the facts and, time and again, she came back with only one solution that made sense. But, if she was right, then it was all too fantastical for words. No, she must have got it wrong, she told herself, giving a mental head shake. But the strands fit. Well, sort of fit. Well, up to a point. And they all definitely pointed one way. Yet, that simply could *not* be right, because what should have happened, hadn't, in fact, happened.

She frowned, and was so deeply engrossed in going over her theory and pulling huge holes in it, that she missed Peter Trent's return. It was only when he started to talk, that she pulled herself out of her reverie, and began to listen.

'So, what's the set-up like over there?' Trevor began briskly by asking his sergeant.

'Mr McIntyre has one of the ground floor rooms in the Cotswold stone building down by Walton Street,' Peter Trent said. 'Most of the admin offices are in there, apparently. It's one of those set-ups whereby you have to go through his secretary's smaller, outer office before you get into his. The toilet they both use is off her room. I had a word with her, and she swears up and down that our friend never left his office after he started work at his usual time of eight-thirty that morning.'

Trevor sighed. 'She strike you as reliable?'

Peter Trent grinned. 'My granny wouldn't have been able to find fault with her, guv,' he said sadly. 'In her early sixties, and devoted to her hubby and three cats. I'd say she likes our Mr McIntyre all right, but she's hardly that fond of him that she'd perjure herself.'

'Right. And the loo's in her office you say, and they both use it?' Trevor prompted.

Trent, with all the weight of his years working with this man behind him, easily read his thought process. 'Yes. So even if he had left his office for a few minutes, say, with the excuse of a call of nature, he'd still not have left her sight.'

'No windows in the loo, I suppose?' Trevor asked despondently.

'Only one of those small, high up ones, that you'd need to be as lithe as a weasel to get through, guv,' Trent confirmed, unhelpfully. And both men grinned at the thought of the short, fat Art McIntyre trying to wriggle through such an aperture. Then the inspector's face tightened.

'You said his office is on the ground floor, was the door between the secretary's office and his shut when you went in?'

'Yes, and it usually is kept shut; I checked,' Peter said, and then added, 'but if you're thinking that he might have climbed through the window in his office and out into the garden, I don't think so, guv,' he added regretfully. 'Granted it is one of those much bigger, sash-window affairs, so it's big enough, but I checked, and right outside is a well-planted flowerbed. Mostly roses too, with a few pretty bushes and marigolds for good measure. None of them has been trampled down. I'd be willing to bet a month's wages he never waded through them.'

'So, unless our little bursary man launched himself from the window ledge and managed to sail unseen over the shrubbery, there's no way he could have got out of his office and stuck the knife into our murder victim,' Trevor concluded.

'Seems not, guv,' Peter Trent said sympathetically. 'And I can't believe that somebody wouldn't have noticed him either. It's not often you see a grown man clamber out of a window! And there's always people milling about inside and out around this place, what with it being open to the public and all. So another perfectly good contender bites the dust,' Trent finished in disgust.

'It makes our little Mrs Dawkins mystery man look better and better by the minute, doesn't it?' Trevor mused. 'Even if he wasn't conveniently bloodstained. But if, by some chance, he isn't the killer, what's the alternative?' He threw the question out to the floor. 'He was there during the right time-frame, and so far we haven't a clue who he is.'

'Perhaps our Mr X came across Maurice's dead body just shortly before I did,' Jenny took up the call to play devil's advocate, 'and simply wasn't as public-minded as me, and decided to just skedaddle instead of reporting it. People do that, don't they? Panic, I mean?'

And, she added silently to herself, especially if they had a good reason to want to keep out of it all, as she strongly suspected their Mr X would have wanted to do. Supposing her fantastical theories were correct of course, she reminded herself ruefully.

'Always possible,' Peter Trent acknowledged. 'People do do funny things if they have a sudden shock. And if our Mr X had dodgy reasons of his own for being out and about, he'd not want to come to our attention, that's for sure.' Like his boss, it had occurred to Peter Trent to wonder if their mystery man had been someone checking out the place with possible burglary in mind. There had to be many pieces of art and other goodies that would attract the seriously light-fingered in an Oxford college, after all.

'You don't think that the man Debbie Dawkins saw is our killer, do you?' Trevor said flatly to Jenny, making his sergeant regard the cook thoughtfully.

But once again, Jenny Starling was thinking hard, trying to put herself in the killer's place, and, whilst it all fit, there was one little piece that didn't.

'You didn't find a second mobile phone anywhere in Maurice's room, did you?' she asked, seemingly out of the blue.

Peter Trent quickly consulted his notes, but was

pretty sure that he already knew the answer. 'No, we didn't,' he said. 'But then, we found his mobile phone on him.' The older man was sure that the cook had been present when he'd told Trevor as much. 'Perhaps you'd forgotten?' he asked kindly.

But Jenny hadn't forgotten. And it was not the victim's own mobile phone that interested her.

Trevor, who didn't for a moment believe that the sharp-witted cook forgot a single thing, opened his mouth to ask her just what she was getting at, but Jenny forestalled him.

'There's something else,' Jenny said. 'About the coffee. I think you'll find that it—'

Just then, one of the constables who'd just taken a telephone call, came rushing over, obviously in a lather of excitement, and waving a piece of paper in the air. 'Sir, that was labs. Forensics have just got some results through, and the man in charge over there thought you'd like to know. One of the cups of coffee, found next to the victim, had enough drugs in it to kill an elephant!'

SEVEN

INSPECTOR GOLDER FROZE for a second, and then slowly reached out to take the piece of paper from the young constable's hand, and read the message for himself.

'I don't speak scientific, but it seems clear enough,' he said at last to his intensely interested audience. 'One of the coffee cups contained nothing but coffee, milk and sugar, and the only potentially deadly thing in it was the usual amount of caffeine. The other had…er….' Trevor squinted at the multi-syllabic chemical formula that the constable had conscientiously written down and grunted. 'Says in the summary, that it's something that's available on prescription and is usually given out to people, mainly the elderly it seems, with a certain heart condition. Administered in the form of a drug called digi—something-or-other.'

Jenny nodded, without surprise. She'd been about to say that she thought one of the coffee cups must contain some kind of poison, but she didn't think that it was politic of her to say so now. Not only would it smack of boasting—a proclivity that had never been one of her favourite pastimes—but it wouldn't do to interrupt the inspector in full flight.

However, she did need to tell Trevor Glover something very important and cleared her throat to get his attention. When she had it, she smiled briefly, almost as if in apology. 'When I was at breakfast, I overheard

Maurice Raines say that his mother had a bad heart condition,' she said. 'You might find it useful to contact her GP and find out if she was prescribed the same drug.'

'You think Mrs Raines, the wife, I mean, might be in the frame then?' Trevor said sharply. 'She'd probably have access to her mother-in-law's medication all right. Providing they were on visiting and speaking terms, that is,' he modified, after a moment's thought. Not all in-laws got on, as he well knew.

Jenny Starling opened her mouth to speak, then thought better of it. After all, having an outlandish and unproven theory was one thing; sticking her neck out without more proof to back it up was another.

'It makes sense in one way,' the inspector carried on, not noticing the cook's hesitation and waving the still-hovering and excited constable away. 'The spouse and immediate family are always the first suspects when it comes to killing your nearest and dearest. But in this case, we've seen neither hide nor hair of the lady,' he added grimly. 'And I would imagine that most of the conference-goers here probably know their chairman's wife by sight and, if she had been sneaking around, surely she'd have been spotted?'

'Not necessarily, guv,' Peter Trent pointed out. 'Not if she picked her time. When Maurice Raines was killed, everybody was out of the way doing their own thing, remember? The conference people at lectures and whatnot, and the college staff doing their cleaning rounds and so forth.'

'Yes, but how would she know when the time was right unless she had access to some sort of timetable, or was holed up somewhere waiting for her opportunity?' Jenny felt compelled to point out. 'I find it hard to believe that she could have even found her way around college without thoroughly checking it out first, let alone manage to find the one time that her husband was on his own, without either a lot of luck, or the sort of planning that would be bound to leave traces. And you haven't found anyone who admits to seeing a strange woman hanging about, have you?'

'No. But she might have come down to Oxford before the conference began and pretended to be a tourist or something, and checked out the lay of the land then,' Trevor said stubbornly. 'Peter, find out if Mrs Raines, the victim's mother, that is, was on this digi-whats-it, and if she is, get a current photograph of Mrs Raines, the wife, and start showing it around college, and see if any of the scouts or anyone else for that matter, recognizes her.'

'Right, guv,' the sergeant said, and was about to leave when the constable came back again.

'Sir, line four. The PM report is in.'

Trevor nodded and reached for the telephone. He listened to the steady voice on the other end, and unhurriedly made notes, ignoring Trent and Jenny, who watched him and tried to guess clues from his reaction. It was a pointless exercise however, and Jenny, with an inner smile, suspected that the inspector would make a demon poker player. His face was, in fact, still expressionless when he finally hung up and turned back to them.

'Well, no big surprises really. Death was due to the knife in his neck, and the pathologist says the shock probably brought on a heart attack, although he would have died anyway from the loss of blood. He had a fairly

healthy liver and heart, for his age, and would have gone
on to live for another good few years yet, apparently.'

Peter grinned at his boss. 'Come on, guv. We're
dying to know, was he poisoned as well?'

'Of course he wasn't,' Jenny murmured automatically, her thoughts already wandering. She was simply
going to have to do something about that mobile phone.
She had half a mind to ask the inspector to see to it, but
he was obviously busy right now. Perhaps, with the bursar's endorsement of her still ringing in their ears, the
scouts would search for it if she asked them.

She nodded, making a mental note to ask Debbie
Dawkins's mother to head the search. She could only
hope that the contents of the waste bins were all stashed
in the bigger refuse bins which hadn't been emptied yet.

Unless, of course, he'd gone to more pains to get rid
of the phone than by simply binning it, Jenny mused.
In which case…. Jenny's thoughts came to a sudden
halt when she realized that both of the policemen were
positively glowering at her.

'What?' she asked defensively.

Trevor Golder sighed at her obviously genuine confusion and ran a hand over his eyes. Well, all of his predecessors who'd worked with her before had, in their
own various ways, tried to warn him to get used to this
feeling that the blasted woman would always be one step
ahead. Now he was beginning to appreciate for himself
just how aggravating that could be.

'How did you know that the victim didn't have the
drugs in his system, Miss Starling?' he asked flatly.

Jenny opened her mouth, then shut it again. No, she
simply wasn't ready yet to come out with the way her
thoughts were heading. These seasoned policemen

would only laugh at her and, more than likely, accuse her of letting her imagination run wild. And who could blame them? Seeing that they were still patiently waiting for an answer, she thought about it for a second, and came up with the obvious solution.

'Well, the coffee cup was still full, wasn't it?' she said sweetly. 'So obviously, he hadn't drunk any of it.'

'It could have been his second cup,' Trevor pointed out icily.

'Oh,' Jenny said. Then looked at him thoughtfully. Perhaps giving him a gentle hint about how the land lay, and then letting him figure it out for himself was the way to go? 'You know, now that I think about it, I remember Maurice saying to some woman at the conference that he was strictly a tea drinker. He liked a special blend, I think he said, and always brought his own supply,' she relayed with clear emphasis, willing him to pick up on it and run with it.

'That's right, I've got a note of that too,' Peter Trent said at once. 'Several people in the initial interviews mentioned Maurice asking for it to be made especially for him after dinner their first night. You know, when everyone else was having the coffee the scouts served afterwards.'

'Hmm,' Trevor said, not willing to let the cook off the hook yet. 'But you were about to say something about the coffee cups before the constable interrupted us. Just what were you about to say?' the inspector challenged. Because he was beginning to get the alarming feeling that the Junoesque cook had already realized that the coffee cup had been poisoned.

Which meant, damn it, that she really *was* way ahead of them.

'Was I?' Jenny said innocently. 'I don't—'

'Oh, there you are, Inspector,' a somewhat imperious female voice interrupted Jenny's need to start telling wholesale fibs, and the cook looked up at the fast approaching Vicki Voight with a smile of sheer gratitude.

But if the treasurer of the Great Jessies noticed it, or even her presence, she gave no sign. 'I wondered if it was possible to have a word. Only, I've been thinking you see, and I'm not sure if anybody else would have thought to tell you. Not that I like to come bearing tales myself, and it almost certainly isn't important, but I thought you'd better know.'

Trevor, dragging his fulminating thoughts away from the aggravating cook, turned to Vicki Voight thoughtfully. Her mass of carefully coloured honey-gold hair had that tint of red in it that he liked, and her figure, although rather fuller than the lady herself would probably have wanted, was the kind that appealed to him. If he hadn't been content in his marriage, she was the sort of woman a man might find tempting.

Which led to the question: Had Maurice been tempted? Perhaps the affair he was having was closer to home than they realized. But there hadn't been even a whisper of it from the rest of the conference-goers, and surely it would have been hard for them to keep it a secret under so many knowing and prying eyes? Besides, when he'd interviewed the lady about Maurice Raines he simply hadn't got that vibe. In fact, he thought he'd detected a certain hint of coolness there.

'Perhaps you could be a little more, well, coherent, Mrs Voight,' Trevor said. 'What is it, exactly, that you think we should know?'

'Well, it's nothing much really. It's about Pippa Foxton actually. You do know she's not one of us, right?'

Trevor blinked. *Not one of us? What the hell was that supposed to mean? Not straight, not a white, Anglo-Saxon protestant; not of the middle classes? What?*

Seeing his confusion, Jenny stepped in smoothly. 'You mean, she's not a paid-up member of your taxidermy society, Mrs Voight?' she asked smoothly.

Vicki glanced at her briefly, then fixed her eyes on the inspector once more. Jenny wasn't insulted. She'd already long since realized that Vicki Voight was a man's woman, so to speak.

'Yes. She's here with Ian as a bit of a lark, obviously. Not that that's what I wanted to point out. So long as she—well, more likely Ian—has paid the fee, what the hell!' Vicki smiled briefly. 'We're not such a stickler for the rules that we would make anything about that! No, it's just about the way she was with Maurice.'

Trevor Golder sat up straight. 'And just how *was* she with Maurice?' he asked quietly.

Vicki, now that it had come to it, looked momentarily unsure. 'Well, that's just it,' she said, somewhat helplessly. 'She was really odd with him.'

'Odd?' Trevor savoured the word thoughtfully. 'In what way, Mrs Voight?'

Vicki sighed. 'Well, it's hard to put into words. You've all met Pippa, right?'

They all nodded. 'A good-looking girl, bit of a fashion *aficionado*, ambitious, and all the rest, yes? The sort that likes to flirt a little, have some fun. And no harm in that, right? Especially with that boyfriend of hers, so smitten and jealous and possessive, it's not surprising that she goes out of her way to wind him up sometimes.'

'Ah,' Trevor said, suddenly seeing the light. 'You mean she was flirting with Maurice? Yes, we have had several reports of that in our interviews, Mrs Voight. One or two of the other members of your society mentioned that she liked wrapping the chairman around her little finger, as I think one of them put it.'

Vicki sighed in obvious impatience. 'Yes, but that's just it, Inspector, it wasn't quite that innocent. I mean, that wasn't all there was to it. I can't explain it, exactly, but it wasn't…normal.'

Trevor shot a quick glance at Jenny to see if she had any clue where this was going, and Jenny gave a quick shake of her head to show that she didn't.

'Not normal?' When in doubt, the inspector had learned that it often paid to simply parrot a phrase and see what came back at you.

Vicki gave another heavy sigh. 'Oh, I knew this was going to be hard to explain. Look, it's normal enough for a pretty girl with a jealous boyfriend to maybe play with fire a bit and flirt with a handsome enough, middle-aged man. I know I used to do it, back when I was Pippa's age. Flirting is fun, and lighthearted, and everybody more or less knows the rules and nobody gets hurt. That's all well and good.'

'I'm with you so far. Are you saying that Pippa took it too far? Did her boyfriend….' Trevor glanced at Trent, who quickly helped him out.

'A Mr Ian Glendower, sir.'

'Right. Did he not, perhaps, see things quite so lightheartedly?'

'Well, no, he didn't as a matter of fact,' Vicki said, with the air of someone who's been distracted. 'He's in that first flush of obsession whereby his sense of balance is all off kilter,' she carried on. 'I know for a fact that he's warned her off Maurice a number of times.'

'Did he make any threats towards Mr Raines himself?' Trevor asked, trying not to sound too eager.

'He might have done, but I never heard him do so personally,' Vicki said vaguely. 'But he's a bit of a hothead, so I wouldn't be surprised. But it's not Ian that's at issue here,' she swept on impatiently. 'His reactions are just what you'd expect from a young man in love: it's Pippa that's not quite right.'

Vicki looked from one of the men to the other. 'There was just something…off, about the way she flirted with Maurice. It wasn't quite…natural. The first time I saw them at it, I hardly paid any attention. I knew it didn't mean anything on the girl's part, and Maurice was too wily to make anything of it for himself, so I never gave it another thought. For all he liked the ladies, Maurice was savvy enough to know when he was being played. Besides, he is…sorry, *was,* always careful to keep his little adventures strictly from the wife. She's the one with the money, you know,' Vicki added, a shade spitefully. 'No, Maurice could see that Pippa was too unpredictable and wild to play away with. So, like I said, I never gave it much thought. But then I began to notice the way she was with him just didn't quite ring true. She was tense, and sometimes the things she said seemed to have some double meaning that she found grim or savagely funny. Once or twice, I could see even Maurice didn't get it, whatever *it* was.'

She was obviously and, to Jenny's mind at least, genuinely struggling to convey the impression she'd received from watching them. The trouble was, she wasn't really succeeding.

'I'm still not sure I know what you mean,' Trevor said cautiously. His copper's instinct was definitely quivering now, but Jenny for one didn't blame him for being uncertain.

She leaned forward slightly, saw the inspector tip her the wink to go ahead and try and sort it out, and began cautiously, 'Do you think Pippa Foxton was genuinely pursuing him?'

'Oh no. That's just it. Sometimes, even when she was flirting with him and at her most outrageous, I couldn't help but feel as if there was some real antipathy there as well.'

Jenny nodded. 'Do you think she might be unbalanced shall we say?'

'Oh, I wouldn't go that far,' Vicki said, sounding a shade alarmed now. 'I'm not a shrink, and I'm not saying that she's touched in the head or anything like that. But…there was just something about her when she was around Maurice that made me uneasy. I just sensed that something wasn't quite right, there.'

Vicki shook her head and held up her hands. 'Look, I can see now that this was a mistake. After all, you're not likely to be interested in my "feminine intuition", are you?' she said, using her fingers to make quote marks in the air. 'It's hardly evidence is it? Just forget I said anything, all right?' she said and, giving them all a general all-purpose apologetic smile, she said goodbye and left.

After she was gone they were all silent for a while. 'And just what was that all about?' Peter Trent finally broke the silence. 'You think she's jealous of this Foxton girl and just wanted to dob her in it?' he asked, but without much conviction.

'No, I don't think so,' Trevor said.

'I think she was genuinely trying to tell us what she knew,' Jenny concurred. 'And a woman like that usually has good instincts,' she added thoughtfully. 'If she thought something was amiss, it probably was. Of course, it might have nothing to do with the case,' she pointed out. 'Perhaps Miss Foxton just has father-figure issues or something. She does have an alibi, doesn't she?' she asked casually.

'Oh yes. With her boyfriend's class all morning,' Peter Trent confirmed.

'Hmm. But she was first on the scene after you'd discovered the body,' Trevor said to Jenny. 'We'd better have her back in and see what she has to say for herself, just in case there's something in it. Peter, see if you can find her and send her down, will you? And get on with those other things too. Time's a-wasting.'

Trent nodded. 'Yes, guv.'

THAT MORNING, PIPPA Foxton was wearing a long, light-weight turquoise and silver-coloured flowing poncho over white stretch skinny jeans. She was wearing her obviously much-adored Jimmy Choo shoes, and was in full make-up. Jenny, who had never seen her in the same outfit twice, wondered about the size and quantity of the luggage she must have brought with her.

'Hello, everyone,' she said cheerily, shooting Jenny a surprised look as she sat down in the seat offered by Peter Trent. 'You were lucky to catch me—I was just about to go to lunch with Ian. He says there's this really recommended little café in St Aldate's that we must try.'

Peter smiled and left to do his boss's bidding, and

Jenny, despite the continued curious glances sent her way by the younger woman, settled herself down more comfortably.

'I have just a few more questions, Miss Foxton,' Trevor began. 'I hope you don't mind Miss Starling's presence, but sometimes we've found that it helps to have an impartial female to sit in on interviews,' Trevor flimflammed with a smile.

'Oh, that's fine. Really, I'm not the nervous type.' Pippa waved a hand vaguely in the air, and Jenny noticed, with some amusement, that her fingernails had been painted a matching turquoise colour. The girl's make-up was flawless as well, and she wondered just how long it took her to get ready in the mornings. Hours, probably, Jenny surmised without envy.

'That's nice to hear,' Trevor said, and hoped she meant it. 'We just want to go over your movements the morning Maurice was found dead,' he said, not quite truthfully.

'Oh, I thought I said.' Pippa batted her lashes at the inspector. 'I had breakfast with Ian and the others, we listened to the opening speeches, then I went to Ian's first lecture/demonstration for all the newbies. Then I left, and bumped into you on the way back and…well… that's that.'

Jenny's eyes narrowed as she wondered if she should warn Pippa that she needed to be more comprehensive and accurate in her details. Then decided that the inspector probably wouldn't appreciate her interrupting the flow of the interview and decided it would probably be best not to butt in.

The inspector, unaware of the cook's thoughts, nod-

ded absently. 'Yes. Were you surprised when you realized that Maurice was dead?' he asked mildly.

Pippa frowned. 'Well, of course I was. I mean, why
wouldn't I be? You don't expect people you know to
just die, do you?'

'No, of course not. And I understand that you had a,
shall we say, somewhat complicated relationship with
Mr Raines, so you must have been upset to hear of his
death?' he persisted gently.

Pippa stiffened a little on her chair and Jenny was
sure that, underneath all that camouflaging make-up,
she had paled. 'Well, I was upset. I mean, I'm human,
the same as anyone else. And just what do you mean,
complicated? There wasn't anything complicated about
it. I hardly knew the man.'

'Ah, but we've had several accounts from people who
said that you and he were pretty friendly.'

Pippa's pretty face tightened ominously. 'There's
some people around here with very dirty minds then,
that's all I can say. I wasn't any more friendly with
Maurice than I was with anyone else, and don't you let
Ian go hearing you say otherwise,' she said grimly, 'or
he'll go mad.'

'So you're denying that you liked flirting with him?'
Trevor said gently, and allowing himself to sound faintly
surprised.

Jenny, listening and watching, silently admired his
technique.

Pippa gave a sudden, nervous laugh. 'Oh, *flirting!*
Well, yeah, I flirted with him a bit. He was good-looking and expected it. But it was just a bit of harmless
fun, that's all. Nobody took it seriously. Or rather'—
she frowned grimly again—'nobody should have.

Look, what's this all about then? Who's been saying stuff against me?' she demanded belligerently, her small chin jutting out in pugnacious petulance.

'It's been suggested though,' Trevor said, ignoring her question, 'that there was something a bit darker than mere flirting going on between you.'

Pippa looked flummoxed for a moment. 'Darker? What do you mean, *darker*?'

'It's been suggested that you might have felt some antipathy towards Mr Raines.'

Seeing that Pippa didn't understand the meaning of the word antipathy and obviously didn't want to show it, Jenny coughed slightly, and said helpfully, 'Someone thought that, although you flirted with Maurice, under-neath, you didn't really like him,' she clarified quietly.

'Oh,' Pippa said. Then shrugged. 'Well, that's daft, isn't it? I just told you, I didn't really know him. He was just the sort you flirted with, you know? An old cod-ger who thought he could still pull the birds. It seemed kinder to play along, that's all. He used to call me "foxy lady" because of my surname, right, and thought it was really clever and nudge-nudge-wink-wink. As if I hadn't heard that a thousand times before!' Pippa rolled her eyes. 'Besides,' she said, her face flushing darkly with sudden anger, 'I'll bet I know who's been saying all this rubbish. It was that woman who's in charge of the money, wasn't it? That Vicki cow.'

'No need to get personal, Miss Foxton,' Trevor said, whilst Jenny thought that it was very interesting indeed that Pippa had got it right first time. She might give the impression of being a bit of a dumb bimbo at times, but clearly she was very astute when it came to social interaction and reading people.

'Well, she's a one to throw stones,' Pippa muttered rebelliously. 'Especially since Maurice was on to *her*, all right.'

Trevor felt his hackles rise. This was the first he was hearing of his murder victim being suspicious of one of his fellow conference-goers. 'Sorry? On to her how?'

Pippa sighed. 'I'm not really sure, to be honest,' she admitted, clearly annoyed to have to admit as much. 'It's just something Maurice said about her once, that's all. I never listened to him half the time; he could talk the hind legs off a donkey, he liked to hear his own voice that much.'

'Can you think what it was about, exactly?' Trevor prompted patiently. 'It could be important.'

Pippa sighed. 'Well, he said something about knowing what she'd been up to, and that she wasn't the only one good with figures. 'Course, then he had to go on and comment about mine.' Pippa smiled, pulling the poncho down over her generous curves to show what she meant. 'But he was talking about financial figures, I think. I got the impression that that Vicki woman might have been cooking the books or something, and he was on to her. She is the one in charge of the money, right? I daresay she just helped herself to some petty cash or something, and he found out about it. It couldn't have been any big deal, anyway, could it, since she was still the treasurer?'

Jenny caught Trevor's eye and raised an eyebrow.

Trevor nodded thoughtfully. 'Interesting,' he said quietly.

Pippa smiled, clearly pleased to have sent the ball slamming back into her opponent's side of the court.

'And you're sure you yourself had no serious issue

with Mr Raines?' Trevor said, catching her self-satisfied smirk.

'No,' Pippa said flatly.

'And you never argued with him?'

'No, I never.'

Trevor nodded. 'All right, Miss Foxton. Thank you for your time.'

Pippa nodded, clearly not sure whether to be relieved that the interview was over, or indignant over the aspersions cast on her character, and in the end simply stalked off in a wave of expensive perfume.

'Well, that might be an interesting little tidbit, if true,' Trevor said, and reached for the telephone. Jenny listened, with only half an ear, as he ordered someone with financial savvy to check over the society's books as a matter of urgency and get back to him straight away.

'Don't forget Vicki Voight has an alibi too,' Jenny reminded him absently. She really was going to have to get the search for that mobile phone underway. She slipped down off her stool. 'I'll get going, if you don't mind, Inspector,' she began, and then shot around as Peter Trent all but ran into the room.

He excitedly beckoned his chief over towards the door and Jenny, following on more slowly, was just in time to hear the sergeant's words.

'Guv, she's shown up at last. Raines's wife. She just walked into the police station in St Aldate's, asking to speak to the officer in charge.'

Jenny watched the two happy men rush away, and frowned thoughtfully.

She wondered what Mrs Maurice Raines would have to say for herself.

And then she wondered just how long it would take the inspector to arrest her for the murder of her husband.

LAURA RAINES LOOKED up as the door to the interview room opened and two men walked in. Her eyes went between them, lingered for a while on the older of the two, but then went back to the weighty man with brown hair and curious brown eyes.

'Are you the one in charge of my husband's case?' she asked calmly, and Trevor, taking a seat, nodded. He introduced himself and his sergeant, for both the recording device and the widow's benefit, stated the time and then folded his hands comfortably in front of him on the table. He looked at her mildly.

'First of all, Mrs Raines, let me say that I'm sorry for your loss. Perhaps we can just go over the preliminaries and get things in order before we start. You are the wife of Mr Maurice Raines, I take it.' He cited the victim's address, and Laura nodded. Then she cleared her throat.

'Yes.'

Trevor nodded, trying to get the measure of this witness and potential suspect. She was still a very attractive woman, with fair hair and big grey eyes and a slender figure. Her make-up was discreet, and she was wearing a skirt and jacket of moss green, with a cream blouse. She wore little jewellery—just a plain gold watch, and pearl stud earrings, but both looked to be of high quality. She was, in his opinion, typical of the kind of woman who'd always known money, and was sure of her status in life.

'Can I ask, Mrs Raines, where you have been for the last few days?' he inquired quietly.

Laura took a deep breath. She'd discussed what they

must do with Simon earlier this morning, and they'd both agreed that they needed to get back to Oxford and see what was happening. And, as the victim's wife, it would look very suspicious indeed if she didn't come forward. Not that it hadn't taken all her nerve to walk into the police building in this unknown city, not knowing what might be waiting for her on the other side. It had been awful waiting for this moment to arrive, and now it came as something of a relief to her to be getting it over with.

But she'd never lacked nerve, and now she needed to be both calm and clearheaded.

'Yes, certainly,' she began, taking a slow, long breath. 'When my husband goes away on these interminable conferences of his, I take the opportunity to have a little holiday of my own. This time, I decided to spend some time on the south coast. Hayling Island in fact.'

She didn't volunteer the name of the inn, but she knew she'd have to, eventually. And, of course, the staff would confirm the presence of that hoary old chestnut, 'the other man'. But she was in no hurry to start volunteering information just yet.

Well, none that would be of any use to the police, anyway. She needed to find out as much as she could about what had been going on first.

'This morning, I rang my children, just to check in, and they told me about…about what had happened to Maurice. Naturally, I came here straight away.' She stared down at her hands in her lap, noticed her wedding ring and quickly looked back up at the inspector.

'Yes, we notified your children as soon as we could,' Trevor agreed. 'But we had trouble locating you. Your children tried your mobile number but couldn't get an answer.' His tone made it more of a question than a statement, and she gave a slight grimace.

'Oh, no they wouldn't,' Laura said vaguely. 'I'm afraid I'd just lost the damn thing. Only a matter of a day or so, but it meant I had to buy a new one, and I hadn't given them the new number yet. I daresay the old one will turn up at home down the back of the sofa or something; they usually do, don't they?' She shrugged. 'I suppose I should have phoned them to tell them I'd arrived safely, but I just didn't think of it at the time.'

She cleared her throat and then looked Trevor squarely in the eye. 'They told me he'd been found dead in the college where the conference was being held. At first, I thought it must have been a heart attack, or stroke or maybe some kind of an accident. But they seemed to believe, that is, they had been *led* to believe by one of your people, that that wasn't the case.' Unconsciously she leaned forward a little against the table. 'But is that really true, Inspector? Isn't it possible there has been some kind of bad accident? Maybe something freakish, and unusual, but accidental nonetheless?' Her voice, although still even and calm, had a hint of wild hope in it.

'I'm afraid not, Mrs Raines. It's a clear case of unlawful killing,' Trevor contradicted gently but firmly.

Laura swallowed once, then nodded. Yes. She expected as much. Simon had been very clear on that. Even so, she'd been hoping against hope, all the way on that hellish drive over here, that he'd got it wrong that there must be some other explanation, no matter how bizarre.

'I see,' she said flatly.

Trevor saw her shoulders sag infinitesimally, and sighed. He never knew how people were going to react to the loss of a family member, and he'd been prepared for floods of tears, anger, disbelief, shock or a combination of all three. But he'd seen at once that Laura Raines was a member of the old-fashioned breed who still believed in maintaining a stiff upper lip.

Whilst that could be useful in some ways, in getting a coherent and logical statement, for example, a bit of honest, spontaneous emotion often told you a lot more, but he was well aware that he'd be getting no such helping hand from the lady in front of him now.

'When did it happen?' Laura asked.

It was a reasonable question, but Trevor hesitated before answering it. Would it give her a chance to concoct an alibi? If she were his number one suspect, he'd be inclined to give out as little information as possible, but at the moment, he had no real reason to suspect her any more or less than anyone else. On the other hand, he would have to find out where she was at the time anyway, so there was little point in keeping it from her.

'Yesterday between eleven-thirty and twelve noon, Mrs Raines.'

Laura nodded, without any sign of emotion. No relief, no anger, and no fear, which surprised Trevor Golder quite a bit. Of course, she could just be numb, or going into shock, he surmised. In which case, he needed to push the interview on.

'May I ask where you were at that time?' Trevor asked, as delicately as he could.

Laura nodded slowly. 'Yes, of course. I think I was arriving at the hotel about then. It must have been, as I remembered thinking it was still a little too early for lunch, and that I should have time to unpack before….' Her voice trailed off. 'So it was then that he…went.

Funny, to think that I was blithely unpacking. You're supposed to have premonitions, or something, aren't you, when something bad's happening to an important member of your life? But I hadn't a clue.'

Her voice had become softer as she spoke and, as if suddenly realizing that she was in danger of sounding maudlin, she seemed to give a mental shake, and her voice rose back to its normal, no-nonsense volume again. 'You'll be wanting to know the name of the hotel, I expect. To confirm what I'm telling you?'

She said it without resentment, but it was clear that she was not particularly happy about it either.

'I'm afraid so.'

Laura nodded once, and recited the name and address of the hotel. She wondered how long it would take them to question the staff and learn about Simon. Not long, she was sure. An hour or so? She'd signed them both in under her name, and using her credit cards, so they wouldn't have Simon's details. But she'd have to tell them, when asked.

But Laura was in no hurry.

'Do you have any leads, Inspector?' she demanded briskly.

'I find it impossible to think that anyone would want to kill Maurice. Oh, I know that he could be a bit of an autocrat at times, and many people in that awful little society of his probably wanted to throttle him from time to time, but not literally.'

She paused and sighed. 'Was it someone at the college itself? Or a random thing? How, exactly… I mean, can you tell me what happened?' Her tone was somewhere between a demand and a plea.

Again, Trevor hesitated. He was certain that Laura

would be too intelligent to supply him with a false alibi that could so easily be checked, which meant that she was certainly not the killer of her husband. On the other hand, she was not altogether in the clear yet, and he needed to know much more about her movements and the state of her marriage before he started giving away details.

He was also aware that the woman's husband was dead, and that she was entitled to certain human dignities.

'I'm afraid your husband was killed with a weapon in the hall of the college where he was staying,' Trevor said carefully. 'As of yet, we've found no witnesses to the crime, and have uncovered no reason why anyone would want him dead.'

Trevor watched her carefully, but the pale, composed face, remained pale and composed.

'I see,' Laura said. Then she took a long, slow breath. 'I suppose, in questioning the other people in that silly little society, that they must have told you something of Maurice's reputation. With women, I mean,' she said with total aplomb, and again, looking him squarely in the eye.

Trevor, who hadn't been looking forward to bringing up just this subject, felt a small spurt of gratitude to her for easing the way.

'It had been mentioned that he was something of a man with the ladies, yes,' Trevor said cautiously. 'Although no one was able to say with any authority that it amounted to anything more than his manner and some flirting.'

Laura smiled slightly. 'I see. Nice of them to be so discreet.' Again, she and Simon had discussed how

much and what she should tell the police, and they'd
agreed that keeping Maurice's affairs a secret would be
counterproductive. Indeed, when it came time to admit
to their own love affair, it could only help them to have
laid the ground in their favour.

'I have to tell you, Inspector, that the rumours were
true. Maurice and I…our marriage, that is, was, well,
to all intents and purposes, more or less over.'

Trevor nodded. He showed no signs of excitement
or suspicion and Laura was to some extent reassured.

'Yes. Once the children were well into their teens,
things between us just seemed to peter out,' she explained simply. 'Oh, it was nothing dramatic. There
were no big scenes, or recriminations, or anything like
that.' She smiled briefly. 'It was just a question of a
gradual widening of the gulf between us, I suppose.
Maurice had always had his outlandish work, which
seemed to make him happy, and I had my hobbies and
interests too. My family has always had money, you
see,' Laura said matter-of-factly. 'It was my money that
started up Maurice's firm, and I've kept up my own social circle of friends and activities. Art, mainly. I'm on
the board of several galleries. Anyway, you don't want
to know all about that,' Laura said practically. 'You
want to know about the other women.'

She leaned back in the seat and sighed. 'Maurice's
women,' she said thoughtfully. 'I was inclined, looking
back, to think that he started with them when the children were almost fully grown, but I think it more likely
now that they'd always been there, more or less right
from the start; I was just too busy to notice. When I finally did…well, they just didn't seem to matter much.'

Laura paused and looked at the two policemen

thoughtfully. 'Of course, I have no way of proving that's true. For all you know, I might be one of those pathologically jealous women who are desperate to keep their men, and react violently to any woman who tries to steal them.' She stopped, thought about it for a while, and then shrugged. 'I imagine you can ask our mutual friends and neighbours and what-have-yous. If they're honest with you, they'll probably paint the same picture that I am. I mean,'—and here she gave a sudden bark of laughter that was not exactly lacking in irony—'I suppose Maurice and I were a common enough, trite little story. A marriage slowly dying on its feet out of boredom and indifference. It would have ended in divorce, sooner or later,' she said sadly, then added vaguely, 'They always do, don't they? It was just that neither one of us had got around to making the effort yet.'

She reached for the jug of water on the table and poured herself a glass. It was dry in the little interview room and she suddenly felt thirsty. She felt drained and tired, and longed to go to Simon and have him hold her and tell her that it would be all right, even if he was lying.

This feeling of constantly walking a tightrope was taking it out of her, and she hoped the interview wouldn't go on much longer.

'Thank you for your candour, Mrs Raines, we appreciate it. Now, just a few more facts, if you don't mind,' Trevor said.

'Of course. Whatever you like,' she forced herself to say with a grim smile.

'Do you have much contact with your mother-in-law?'

Laura stared at the policeman for a second, looked totally nonplussed and then smiled uncertainly. 'Not really, no. She's not very well, and I think Maurice was thinking of arranging for her to go into a home soon. But we got on all right, as mother-in-law and daughter-in-law I mean. I'm sorry, but I don't quite see how that's relevant?'

Trevor nodded. 'Just bear with me a bit, Mrs Raines. When was the last time you visited her at her home?'

'Yonks ago. Maurice called on her regularly, and sometimes we'd have her over to our home for Sunday lunch. But not so much recently, as I said, since she's getting rather frail.'

Clearly, Laura Raines seemed to be struggling to see where this line of questioning was going, and Trevor didn't want to push it. If the lady had had access to her mother-in-law's heart medication, she wasn't going to give the game away easily. If she was somehow responsible for that poisoned coffee cup, he didn't want to alert her to her danger unduly.

'When was the last time you saw your husband?' he asked next.

'The day he left to come down to Oxford.'

'Did he seem normal in his manner? Worried about the up-coming conference perhaps?'

'No, he seemed the same as usual,' Laura said.

'He never mentioned any threatening phone calls, or that he'd made an enemy of someone in the society perhaps?'

'Good grief, no,' Laura said, again sounding clearly astonished.

'Did he mention to you anything about Mrs Voight, or the finances of the society? Did he voice any suspicions about anyone?'

'No. But then Maurice wouldn't, even if that was the

case,' Laura assured them. 'He was the sort of man who liked to handle things himself.'

For a moment that thought hung in the air, and all three people in the room were clearly thinking the same thing. Namely, this time, Maurice Raines had taken on more than he could handle.

Trevor broke the silence with a small sigh. 'All right, Mrs Raines, that's all for now. I take it that you're going to be staying on in Oxford for a while?'

'Yes, I've taken a room at the Randolph.' She named the famous, first-class hotel in the centre of town.

Trevor saw Peter Trent take a note of it, and nodded. 'We'll be in touch again soon,' Trevor said. 'Perhaps you could give my sergeant the number of your new mobile phone, so that we can remain in contact?'

Laura Raines did so, rose steadily, gave a brief smile to each of the men, and left.

When she was gone, they were silent for a moment. Then the sergeant stirred.

'Formidable woman, that,' he remarked at last.

'Yes,' Trevor agreed thoughtfully.

'She was hiding something,' his sergeant remarked.

'Yes,' Trevor again agreed thoughtfully. 'Get on to the hotel in Hayling Island. I want her alibi confirmed.'

The sergeant nodded, snapped his notebook shut and left.

Trevor continued to sit in the empty interview room for some little time, tapping his forefinger thoughtfully against his lips. For all her apparent frankness, calm equilibrium and her smooth co-operation, the experienced policeman was convinced of one thing: Laura Raines was a woman desperately afraid.

EIGHT

THE NEXT DAY, the two policemen drove through the college gates almost in tandem. Trevor parked first, then waited for his sergeant to join him before turning and heading towards the incident room. As they walked, they caught up on yesterday's findings.

'You've got the last of the uniform reports in on any sightings around the college of anyone acting suspiciously, right?' Trevor asked, nodding at one of the scouts who looked vaguely familiar and who scuttled past them pushing a laundry trolley.

'Yeah, no real joy, though,' Peter Trent sighed. 'Just the usual—a few troublemakers who wanted to make life difficult for someone they've got it in for. One even claimed that he saw his neighbour walking past the college with a machete! Nothing in it, of course. We're thinking of doing *him* for wasting police time.' The sergeant snorted in disgust. 'We had two reports of a street person, who turned out to be well known to the locals, and who'd spent the morning of the murder sleeping it off in the cells before being released just before eleven. Apparently, the bottom end of the college grounds was a regular begging spot for him. But his clothes were clean—well, not clean obviously,' the older man said with a wide grin, 'but free of any blood spots anyway.'

'And nobody reported seeing any dark-haired, thirty-something man leaving the college at any of the exits

or entrances wearing bloodstained clothing, I suppose,'
Trevor interrupted the woeful listings wearily.

'Sorry, guv, no. Nearest we got was one bloke of Oriental appearance, who seemed to be wearing a dark, stained T-shirt. Turns out he was a cook at a local Chinese takeaway, and the stains in question were mostly soy-sauce. Gave the lucky plod checking that one out a free meal, apparently.'

Trevor snorted. 'Right.' He filled in his sergeant on the latest forensic findings, which were equally unhelpful. There had, of course, been a lot of fingerprints and trace evidence found in hall around Maurice Raines's body, but then there would be. Half the college and all the conference-goers had been in hall at some point.

'We also heard back from the victim's solicitor,' Trevor concluded. 'Seems the will is straightforward enough. Some gifts of various stuffed creatures to people in the taxidermy society, and the bulk of his money left to his two kids.'

Trent frowned thoughtfully. 'Nothing to the wife then. Significant, you think?'

Trevor shrugged. 'Not really. According to the solicitor, Maurice Raines's estate wasn't that big. Although he lived in a big house, ran a nice car and owned his own business, the bulk of the money in the marriage belonged to the wife. Her money's tied up in trusts. The house is in her name, the cars likewise. Insurance policies, ditto. She even owns half his taxidermy business, since it was her money that financed it, and Daddy's solicitors made sure she wasn't ever shortchanged. So Maurice himself had very little in real assets to leave.

No, I don't think we can argue the case that the widow had any financial reasons for having him bumped off.'

'Well, let's hope something breaks today,' Peter said philosophically. 'And speaking of the widow, do you want to tackle the lady about her hotel-mate today?'

Trevor pushed open the door to the incident room and thought about it. 'Possibly.' On the face of it, the fact that Laura Raines had spent the time of her husband's murder on the south coast with another man was definitely a meaty morsel to get your teeth into; on the other hand, she'd already admitted in her initial interview that she and her husband had pretty much lived openly in a dead-end marriage. So, presumably, each partner felt able to stray without worrying too much about what the other thought of it, or any nasty little consequences that might ensue.

Also, it had been confirmed by the management and staff that Laura Raines had been checking in at the time of the crime, and had shortly been joined by her lover so there was no hurry to confront either one of them yet.

'The fact that she kept quiet about him might mean there's something there, guv,' Peter said thoughtfully.

'Possibly. Mind you, there needn't be anything in it for us just because she was being cagey about him either. She struck me as a private sort of person. And not volunteering information isn't the same as lying: she might just have seen keeping quiet about him as a good idea at the time. Still, we need to speak to them both at some point. You've got people running him down?'

'Yes, guv. I ran a computer check last night: he's got no record, not even a speeding fine. He's younger than her by a fair bit, and a good-looking bloke as you might expect according to his driving licence photo.'

Trevor grunted, but said nothing. At his desk, he took off his jacket and reached for the laptop to check his emails. 'Well, let's see what today brings. I can't help but wonder what that damned cook's up to,' he muttered quietly, so that none of the others working in the office could hear him. So far, word hadn't seemed to have spread amongst the troops about her, and he wanted to keep it that way.

Peter grinned. 'I know what you mean. Sharp, isn't she?'

Trevor smiled grimly, but said nothing as he opened his first electronic message.

Peter Trent decided to prod him gently. 'And she has been useful, sir,' he added mildly.

'Oh yes, she has been that,' Trevor agreed flatly.

AT THAT MOMENT, the Junoesque cook was being helpful to the police investigation once again. Or rather, a scout named Dorothy Greening was being helpful, and Jenny was listening closely.

Jenny had just overseen the breakfast rush, and was sitting in a quiet corner of the vast kitchens enjoying a much-needed cup of tea, when a white-haired, slightly nervous woman in a pink overall slid inside and glanced around timidly. Since most of the kitchen staff were busy washing up, the scout was able to pick out the woman she needed easily, and she approached quickly.

Jenny watched the sixty-something woman approach and smiled her friendliest smile. The woman, who was barely five feet tall, had the petite person's brisk way of walking, like she had energy and more to spare for everything that she did. But she was looking uneasy, and Jenny wanted to reassure her. So, as she arrived, Jenny pushed out another chair.

'Hello, have a seat. Want a cup of tea?' she offered amiably.

'Oh, er, no thanks,' the older woman said, a little wrong-footed by the offer. 'You are the cook, right, that Mavis said we needed to see? About the phone?' She sounded uncertain now, as if she doubted that this large, young but friendly woman could possibly be the liaison between the college staff and the coppers.

Jenny nodded, although she had no idea who Mavis was. She'd asked Debbie Dawkins's mother to spread the word around the scouts, asking if a mobile phone had been found or discarded since the taxidermist's conference had started. No doubt she had passed that message on to the mysterious Mavis, amongst others.

'Yes, that's me. Found it, have you?' she asked casually.

To her surprise, the older woman looked abruptly miserable. 'I don't want to lose my job, miss,' she said, whispering it so that none of the others in the kitchen could hear. Not that they were paying any notice. 'I didn't mean to do nothing wrong, honest. Only it were in the bin, see. Obviously, nobody wanted it. If it's been chucked out, it isn't stealing, is it? Not if it was in the bin,' the scout reiterated in a nervous, sibilant rush.

Jenny instantly twigged. 'No, of course not. If it was in a bin it was rubbish, and discarded. You just found it and decided to recycle it, instead of just tossing it away, and why not? A perfectly good mobile, was it?' she asked sympathetically.

The older woman looked relieved. 'Right. I thought at first it must be broken, see, otherwise why chuck it?'

Her little head tilted a bit to one side, reminding Jenny of a curious bird contemplating a worm. 'But when I turned it on, it lit up and everything. And had a dial tone. Not that I know much about them—I never use 'em myself. But my Sheila said she needed a new one, but couldn't afford one, so I thought, why not? It doesn't matter, not if someone's thrown it away, like you said.'

'Oh, absolutely,' Jenny agreed, with another reassuring smile. 'It's amazing what perfectly good stuff people throw away nowadays, isn't it? By the way, what's your name?'

'Oh, Dotty. Dorothy Greening, that is,' she said, suddenly remembering that the bursar himself had told everyone that they had to tell this woman anything that they might know. 'I work over there.' She pointed through a small side window out across the quad towards one of the residential buildings where the majority of the conference-goers were being housed. 'Cleaner, see? I found it in one of the big wastepaper baskets in the entrance hall, underneath the pigeonholes. Where they picks up their mail and messages and whatnots.'

So saying, she reached into the pocket of her voluminous pinafore and brought out a smart-looking, up-to-the-minute mobile in a dark plum colour. 'A beauty, ain't it?' Dotty said admiringly. 'Luckily, I hadn't got around to seeing Sheila yet, so I hadn't given it to her. So she won't even know she might've been able to have it. If you see what I mean.'

Jenny did. She glanced at the phone, wondering if she should try and get a napkin to preserve any fingerprints that might be on it, but then realized that Dotty had probably handled it thoroughly. Even so. She reached for a paper napkin, and held it out to the older woman. Not surprisingly, Dotty's eyes widened in dismay.

'Oh crikey, you really think it's important then? To do with that poor sod what got done in?' she asked unhappily, as she dropped the mobile gingerly into the big cook's now protected hand.

'It's possible, Dotty, yes. We need to get it to the police. Don't worry,' she added quickly, as the older woman reared back. 'You don't have to do it alone; I'll come with you,' she soothed, guessing that the other woman had probably never had anything to do with the police in her life. 'And we needn't say anything about you taking the mobile phone home and maybe giving it to Sheila, hmm?' she encouraged brightly. 'We'll just tell them where you found it and that you handed it over to me when you heard that the police were looking for it. That's simple enough, isn't it?'

The old scout looked relieved at this, if not much happier, but she nodded glumly and gamely, and, with a resigned slump of her shoulders, followed the cook out of the kitchen.

PETER TRENT WAS the first to spot them as they entered the incident room, and nudged Trevor on the arm. Trevor took one look at the glum-faced and clearly nervous older woman, and read the situation in a nano-second. As they approached, he asked Peter loudly to go get them all a nice cup of tea, whilst at the same time feeling a distinct sense of *déjà vu*.

This was the second time that Jenny Starling had brought one of the scouts to them with something interesting to relate. He wondered what it would be this time.

It took little time for Dotty to tell her—slightly

amended—tale about finding the mobile phone in the wastepaper basket. Gentle questioning by the patient Peter Trent produced the information that Dotty emptied the bins every day, and that the phone had been found on the morning that the 'poor man had died', around her usual time of doing the hall, which was between half past ten and eleven, which meant it could have been dropped in there at anytime from the same period the day before.

Trevor thanked her, took the napkin-wrapped gift with enthusiasm and told the relieved old woman that she could go.

When Dorothy had all but skipped like a spring lamb from the room, he stood for a few seconds staring down at the mobile, then looked at the cook curiously.

'I take it from all that, that you'd actually asked the scouts to search for a discarded mobile phone?' he asked calmly. Very calmly, he thought, since this was the first he'd heard about it.

'Yes,' Jenny agreed, not liking the very patient tone of his voice much. Rather belatedly she realized that she'd managed to get into the inspector's bad books. Again.

'And just what made you do that? I mean, what made you think that there'd even be one in the first place?' he demanded, still with the same tone of dogmatic patience.

'Well, it seemed to me that there might be one,' Jenny said cautiously. 'And if there was, I thought it best to find it before the dustbin men came.'

Peter Trent, sensing that his superior's blood pressure was probably rising too much for everyone's good, reached for the phone and, using the napkin to keep his own prints off it, turned it on and began to explore.

'Yes, but what made you think—' Trevor persisted through gritted teeth, when he heard his sergeant suddenly draw in his breath.

'Bloody hell,' Peter whistled under his breath. Then, looking up, said excitedly, 'Guv, do you know who's phone this is?'

Trevor scowled. 'Obviously not, Sergeant, since you're the one looking at the log of its calls,' he pointed out with heavy sarcasm. Then he shot an equally none-too-friendly look at the cook. He'd have bet a month's salary that this bloody woman not only knew whose phone it was, but probably knew what it had been doing in a wastepaper bin in the first place and who had put it there.

'Miss Starling, I want a word with you, and I think—' he began aggressively, when once again his sergeant interrupted him.

'Guv, it's Laura Raines's phone!' he said, the excitement in his voice making several heads turn their way. Including the inspector's.

'The widow's phone? That's right, she told us she'd lost it just recently,' he said, then quickly walked behind Trent and stared down at the mobile over his shoulder. 'What was the last call made on it?' he demanded abruptly.

Peter fiddled with it, a shade clumsily since he was still using the napkin to preserve prints. He read it out.

'That's Simon Jenks, guv, I recognize the number. That's the bloke she was staying with in Hayling Island.'

'And the time and date?' Trevor pressed.

'Hold on, I've got to go back to the menu…here it

is… The night before Maurice Raines died. It was a text message.'

'Well, pull it up,' Trevor barked.

His sergeant did so and both men's faces went tight with excitement as they read it. 'At last,' Trevor hissed. 'Finally, we're getting somewhere. Right, let's get the widow Raines back in. This time she has some real explaining to do.'

Jenny said nothing as she watched both men leave hurriedly. She sighed heavily, then got up and made her way back to the kitchen. She had the evening menu to prepare.

She wanted to start with a nice watercress and Stilton soup. Except her budget wouldn't stretch to Stilton, so she'd sourced a locally produced blue cheese that was a fraction of the cost but would be, almost, equally delicious.

Now she needed to think of a good main course to go with it.

But, as she worked, her mind kept going back to Laura Raines and the two policemen. She knew what they were thinking of course—and she was almost sure that they were wrong.

It would be pointless trying to tell them that at this stage, though. She needed much more proof than mere theories, no matter how well they fitted with all the evidence.

She sighed, and decided she'd better get on with it. She'd already got a few odds and ends sorted out to add weight to her working hypothesis, but she was still a long way from producing anything like the proof needed to convince the police.

There was someone though who might just be able to help her out.

Leaving the kitchen and her menu only half-planned, the cook made her way to the same residential building where Dotty had found the mobile. She'd had the list of room numbers from Art, which showed where everyone was staying, but so far she'd avoided bearding anyone in their den, so to speak. Now she had no choice.

It was nearly lunchtime and, with a bit of luck, the conference-goers wouldn't be at lectures or buying goods from the tables that were set up in hall, so she might just catch him in.

She climbed to the second floor, passed a stuffed roe deer that had been deposited on the half-landing, and knocked on the second door on the right.

It opened after just a few moments, and Ian Glendower stared out at her.

'Yes?' he said sharply, his eyes narrowing on the cook.

Jenny smiled mildly. 'Oh, hello, Mr Glendower, I don't suppose you remember me? I'm Jenny Starling.' She held out her hand firmly in the face of his continuing silence and forced him to shake it. 'I'm the cook here. I wondered if I could just ask you something?'

Ian Glendower frowned. 'What about?' he asked suspiciously.

Jenny knew right there and then that she was going to have to be very careful now. 'Well, actually, it's about stuffing a tiger,' she said, with a bright, warm smile.

DEBBIE DAWKINS ALWAYS enjoyed her lunch hour. It wasn't that she particularly hated working at the department store, but doing two jobs meant that every free hour was especially precious to her.

Today, she was meeting up with her oldest pal Tracey at a little snack bar just off New Inn Hall Street that had a good reputation with vegetarians. Not that she was that way inclined herself, but it was Tracey's latest fad, and she didn't mind giving it a go.

The two friends had just ordered various salads, and were busy gossiping about the latest scandal to afflict an old school friend, when Tracey noticed that Debbie kept staring at someone over her shoulder.

Naturally, she turned around curiously, but saw no one that she knew. 'What's so fascinating behind me?' Tracey, a round-faced girl with untidy blonde hair and wide-spaced brown eyes, asked with a small grin. 'Seen someone you fancy have you?'

'That bloke over in the corner. Talking to the ash-blonde,' Debbie said, her mouth going dry.

Quickly her friend checked him out and turned back, grinning. 'Very nice. Bit out of your league though, girl, if you don't mind my saying,' Tracey said cheekily. 'And that woman he's with is wearing a couple of thousand quid in jewellery or I'm a monkey's uncle. Think he's her toy boy?'

'No, that's not it,' Debbie hissed. 'I think that might be him.'

'Him? Who?' Tracey said, then suddenly paled. 'Oh. You mean *him?* Bloody hell, Debs, are you serious?'

Of course, Debbie had told her best friend all about the excitement at the college and, since it was all over the news, Tracey had been eager to get the full low down on the college killing. So she knew all about her friend seeing someone leave the murder site at around the time of the killing.

'Do I look like I'm joking?' Debbie said, nervously, crumbling away at the bread roll on her side plate.

Tracey felt slightly sick. 'Oh, Debs, are you sure?' she leaned forward and reached a hand shakily over the table, stopping her friend from shredding the bread. 'Act cool, yeah?' she whispered nervously. 'I don't think he's seen us or anything, so don't worry. Are you sure it's him though?'

'No. How can I be sure, not a hundred per cent sure?' Debbie said slowly. 'But it looks awfully like him. I saw him mostly from the back, remember, and briefly, the side of his face, not head on, like now,' she whispered back. 'But it really looks like it could be him.'

The scout bit her lip. 'Or am I just thinking it must be him because he's the first man I've seen that fits? I mean, right sort of hair, right sort of build? I don't know. Oh, Trace, what do you think I should do?' she implored.

Tracey's big brown eyes widened even more as she thought about it for a second or two. Then, 'You ought to phone the cops, I reckon,' she whispered, so quietly that Debbie almost didn't hear her. 'You got the number of that cop who talked to you? Inspector what's-his-name?'

'Golder. No,' Debbie whispered back. 'But I'll call the college, shall I? The switchboard in the lodge will be able to put me through to him. They've got an incident room there. You really think I should? What if it's not him? I'll feel such a prat, Trace.'

'Yeah, but on the other hand, what if it *is* him?' Tracey responded pragmatically. 'I mean, they can't fault you for it, can they, even if it turns out to be a false alarm? I mean, it would be an honest mistake, wouldn't it?'

Debbie reluctantly phoned the college, and within a few minutes, she was talking to Peter Trent, and telling him where she was and what was happening.

Her friend listened, pale-faced but clearly excited, to her friend's one-sided conversation.

'Yes, Sergeant, it really looks like him. But I can't say for sure. He's sitting in the back of the café, and it's a little dark in the corner... What?... Yes, he's with a woman. Older, dressed really nice, a lady, with pale blonde hair... No, he hasn't. I don't think so anyway? Should me and my friend leave?... OK... Yes, we'll wait outside. Right. Yes.'

She hung up and rose. 'Come on, we've got to wait outside. They're coming over,' she whispered down at her friend, who shot up eagerly and grabbed her bag.

It was easily the most exciting lunch Tracey had ever had.

PETER TRENT AND Trevor Golder arrived about five minutes later.

Debbie quickly described to the inspector where they had been sitting, and what the man was wearing, but already Peter Trent was looking through the window. When he walked back to Trevor, he said quietly, 'The lady is Laura Raines, sir.'

Trevor nodded, thanked Debbie and told her that they would be needing a formal statement later, but for now, she was free to get back to work. He watched the excitedly chattering, but slightly shaken girls, walk away, then turned to Trent.

'Right then, let's have them in,' he said, with quiet satisfaction.

Laura Raines was the first to spot them, and Trevor saw her lean forward and quickly say something to her companion. A moment later, the man looked over at them, clearly going pale and looking alarmed. He saw Laura Raines reach out and put her hand over his and say something urgently.

The man nodded, but licked his lips nervously. When the two police officers arrived at their table, Laura smiled a shade grimly at them.

'Inspector Golder. I take it you want to speak to me again?' she asked, her chin coming up in definite challenge.

'Yes, Mrs Raines. And this is Mr Jenks, I presume? Simon Jenks?' Trevor said, not letting her get the upper hand. If she thought she could control this process, she needed to know better.

The handsome younger man seemed to flinch, but he managed to nod his head wordlessly.

'In which case, sir, I really need to speak to you as well. Perhaps you could both come down to the St Aldate's station with me?' Trevor asked blandly.

Simon Jenks went even paler than ever and, when he rose, Trevor would have bet a month's salary that his legs were shaking so hard they felt barely able to support him. He wasn't surprised when the younger man actually reached out to steady himself against the back wall of the café as he stood up.

He also shot Laura Raines a quick look that Trevor found hard to place exactly. It had an element of pleading certainly. And fear, definitely. Also one of bafflement and, perhaps, a touch of uncertainty? It was as if he was looking to his lover to both save him, and yet, at the same time, he seemed to be trying to understand exactly what it was that he needed to be saved from.

It boded well for an interesting interview ahead, but as they drove the short distance to St Aldate's, Trevor wasn't entirely sure that things were going to go quite how he expected them to. There was something about the pair of them that wasn't quite right—that didn't quite fit the pattern he was expecting.

And it worried him.

THEY SEPARATED THEM at St Aldate's, with Peter Trent taking the widow to one interview room, whilst Trevor took the widow's lover to another.

Simon Jenks followed the heavy-set slightly older man into the small room with a feeling of vague numbness, interlaced with rolling waves of nausea. He'd known this moment had to come, but he'd never expected it to come so soon. Or that he'd be taken from an inoffensive little café in the middle of the day, and abruptly thrust into an environment like this.

He looked around the brick room, with its dirty whitewash, high, barred windows and scuffed tiled floor, and it was as if he could almost hear a cell door clang shut. He forced himself to take a deep breath, and very happily accepted the wooden chair that the inspector indicated. He all but fell into it, glad to take the weight off his feet.

He felt curiously light-headed.

He had to force himself to remember what he and Laura had discussed. He had to make sure he got it right. But as he faced the bland-faced man in front of him, he wasn't sure that that was the right thing to do.

He wasn't sure how much he could trust Laura, that was the trouble. Worse, he was assailed with the terrible, lemming-like compulsion to just tell this quiet, almost friendly-looking man everything that had happened and get it over and done with.

But disaster lay that way, didn't it? Laura was right: innocent people got sent down for things they didn't do all the time. Telling the truth was no guarantee that you'd be safe.

Instead, he had to follow the plan.

He cleared his throat. 'I think I should have a solicitor present,' Simon Jenks said flatly.

Trevor felt his heart sink. That was the last thing he wanted, but he knew he had to tread carefully. 'You are entitled to have a solicitor present, sir,' he said mildly, 'but I must point out, that, as of this moment, you're not being charged with anything. We simply want to ask you a few questions with a view to eliminating you from our inquiries.'

Simon took a shaky breath. Yes. That's just what Laura had said they'd say. But it was all right for her. She had an alibi.

'Even so, I think I would prefer to have someone with me who knows the ropes. I've never been questioned by the police before, and I realize I might be in a…well, in a rather precarious position. Not that I've done anything,' he said, then abruptly stopped. No, he mustn't let himself be cajoled into speaking. Laura had warned him about that as well.

Slowly, he leaned back in his chair. 'I have a number that you can ring.'

Trevor smiled blandly. 'A local number, is it, sir?' he asked mildly.

Simon frowned then nodded slowly. 'That's right.'

'Only, with you being from up north, I thought your solicitor might have to come down from Leeds or something, but if you already have someone local lined up...well, I think it's splendid that you had the forethought to find someone else on the doorstep, so to speak.'

Simon paled even further. 'Laura... Mrs Raines thought it was a good idea,' he managed to say faintly.

Trevor nodded. Yes. He was beginning to understand now that in this relationship it was definitely the widow who was the driving force, and the one to be reckoned with. Still, it was the lover boy who'd been seen at the college leaving a dead body behind him. Trevor, although worried by the less-than-emphatic identification by Debbie Dawkins, was nevertheless sure that the man in front of him was the one with all the answers.

Now all he had to do was get them from him.

'So, if you'd give me your solicitor's details, we'll get him down here, shall we?' Trevor said with a brief smile. 'I'm sure we'll have a lot to talk about, so it's best we get started. Right?'

IN HER INTERVIEW ROOM, Laura Raines had not asked for a solicitor. Indeed, Peter Trent had only basic questions for her, mainly confined to confirming that she knew the contents of her husband's will, and repeating her movements on the day that her husband died.

Most of it was routine, and a question of playing for time whilst his boss got the chance to learn what Simon

Jenks had to say for himself. Trent wouldn't have been human if he hadn't felt that he'd drawn the short straw.

WHILST THE SERGEANT was exercising patience, Jenny Starling was in hall, looking at a big black stuffed bear. Since Maurice's opening speech, it had been left standing with its back to a wall, where it was periodically admired by the taxidermists. Even the scouts serving dinner had grown fond of it. The trolley that had wheeled it in had been put away somewhere, but, as Jenny met the brown glass-eyed stare, she nodded.

OK. It all fitted. The bear. The medication found in the coffee cup, which would turn out to be the same sort as that being taken by Maurice Raines's ailing mother. There had obviously been something on the mobile phone that had excited the police's interest, and she could make a good educated guess as to what that would be. So either Laura Raines, or her lover, or both, would be arrested for the murder before long, Jenny supposed with a sigh.

The timing of that morning's scheduling when Maurice Raines was killed was now perfectly understandable under the circumstances, as was the out-of-character behaviour of one of the main players.

Jenny nodded. Yes, it all fitted. She knew exactly who had planned such a meticulous murder, and she could see quite clearly how it was all supposed to have gone down.

The trouble was, not one bit of that knowledge was going to help her in finding out who had killed Maurice Raines or why.

She sighed, patted the bear on his stuffed paw—after

all, it was hardly his fault was it?—and went back to her kitchen.

She still had a main course for tonight's dinner to arrange.

SIMON JENKS'S SOLICITOR arrived promptly. He was somewhere in his mid-forties, with a slight paunch, slightly thinning hair, and wore a pair of narrow spectacles. He asked for and was granted some time alone with his client, and then Trevor was allowed back.

This time he had Trent with him and the interview was formally recorded. The inspector knew from the quick debriefing with his sergeant that he'd got nothing of interest from the widow, and that she was now waiting downstairs in the police station's foyer, fully expecting her boyfriend to be joining her soon. Peter had not been able to tell whether that was bluff on her part, or genuine belief.

It had been agreed between them that Peter Trent would not, at that point, mention finding the mobile phone, or the text message that had been on it. They wanted to spring that, fully formed, on Simon Jenks and see what rewards it would reap.

Now Trevor smiled gently across at the pale-faced photographer, and 'other man' in the Raines's marriage and arranged his thoughts.

'So, for the record, sir, could I have your full name, address, age and occupation?' Trevor began.

Simon Jenks coughed, but managed to clearly supply it all.

'And how long have you known Laura Raines, sir?' Trevor began gently.

'Over six months now.'

'And you are in an intimate relationship with her?'

'Yes.'

'You knew she was married?'

'Yes. But she told me that the marriage was defunct. Her husband regularly had relationships with other women, and divorce was inevitable.'

Trevor nodded. 'Ah. I understand that it is Mrs Raines who has the money in that marriage?'

Simon flushed, but said flatly, 'I never knew that until quite late on in our relationship. And that's nothing to do with me. I mean, it's no concern of mine. I run my own business. That is, I'm self-employed.'

'Yes, we know,' Trevor said pleasantly.

'Can we please stick to the point, Inspector?' the solicitor spoke for the first time.

'Of course,' Trevor said mildly. 'Whose idea was it to spend five days in Hayling Island?' Trevor quoted the dates, and jotted something down in his notebook.

'Laura. She said her husband was away, so we might as well have a little holiday too.'

Trevor nodded. 'Have you ever met Maurice Raines?'

'No.'

'But you know what he looks like?' For the first time, Simon Jenks looks confused. 'What do you mean?' he asked nervously.

'Had you seen the two of them out and about, say, in Harrogate, where you all live? It's a small town, you might have come across them together in a supermarkets, or in a restaurant? Or had Mrs Raines shown you a photograph of her husband perhaps?'

'No, of course not,' Simon said, after a noticeable pause. No doubt he was trying to see where the policeman was going with this, and failing to do so. From the frown on his solicitor's face, he was wondering the same thing.

Which pleased Trevor Golder considerably. Things had been feeling too glib by far up until now. He had a feeling that Simon Jenks had been following some pre-arranged pattern, and he needed to break it up.

'So, if you had passed Maurice Raines on the street, you wouldn't have known who he was?' he pressed.

'No,' Simon said, a shade reluctantly, Trevor thought.

'Tell me about your journey from Yorkshire to Hayling Island. A bit of a long haul, that, wasn't it?'

Simon nodded. 'It was, but I took it slow and steady.'

'You must have left early,' Trevor prompted.

'Yes.'

'But you and Mrs Raines decided to drive separately. If you'd gone down together, you could at least have shared spells behind the wheel, couldn't you?' he pointed out.

Simon nodded, looking happier. Obviously, this was a question he'd expected and knew the right answer to give.

'We wanted to have our own separate cars, Inspector, just in case. I might have had to come back earlier, if a job had come through. Being self-employed, I can't always pick and choose when I work. It would have meant that Laura could have stayed on for the full five days, if that had happened.'

Trevor nodded. 'I see. And you went straight from Yorkshire to the south coast? You didn't detour to Oxford? Bearing in mind that traffic cameras are very prevalent nowadays, sir, if I authorize a search for your car number plate, will I find it present in Oxford on the morning of Mr Raines's death?'

Simon Jenks went very pale.

His solicitor stirred himself. 'If you have evidence that my client was in Oxford, Inspector, please say so.'

Trevor smiled.

'On the morning that Mr Raines was murdered, a man was seen, leaving hall, by one of the cleaners at the college. She was able to give us a very detailed description. The man she described fits you perfectly, Mr Jenks. Would you be willing to take part in an identity parade, sir?'

'No, he wouldn't, Inspector,' the solicitor spoke sharply, before his client could do so.

Trevor wondered for a moment if Simon Jenks was actually going to pass out. He wouldn't be the first suspect to do so, not by a long shot. And he had gone that slightly sickly green colour around the corner of his mouth that usually meant something of that kind was in the offing.

'I'm showing Mr Jenks an object,' Trevor said mildly for the tape, and nodding to Peter Trent. He waited whilst his sergeant handed over the distinctively coloured mobile phone.

'I'm showing Mr Jenks a purplish-coloured mobile telephone. Do you recognize it, Mr Jenks?' he asked.

Simon glanced at the object in the plastic bag, and quickly licked his lips.

'It looks like a mobile phone,' he heard himself say helplessly.

'Does Mrs Laura Raines have a phone like this?'

'I think so,' Simon whispered.

'I'm going to show Mr Jenks a text message that is stored on the phone,' Trevor went on carefully. Using gloves, he removed the mobile and called up the message. He then turned the small screen around so that Simon Jenks could see it.

'Can you read the words on the screen, Mr Jenks?' he asked.

The solicitor squinted and looked at it closely.

'Yes,' Simon Jenks whispered.

'Is the message addressed to you?'

'Yes.'

'Is it from Mrs Laura Raines?'

'Yes.'

'Does it ask you to meet her in the main hall of St Bede's College at eleven-thirty on the morning of the second of July?'

'All right, this interview is terminated,' the solicitor said firmly. 'Inspector, I wish to consult with my client.'

Simon Jenks stared at the mobile phone, but said nothing.

Trevor rose from the table. He indicated on the tape that he and his sergeant were leaving the room, and the two men left in silence.

Outside, Trent slowly let out his breath. 'What story do you suppose those two are going to concoct now, guv?' he asked, nodding back towards the interview room. 'I thought Jenks was going to pass out once or twice back there—that or lose his breakfast. I reckon he's got jelly for a backbone, that one. Wanna bet he'll cop to it before the day's out?' he crowed.

Trevor looked at his sergeant's smiling face, and grunted.

Somewhat belatedly, becoming aware that his superior didn't share his confidence, Peter Trent's smile gradually withered.

'Go and get the widow back,' Trevor said quietly after some moments had passed.

The sergeant looked surprised, but quickly jogged downstairs, relieved to see that Laura Raines was still there, waiting patiently, and pretending to read a magazine. She got up when she saw him, and looked over his shoulder, as if expecting to see her lover.

When she didn't, her eyes fastened back on him. She nodded without comment when he asked her if she would mind returning with him to the interview room. He didn't understand why the boss wanted to have another go at her when it was obvious that Simon Jenks was their killer, but he'd learned over the years never to underestimate Golder. Perhaps he was sure that, though Jenks might be the actual killer, it was the black widow who was the brains and the motivating force behind it. He was inclined to think that way himself, and was looking forward to see how he set about proving it.

Laura Raines hesitated briefly when she stepped into the interview room and saw that the inspector was already seated there. She took a seat calmly though, and watched and listened without expression as Golder went through the routine with the recording device, and then sat, waiting tensely for him to begin.

For a moment or two, Trevor simply looked at her, wondering how best to crack the veneer of her control. Then he decided that finesse wasn't needed.

'We believe that Simon Jenks was in Oxford on the morning that your husband was killed, Mrs Raines,' he said flatly. He saw her hands tighten on her bag, which she'd set in front of her on the table, but other than that there was no reaction.

'We have a witness, a cleaner at the college, who saw

a man matching Mr Jenks's description, leaving hall at around the time of the murder.'

Her knuckles went white, but again she said nothing. Trevor had the uncanny feeling that she was waiting for something, but he had no idea what it could be. The two statements he'd just made should have been enough to poleaxe her, and the fact that they hadn't left him feeling extremely wrong-footed. A cold, hard feeling was beginning to claw its way up his spine, as he began to wonder just what the hell was going on.

'For the tape, please, can you identify this?' Trevor plugged on relentlessly, holding out the plastic evidence bag with the mobile phone inside, watching her closely.

And for the first time, Laura Raines showed emotion. Her shoulders slumped dramatically like a puppet that had just had its strings cut, and she let out a long shaky breath. But the face she turned to Trevor was tearful with relief, and the hand she held up to her mouth was to half-cover a trembling-lipped smile of joy. 'You found it. It was there. My phone! He wasn't lying!' She began to shake. 'Don't you see?' Laura Raines was openly crying now, but also laughing. 'Don't you understand? It's all right now.'

She looked from the gobsmacked face of Peter Trent, to the surprised and confused face of the inspector. 'He wasn't lying!' Laura Raines said simply.

And in her voice was the unmistakable ring of vindication and utter joyous relief.

NINE

JENNY SMILED ACROSS at James Raye and clicked her mug of tea against his in a silent toast to the future. They were in his room at the college, and discussing possible summer holiday destinations. Although the conference was due to end the following day, and he had to drive back to Harrogate, neither one of them were assuming that that would be the last time they'd see each other.

'Of course, you can always come down for the weekends, until my contract here runs out,' Jenny mused.

'Mini-breaks in the city of dreaming spires with you sounds wonderful,' he agreed. 'Mind you, I've got two full weeks due in July.' He let the sentence hang delicately in the air, and Jenny smiled wistfully.

'I wish I did. Unfortunately, I'm here for the season, which doesn't end until Michaelmas term begins, in September.'

James sighed. 'Pity.'

'After that, I'm free and will be looking out for another job somewhere. I could always head vaguely north.' She too let the sentence hang delicately. But she wasn't surprised when he grinned happily, and nudged a bit closer to her on the sofa. 'It's lovely up north,' he agreed. 'We've got York Minster, the dales and rugged coastline. And me.'

Jenny's eyes sparkled. 'The rugged coastline sounds good.'

They were still laughing when a knock came at the

door and Jenny, who'd been anticipating a nice, long, lingering kiss, sighed instead. James, frowning, put his mug down and got up to answer the summons.

Norman, who'd escaped from his tank yet again, sauntered very slowly and hesitantly across the glass-topped coffee table in front of her, and eyed James's steaming mug with one interested eye, whilst his other eye tracked the progress of a spider up on the ceiling.

Jenny was vaguely assessing the arachnid's chances of living to see another day—not good—when she heard a familiar voice coming from the doorway, and slowly rose to her feet. Over James Raye's shoulder, Peter Trent saw the movement and apologetically he coughed into his hand.

'Sorry to disturb you, Miss Starling, but the inspector wonders if he could have a quick word,' he murmured, trying not to look at either of them. Jenny found his diplomacy touching.

She smiled, already walking towards him. 'Of course, Sergeant. James,'—she reached out and took his hand, giving it a quick squeeze—'we'll talk later, all right, and get something sorted out.'

James returned the squeeze and looked at her carefully. 'Yes, we must do that,' he said.

Peter Trent went a shade pink and turned away, and Jenny smiled again as she followed the stiff-backed sergeant to the incident room. Not so much diplomacy as an unexpected streak of shyness, it seemed.

Trevor was sitting at his desk, scowling down at the transcript in his hand. He looked up as the statuesque cook entered, and wondered if this was such a good idea after all. Then he sighed. At this point, he was willing to accept any help that he could get, and he couldn't help but think that Jenny Starling was as good a place to start as any. He'd be surprised if she couldn't add something helpful and, even if she couldn't, it would be good to bounce his ideas and thoughts off someone with her brains and perspicacity.

'Thank you for coming. I can see by the abashed look on my sergeant's face that this might not be a convenient time for you.'

Jenny shook her head, and grinned. Obviously, the inspector was well aware of where she'd been and with whom. Otherwise, how would Peter Trent have known where to come calling?

'It's fine, Inspector,' she assured him. 'You have something to tell me?' she asked, taking a seat and looking around. The incident room was empty of personnel for once, and she didn't think that was necessarily a matter of chance. Clearly, the inspector didn't want to be overheard.

'I want to fill you in on a few developments and get your angle on what's been happening,' he agreed, cautiously.

Ah, Jenny thought. That explained it! He didn't want to be caught out speaking to a mere civilian. 'OK,' she agreed affably. 'Shoot.'

Trevor nodded. 'First, the stuff found in the coffee cup next to Maurice's body was definitely the same brand of pills used by the victim's mother.'

Jenny nodded. 'Yes, they would be,' she said mildly.

'And the mobile phone that you found definitely belonged to Laura Raines, the victim's widow, as we thought. She admitted as much.'

Again Jenny nodded, and Trevor's eyes gleamed.

'And something tells me that you already knew that it would be.'

Jenny nodded, then realized she was probably beginning to look like one of those nodding dogs you saw in the back of car windows, and stopped.

'You've questioned Mrs Raines, I take it?' she said, calmly.

'Yes, and, even more interestingly, we've talked to the man she was having an affair with.'

Jenny let out a long, slow breath. 'Ah. So that's it. I did wonder.'

Trevor's lips twisted slightly. 'Yes, I'm sure you did, Miss Starling.'

'Please, call me Jenny.'

'His name is Simon Jenks. He's a self-employed photographer, a good-looking man, a few years younger than the new widow, and currently unattached.'

Jenny smiled slightly. Nothing surprising there, then.

'The text we found on the telephone, from Laura Raines, was addressed to him. In it, she was asking him to meet her in hall at the college. What's more, he's the man your scout's daughter saw leaving the hall at around the time of the murder,' Trevor said. But if he'd hoped to surprise, or even disconcert her, he was in for a disappointment.

'Yes, it fits,' she said simply. Then she looked at him thoughtfully. 'I take it you've arrested him? And her?'

Trevor shifted slightly on his seat. 'Let's just say that they're currently helping us with our inquiries. We've got some time to go yet before we can charge them with anything. Besides, after answering a few of the more mundane questions, both of them have now clammed up and are discussing things strictly with their solicitors. Neither of them have admitted to anything.'

'And you're being cautious,' Jenny said, beaming a smile of approval at him. 'I don't blame you. With all the problems you'll have making a charge stick, I'm not surprised.'

Trevor caught Peter Trent's questioning eye, and scowled.

'Problems, Miss Starling?' he said silkily. 'I'm not sure that we've got too many of those,' the inspector said with understandable satisfaction. 'We've got means, motive and opportunity.' He ticked them off on his fingers as he talked. 'It seems to me that it's a classic case of its kind.'

Trevor leaned back in his chair and stretched. 'The trouble is, proving that they're in it together. Which is where I wondered if you might have any thoughts.'

Jenny opened her mouth, caught the inspector's puzzled eye, and closed it again. Rapidly, she ran through her options, and decided that it would probably be more diplomatic to approach things obliquely. Let the inspector come gradually to the realization that his case was hardly all sewn up. In fact, far from it.

'I see,' she said cautiously. 'I take it that Debbie Dawkins has been able to confirm that Simon Jenks is the same man she saw that day?' she asked innocently. 'I mean, with a rock solid identification that will make your superiors happy?' She rained as gently as she could on his parade, and genuinely without any enthusiasm.

Trevor scowled. 'No. Unfortunately, her testimony is a bit uncertain.'

'Has he admitted to being there?'

'No, not yet, but he'll crack,' Trevor said. Even as he

heard himself say the words, he was not, in fact, quite so sure. The weak type could be oddly stubborn at times, and Simon Jenks had been adamant at demanding a solicitor and, so far, had yet to be persuaded to make a formal statement.

'But you've found other witnesses, in Walton Street, or in college, who saw him?' Jenny carried on, studying her fingernails.

Trevor again exchanged a glance with his sergeant. 'No one in college admits to having seen him,' he admitted reluctantly.

Jenny nodded. 'But if he killed Maurice, he'd be covered in blood. Yet, Debbie said his T-shirt when she saw him was bright white and spotless. So, you must have witnesses in the city who saw someone matching his description with bloodstains on him, right?'

'No,' Trevor said heavily. 'But Mrs Raines had access to the heart medication, the same kind that was found in the poisoned coffee cup. Oh, I know what you're going to say,' he pressed on, as Jenny once again opened her mouth, and then closed it without actually saying anything. 'A lot of people could probably have got their hands on the same kind of medication. It's a fairly common heart pill, apparently.'

Jenny, who hadn't been about to say that at all, merely smiled slightly. 'And you have an explanation for why the coffee was poisoned with it in the first place?' she asked casually.

'Well, obviously, their plan was to poison Maurice with it. But something went wrong, and Jenks had to resort to plan B. Plan B being an improvization. In the event, he simply picked up the nearest sharp object, which happened to be a very sharp fleshing tool, as we know, and stabbed Maurice Raines in the neck with it.'

'Huh,' Jenny said. 'Except we know Maurice didn't drink coffee,' she pointed out. 'I knew that the first morning I had breakfast with him. Most of the conference people knew about it too. But you think his wife, of all people, wasn't aware that he only drank his own favourite brand of tea?'

The silence went dead and flat. This time it was Trevor Golder who opened his mouth and then closed it again without speaking.

'Damn,' Peter Trent said softly.

Trevor rubbed a tired hand over his eyes, but wouldn't be defeated. 'OK, so perhaps there's something else going on. We know the wife has a cast-iron alibi whilst lover boy does not. She must have arranged it that way. Suppose she didn't tell lover boy about her husband's drinking habits. Perhaps she forgot.'

Jenny shot him her best *are-you-serious* look, and he had the grace to hold up his hands in defeat. 'OK, not that.' He shuffled uncomfortably on his chair for a moment, and then snapped his fingers. 'Perhaps it was deliberate. Perhaps she was playing some other kind of game. What if she wanted to drop Jenks in it somehow? Perhaps she didn't really want to kill her husband, just scare him? Or maybe this was some sort of sick game that Maurice and Laura Raines were in on together, the joke being on Simon Jenks somehow.'

Trevor met her sceptical gaze and knew his arguments sounded absurdly weak and far-fetched, but he was unwilling to give up on his two prime suspects just yet. 'You'd be surprised at the lengths some jaded married couples will go to to spice up their love lives,' he heard himself say insistently. 'Just stay with me for a minute on this. Say this was some kind of fantasy scenario they set up together, Maurice and his wife, I mean. They arrange to get Maurice and Jenks together in the same room, hence the text message from her phone, in order to play out some sick game on the poor sod. I don't know, perhaps Maurice is supposed to tell his wife all about it later, and they'll have a good laugh. Maurice comes across as the outraged husband or what-have-you, but Jenks panics and kills him for real.'

Jenny looked at Trevor, but kindly said nothing.

Peter Trent looked at the inspector and also kindly said nothing.

Trevor Golder grimaced. 'OK. Seriously grabbing at straws there,' he muttered with bad grace. 'But in that case, just what the hell is going on then? Peter, tell Miss Starling about our interview with Laura Raines.'

The sergeant, although clearly uncomfortable with bringing a civilian up to date on police matters, nevertheless obliged.

'And I could swear,' he concluded, 'that when the guv'nor confronted her with her so-called missing mobile phone, she looked positively relieved.'

Jenny nodded. 'Yes, I imagine she would be,' she murmured, unaware that her mild comment had just made the inspector start to grind his teeth. 'I expect she was happy that he hadn't lied to her,' she said, unknowingly further compounding her mistake.

Then she stopped instantly, as both policemen jumped as if they'd been simultaneously goosed. 'How the hell did you know that?' Trevor roared, whilst, at the same time, the sergeant spluttered, 'That's almost what she said word for word!'

Trevor, breathing rather hard now, looked at the cook grimly. 'Do you have someone on my team feeding you information?' he demanded coldly.

'Good grief, no!'

'You don't have one of us bugged, do you?' he asked, not quite totally joking.

Jenny laughed nervously. 'Don't be daft! It's just that it's obvious that that was how Laura Raines would react. She's well and truly head over heels in love with Simon Jenks, right?' she asked. 'You said that's the impression you got?'

'Oh yeah, besotted with him, I reckon,' Trevor confirmed, but not looking particularly mollified by the cook's obvious attempt to mend her fences. 'I've seen it before: a good-looking, middle-aged woman in a dead marriage; they find some young handsome bloke, and it's love's young dream all over again. I think they're trying to recapture their youth, or something. Perhaps they think it's their last chance at romance, or having a last bite of the big, emotional cherry. All I know is, when they get like this, they fall harder than a ton of bricks.'

Jenny winced slightly at the inspector's rather sexist psychobabble but understood well enough what he was saying. It was only what she'd thought herself, minus the smug, superior judgmental aspect of it.

'Well then,' she said simply, and shrugged.

Trevor manfully fought the urge to pull his hair out. 'Well then, what? What exactly is going on with those two?'

'You want my best guess?' Jenny asked guilelessly. The inspector, although grimly coming to the conclusion that the large, beautiful young woman in front of him had somehow suckered him, nevertheless nodded.

'I'd be very interested in hearing your best guess, Miss Starling,' he said, with exaggerated politeness.

Jenny caught it, but let it go. She could be magnanimous that way.

'OK. I think Simon Jenks probably *was* the man that Debbie saw. I think that afterwards, he left the college and went straight to Laura and told her what had happened, stressing the fact that he was innocent of all wrong-doing, naturally. And Laura Raines, a woman very much in love with him don't forget, needed to believe him, and wanted to believe him, but probably hadn't quite *managed* to believe him, until the moment you told her about finding her missing mobile phone. Which confirmed some part of his story. And then, of course, she began to *actually* believe him, which is what made her so happy. Hence, her odd reaction at the interview.' Jenny took a deep breath and smiled radiantly. 'It's really simple and not at all complicated when you think of it like that.'

Trevor stared at her incredulously. Peter Trent simply sat and blinked.

'Now look here, Miss Starling,' Trevor began, but before he could work up a full head of steam, they were interrupted.

The door opened, and a uniformed WPC came in. 'Sir, I've had an urgent message from the financial consultant you ordered to look into the taxidermy society's ledgers. He say's he's uncovered evidence of embezzlement. What's more, he thinks it's likely that our murder victim had discovered it too!'

TREVOR ROSE POLITELY as Vicki Voight was ushered into
the room by his sergeant. Although he had by no means
finished his conversation with the aggravating cook,
he'd decided to postpone it for a short time.

He was very much aware that he needed to work all
the angles now, especially since Jenny Starling had just
pointed out all the flaws inherent in rushing to arrest
either Laura Raines or her lover. Besides, this business
about embezzlement needed to be sorted out. After all,
money was one of the prime causes of murder, as any
good police officer knew. Although the cheating couple
remained top of his list of suspects, he wasn't averse
to having another line of inquiry to pursue. It would at
least keep his bosses happy.

'Ah, Mrs Voight. Thank you for coming. Please, take
a seat. I take it you don't mind if Miss Starling re-
mains?' he greeted her cordially.

Vicki shot the other woman a curious look, and was
clearly not at all sure whether she minded or not. But
she didn't seem in the mood to quibble.

'I was just preparing the closing speech of the conference for tomorrow, Inspector. As you know—or maybe
you don't—that was Maurice's prerogative, but with
him gone, it falls to me now, so...' She let the sentence
trail off, but it was clear where she was going with it.

Trevor smiled obligingly. 'I'll try not to waste too
much of your time, Mrs Voight,' he said with a wide
smile.

Whilst he'd been waiting for Peter to come back with
his witness, he'd been on the telephone to his financial
expert, and had made plenty of notes. An email of his
full report would be on his desk by the end of the day,

but he felt sure he had enough of the facts now in order to take the stuffing out of the impatient treasurer of the Greater Ribble Valley and Jessop Taxidermy Society.

Vicki sighed, but sat down. 'I take it that it is all right for all of us to leave tomorrow?' she asked tentatively. 'We are all due to go, and some of the others have been asking me. They're not quite sure if we're "free to leave town" so to speak.'

Trevor smiled. 'That'll be fine, Mrs Voight. We have everyone's contact details.'

Vicki slowly relaxed. 'Good.'

'But we do have one or two more questions for you,' Trevor said smoothly, and Vicki instantly tensed up again.

'Oh?' She laughed nervously. 'What can I do to help? I've already told you everything I know.'

'Well, you can start by telling me just what it was that Maurice Raines did when he discovered that you were stealing from the society, Mrs Voight,' he said mildly.

The colour slowly drained from the other woman's face, leaving her make-up standing out in stark relief on her face. Jenny glanced away, not wanting to intrude on such a moment, and looked out of the window instead.

'How did…? I mean, I haven't stolen anything. Not really. Only technically. It wasn't a lot, and it only happened a few times when I got really desperate. All the money's back in place now.' The older woman's stumbling voice broke off in a sob, and Jenny turned back just in time to see the inspector hand over a large tissue from a box of them on his desk.

Obviously, he'd been prepared.

Vicki cried into her tissue for a while, big, gulping, unlovely sobs that had to be genuine. Eventually, she composed herself and turned defeated, mascara-smudged eyes back to the inspector.

'It started last year. When the recession really began to bite. My husband lost his post, and it took him a while to find another job. Not as well paid, but....' She shrugged, and then smiled. She began to shred the tissue. 'You don't want to hear about that. Anyway, one month, we just couldn't meet the mortgage payment. It came as a bit of a shock, even though it shouldn't have. We'd already had to sell the second car, cancel the holidays and, well, the upshot was, the bank was forgiving enough, but then, after we were months in arrears, I simply had to find a way to meet the payment and so I borrowed it from the society funds.'

'And Maurice found out, didn't he?' the inspector said, keeping his voice sympathetic and choosing, for the moment, not to take issue with her choice of words. He rather doubted that any of the other society members would see her actions as 'borrowing' anything.

'Oh no. Well, not right away,' Vicki said quickly. 'I had to borrow about four more months' worth of mortgage payments after that, but then my husband got a job, like I said and, after a while, I was able to siphon the money back in again. It was'—and here Vicki snorted with bitter laughter—'ironically enough, it was when I was doing *that,* paying it back *in* I mean, that Maurice twigged as to what was happening. It was a sheer fluke that he did, really, but then again, Maurice was always very smart. He seemed to have an instinct for trouble,' she added, her tone in equal part sad and grim.

'He threatened you?' Trevor asked quietly.

'What? No. What do you mean? Threaten me with what?' Vicki asked, clearly surprised.

Trevor shifted a little on his seat, not happy with her unexpected response. 'Oh, come on, Mrs Voight,' he cajoled heavily. 'Mr Raines was the bigwig of the society, wasn't he? The chairman, or managing director, or whatever you want to call it. The head honcho. He couldn't have taken it kindly to find out that his treasurer had her hand in the till.'

Vicki flushed an ugly red at the deliberately insulting turn of phrase, then sniffed into the tissue again. 'I told you, it wasn't like that. It was only a few times, and the money was back in place. OK, he tackled me about it and, being Maurice, he was infuriatingly smug and couldn't resist giving me a blast of his moralistic lecturing. But he listened to what I had to say, and he understood that times were hard. Even his own company has felt the pinch. In hard financial times, big taxidermy jobs are hardly anyone's top priority. Maybe it made him a bit more sympathetic than he usually is. A bit more human. Anyway, he said that since the money was back, he wouldn't take it any further. Besides,' Vicki forced herself to sit up straighter and go on the offensive, 'it's not as if there were people hammering at the door to take on the treasurer's job. It's not a paid position, you know, and it's a lot of work, and takes up a lot of free time. If Maurice forced me out, he'd have to take it on himself, and if you knew anything about Maurice, you'd know he wouldn't be keen to do that. He liked to think of us as his slaves rather than his unpaid fellow members.' Vicki took a shaky breath. 'Look, the money's back. No harm has been done, and nobody's any the wiser. You don't have to take this any further, do you?'

Trevor sighed. He wasn't particularly interested in the penny ante frauds of an obscure little taxidermy society. 'I'm not sure that it's quite as innocent as you make it sound, Mrs Voight,' he persisted doggedly. 'I only have your word for it, after all, that Maurice was as forgiving as you say he was. Suppose he threatened to expose you, to tell the others, or your husband, or even to call the police in. You might have good reason to try and silence him in that case.'

Vicki again went pale. 'What? You think I wanted to *kill* him?' she squeaked incredulously. 'All over a few thousand pounds? Are you insane? Besides, I told you, he wasn't going to tell on me. Oh, I'm not saying he didn't want something in return—' Vicki said hotly, then suddenly stopped talking as she realized what she'd just said.

Trevor and Peter Trent both snapped to attention and watched her like a dog spotting a running rabbit.

'Oh? And just what was it that Mr Raines wanted in return?' Trevor asked, eyeing Vicki's long, honey-coloured hair and rather rounded figure speculatively. Had he demanded sexual favours, and Vicki, in disgust, had preferred to bury a knife in his neck? 'He was something of a ladies' man, wasn't he?' he said delicately.

Vicki looked in turns appalled, chagrined, and then amused. Finally, she managed to laugh. 'No, it wasn't that. I wasn't quite young enough or thin enough to suit his exacting standards,' she said bitterly. 'No, it was the tiger he wanted.'

Trevor's jaw dropped. He looked at his sergeant, wondering if he'd heard the same thing. For a second, he was utterly incapable of speech.

Jenny, smothering her laughter behind her hand,

coughed gently. 'You mean the contract to stuff the tiger the wildlife park had offered?' she clarified gently.

'Yes,' Vicki said, then seeing the policemen's continued puzzlement, sighed heavily. 'You see, Inspector, our society had been offered the chance to stuff a tiger for an educational exhibit. It was a hotly contested contract, as you can imagine, since such large and exotic animal commissions are few and far between. We had competition not just in the north, but nationwide. Still, we fought hard for it, and got it. Naturally, the choice of who was to take it on was, technically at least, open to any one of the members, but in reality only Maurice's firm, and perhaps a co-op consisting of some of the other members, was in the running. Myself, Ian Glendower, and a few others, were in the co-op. But when Maurice found out about my borrowing the money, he made it clear that he wanted me to drop out of the competition. Which I did, of course,' she added, her shoulders slumping in defeat. 'And when I did so, one or two of the others decided it might be too much to take on, and our bid sort of fizzled out a bit.'

'So Maurice would be almost certain to get the contract to, ah, stuff the tiger,' Trevor said. 'Yes, I see.'

'So he had no intention of dropping me in it over the money, and I had no motive for killing him,' Vicki pointed out, with a return of spirit.

Trevor smiled briefly. 'So you say, Mrs Voight,' he murmured.

Vicki's eyes flashed. 'Oh, for heaven's sake! If you want to harass someone who did have a grudge against him, and really did have one massive argument with him not so long ago, why don't you talk to Ian? He was really mad when I dropped out of the bid. I don't know how he found out, but I know he blamed Maurice for it. If you really want to talk to someone who was angry enough to kill him, you should speak to him!'

Vicki, breathing hard, slumped back in her chair, emotionally exhausted.

Trevor Golder looked at her for a moment, remembered her solid alibi for the time of Maurice Raines's death, and nodded.

'All right, Mrs Voight. I'll do just that,' he said mildly. 'Thank you for your time.'

Vicki needed no second telling and left, rapidly.

Trevor turned wearily to his sergeant. 'Well, we've had one wild goose chase,' he said flatly. 'We might as well go on another.' Because, unless his memory failed him, Ian Glendower had an alibi every bit as solid as that of Vicki Voight.

He eyed the cook sitting quietly in the corner and smiled grimly. 'I suppose you knew all about the tiger as well?' he said softly, and then held up a hand as Jenny opened her mouth to speak. 'No, don't bother,' he said. 'Of course you did.'

IAN GLENDOWER WAS the first one through the door, but right on his heels, and perhaps not totally unexpectedly, came Pippa Foxton. This time the young woman was wearing a pair of sea-green, tight-fitting pants with an intricate silver-thread design, and a floating sea-green, turquoise and cream top with a very low neckline. Large turquoise and silver jewellery gleamed at her neck, ears and on her wrist and fingers. She was wearing as well her beloved Jimmy Choo shoes. Her eye make-up in particular was dramatic: in greens and blues, with heavy black eyeliner laid on to taper to dramatic points, she reminded Jenny a bit of the late Elizabeth Taylor in full make-up for her role as Cleopatra.

'Hope you don't mind me tagging along, Inspector,' she said cheerfully, 'but when *your* man here came along to nab *my* man,'—she flashed Peter Trent a flirtatious grin—'I just had to come along and offer my moral support.'

Trevor shrugged gallantly. 'Not at all, Miss Foxton. It's always a pleasure to see you.'

He ignored the glowering look Ian shot his way, and could well see how the young man would object to Maurice Raines's acknowledged flirting with his girlfriend. The youngster clearly had a thin skin where the vivacious Miss Foxton was concerned.

'I just need to clear up a few details, Mr Glendower,' Trevor began benignly. 'When was the last time you spoke to Mr Raines again?' he asked, deciding to approach the issue obliquely.

Ian rolled his eyes and sighed ostentatiously. 'I already told your people all this: it was just after breakfast on the day he died.'

'Oh yes.' Trevor made a show of consulting his notes. 'It says here you were discussing real estate or something.' He managed to make it sound so unlikely as to be ridiculous. 'Sure you weren't discussing wildlife instead, maybe?' he asked archly.

Ian's already glowering face took on a genuinely puzzled look. 'What? Wildlife? No, we were discussing the price of houses, like I said. Pip and me are looking for a place of our own, out in the country somewhere. I hate Leeds, and Pip was brought up in the country, a nice little place called Wither Sedgewick, and she always said that she wanted to get back to the Dales, so we'd both decided that now might be a good time to relocate. I asked Maurice if he had any ideas on which areas were better value than others. It was the sort of thing he'd know about,' he admitted grudgingly.

Jenny Starling stiffened on her chair and then forced herself to relax. Her mind, however, began to race. Fortunately, the inspector didn't notice and continued his questioning urbanely.

'Ah. See, I thought you might have been asking him about tigers,' he said silkily.

'Tigers!' It was Pippa who repeated the word with a hint of wonder in her tone. 'Did you just say tigers?'

Trevor smiled at her. 'Yes. That was the reaction I had when they were first mentioned. But apparently there's a contract up for grabs to stuff one, and we have information that Maurice was preventing your boyfriend from having the chance of doing just that.'

Pippa bit her lip and cast a quick sideways glance at Ian, who was back to scowling ferociously. Wordlessly, she placed a warning hand on his arm. Her foot began to beat a nervous tattoo on the floor, attracting Jenny's eyes to her shoes. Those quirky, high-heeled, ridiculously expensive Jimmy Choo designer shoes.

Shoes.

Jenny blinked. Shoes. Of course. Shoes.

'Is that true, Mr Glendower?' Trevor said sharply, making Pippa flinch.

'He was trying,' Ian said flatly. 'I suppose you've been talking to Vicki? Well, she might have dropped out of the co-op, but I was rallying others. We were in with as good a shot as Maurice's hot-shot firm to get the contract. So what?' he added aggressively, his jaw thrusting out in defiance.

Trevor found himself echoing the sentiment. Exactly, so what? He'd be laughed out of the office if he tried to put that forward as a motive for murder. Besides, Ian had a rock solid alibi. At the time that Maurice Raines was being killed, he was showing half-a-dozen people just how to stuff a squirrel, or whatever, with his fashion-plate of a girlfriend looking on in admiration.

But he wouldn't go down without a fight.

'Is it true that you had a flaming row with him about it?' he asked straight out.

To the policeman's surprise, Ian suddenly laughed, his hitherto taut body suddenly relaxing, as if somebody was letting the air out of a balloon. 'Sure enough, I did,' Ian admitted with some satisfaction. 'He was so used to being the bee's knees, I just couldn't help showing him that not everyone felt the same way about him. I bloody well enjoyed myself doing it too,' he admitted candidly.

'And just how did Mr Raines react?' Trevor asked, with genuine curiosity.

Ian laughed again. 'How do you expect? He puffed himself up like one of those blow-fish and spouted the usual guff and threats.' Ian shrugged magnificently. 'I couldn't have cared less. He had no power over me—I don't work for his company, glory be, and he can't get me ousted from the society unless I either fail to pay my fees, or he can get the majority to vote me out. And believe me, there are enough of us in the society who didn't respect our late unlamented chairman for me to be sure *that* would never happen.' Again he shrugged. 'So I just let the old sod have it, and that was that. There wasn't much he could do about it in the end.'

'But he would have got the tiger, Mr Glendower, wouldn't he?' Trevor said softly.

Ian went back to glowering at him.

Sensing his change of mood, Pippa stirred beside him, and squeezed her hand, which was still resting on his forearm. 'Is that all now, Inspector? Only Ian has to get ready for his next lecture, don't you?' she said sweetly.

Trevor looked at her with a faint smile. Obviously she knew her boyfriend had a short fuse, and was probably used to by now to trying to keep a tight rein on it. Lots of people had tempers, but it didn't make them killers. Intriguing or not, getting to be the one to stuff a tiger, for Pete's sake, wasn't much of a motive for murder either. He sighed in defeat.

'Yes, that's all for now,' he said heavily.

Once his sergeant had shown the couple out, Trevor turned around in his chair and contemplated his nemesis, but the cook was staring off into the distance, her lovely eyes narrowed in thought.

'Now, Miss Starling, about Laura Raines and her lover boy, and this clever plot to murder her husband. Let's have your thoughts on it, please. And this time, I want it plain and simple, and leave nothing out,' he demanded flatly.

Jenny dragged her thoughts back to the inspector, and looked at him blankly.

'What clever plot to murder her husband?'

Trevor snorted. 'Oh, come on, Miss Starling. Her mobile phone. The poisoned coffee. The text message to get Simon Jenks to come to the college. It reeks of a frame up, or a double bluff, or *something*. It's all such a damned convoluted muddle, you're not trying to tell me that somebody, somewhere, hasn't been up to some clever planning.'

'Oh, yes. No, I agree,' she said, somewhat confusingly. 'Someone obviously planned a cold-blooded and cleverly thought-out murder plot.'

'Exactly what I said,' Trevor agreed smugly. 'So who was it? Who went to all that trouble to kill Maurice Raines?' he demanded impatiently. 'And don't try and tell me you don't have it all figured out,' he added angrily.

'Maurice?' Jenny said, with genuine bewilderment. 'Well, nobody,' she said. Then seeing Trevor gape at her, said, again with genuine puzzlement, 'Obviously, nobody planned all that with the poisoned coffee and the mobile phone and what have you, in order to kill Maurice. Surely, that's clear as day?'

She looked from Trevor to the equally gob-smacked Peter Trent. But it was the sergeant, who asked the obvious question.

'What do you mean? Who was the intended target then?'

Jenny frowned at him. 'Well, Simon Jenks of course. Who else?'

TEN

'WHAT?' TREVOR GOLDER GASPED. 'Tell me you're kidding. We can't have been investigating the wrong crime all this time!'

Then, without even giving her time to reply, he seemed to run through a mental, lightning-fast review of the facts and conceded that they had, for his next question came with barely a pause. 'Why the hell didn't you tell us?'

Jenny reared back slightly, unprepared for such an unwarranted attack. She looked helplessly from one policeman to the other, and said faintly, 'But I thought you understood. It has to be obvious, doesn't it? I mean, from the moment we learned about the poison in the coffee cups.'

Trevor forced himself to take a long, slow, deep breath.

'I'm afraid it's not clear to me, Miss Starling,' Peter Trent, seeing it as his duty, took the blow for his superior, and confessed his ignorance first. 'Can you just spell it out for me, please?'

'Well,' Jenny began doubtfully, casting quick looks between the two policemen, and wondering if they really did want it spelt out for them. 'As soon as we learned that the coffee cup had been poisoned, it was clear that somebody had been meant to drink it and die, right?' she began tentatively.

'Right,' Peter confirmed. 'The doctor's report said that there was a massive dose of the stuff, and certainly enough to render someone unconscious and then dead within five minutes or so. So somebody definitely meant business.'

'Yes. So someone was meant to drink the coffee and die very quickly. Maurice was lying on the floor dead and, as we now well know, there would seem to be any number of people who had ample reason not to mourn the fact,' Jenny agreed. 'So the most obvious conclusion to jump to was that Maurice Raines was intended to drink the poison, but for some reason didn't, thus forcing the killer to go to plan "B" as it were, and improvise. Hence the fleshing tool in the neck.'

'Again, that seems fairly clear,' Peter said again. It was, more or less, what he and Golder had been thinking.

'But then in that case, and almost right away, we come up against a very sticky problem, don't we?' Jenny pointed out reasonably. 'That is, everyone knew that Maurice didn't drink coffee. Everyone knew, in fact, that he was a pedantic old sod in many ways, and made a big thing out of using his own special blend of tea. It was one of the many ways he had of demonstrating himself to be superior to the rest of the plebs, right?'

The sergeant nodded patiently. 'Again, that's all right as far as it goes, Miss Starling. We all know enough about his character now to see how that fits in, but perhaps the killer simply didn't know about it? The killer could have just poisoned the coffee, believing Maurice would drink it.'

Trevor Golder let out a long, slow breath. 'Yes, surely that makes more sense?' he put in, glad of the reprieve. 'More sense, anyway, than the wrong person getting killed?'

Jenny frowned at him. 'Does it? You're saying then that Maurice's killer must be a relative stranger to him and his drinking habits? In other words, not his wife, or a member of the conference?'

Trevor saw the huge flaw at once and was forced, reluctantly, to concede the point. 'It does seem unlikely,' he had to admit.

'Yes,' Jenny agreed gently. 'Quite apart from the fact that it raises the question of why would someone who didn't know him very well want to kill him in the first place. It also makes a nonsense of all the other things that point to the fact that the killer must have been very well acquainted with Maurice indeed—in point of fact, a conference member, or a member of his family, or inner circle of friends.'

'What pointers?' Again it was the sergeant who asked, realizing that it would be much too galling for Trevor to have to keep doing so.

'Well, the poison belonging to Maurice Raines's mother, for instance. That in itself is inconclusive, as we can't actually prove, for certain, that it was hers. It might be a massive coincidence if it wasn't, but coincidences do happen, as we know,' Jenny said. 'But the timing of the murder makes it impossible that someone not already well in place could have committed the crime,' she swept on, with inexorable logic. 'I mean, it's impossible to believe that an outside agency would be able to arrange for Maurice to be alone, at that time, and for everyone else to be safely out of the way.'

Trevor sighed. 'Go on.'

'So, I saw at once that the poison in the coffee cup

couldn't possibly have been meant for Maurice. The killer must have been aware of his habit of only drinking his own special brew. Plus, the fact that there were two cups, one poisoned, one not, meant that there were clearly two people involved. Someone was meant to be with Maurice, and that someone, therefore, was meant to drink the poison. At the time, we had no idea who that was. But now we do. *Ergo.…*' She trailed off quietly.

'Simon Jenks. Yes. I can see how that fits,' the inspector admitted. 'The killer lured Jenks to the hall with the text message from Mrs Raines's mobile number. Everyone nowadays has that little gizmo on their phones that lets them know who's calling, so he had no reason to suppose that it was anyone other than Laura Raines who was texting him. But who would want Jenks dead?' he asked exasperatedly, and saw before him the whole new investigation that would have to be set up. 'It could be anyone! We haven't even looked at his background yet! He could have money troubles, or a drug or gambling habit. He might have done something bad in his past that got him killed, or he might have another woman on the side. Jealousy is always a strong…yes!' Trevor snapped his fingers, beginning to look excited again. 'Perhaps Laura Raines knew about another woman, and was jealous. She'd want him dead then. She's so besotted with him, it would put her right over the edge.'

'And she persuaded her husband to bump him off for her?' Jenny asked sceptically, hating to bring him back to earth with such a bump. But, really, she couldn't have him going off on such a flight of fancy without reining him in. 'She was booking in to the hotel in Hayling

Island at the time, remember? And why would Maurice do her dirty work for her anyway?'

Trevor blinked, and then subsided back onto his chair. 'Damn it, we're right back at the beginning.'

'Hardly that, Inspector,' Jenny said with a smile. 'Cheer up. There's only one person who wanted Simon Jenks dead, and only one person who was in a position to arrange it.'

Trevor felt the hope rise up, cancelling out the sick feeling in his stomach. 'There is? Who?'

Jenny all but gaped at him, then realized somewhat belatedly that she was being rather rude, and forced herself to frown gently. 'Well, Maurice Raines of course.'

Trevor opened his mouth and then closed it again. He looked at his sergeant, who looked at him, and then looked at Jenny Starling, who was looking at him with a mixture of puzzlement and apology.

'But Maurice Raines was the victim, Miss Starling.' Again, it was Peter Trent who fell on his sword.

'Yes, I know, but that doesn't mean that he wasn't the one who planned the murder of Simon Jenks,' Jenny said, perfectly reasonably, she thought.

But Trevor Golder obviously didn't think so, for that worthy policeman was beginning to huff and puff and turn a particularly unbecoming shade of puce.

'That's enough!' Trevor snapped, then took a mammoth breath. 'Miss Starling, I want you to start at the beginning. Explain everything, as if you were talking to two dunces. Leave nothing out, keep it simple, and make it clear. Now, if you please,' he demanded, with ominous firmness.

Jenny responded to the command almost as the

rawest of police recruits might, and stiffened her shoulders, and almost snapped out 'Yessir' in response.

'All right,' she began, not noticing that Trevor had just indicated to his sergeant to start taking notes.

'Imagine that you're Maurice Raines,' Jenny began. 'You've been very comfortably married to a wealthy woman for twenty years or so. You're used to being a big fish in a small pond—that is, the world of taxidermy, running your own company and being the big chief of the Great Jessies. The recession has hit your business a bit, true, but you always have the safety net of your wife's wealth to fall back on, so nothing really to worry about there. Everything is going along splendidly. You even get to indulge in extra-marital affairs without any real qualms, and then, suddenly, disaster strikes.'

Jenny paused, and glanced out of the window. 'You find out that your wife, for once, is the one doing the straying. Worse, she's serious about it!' Jenny turned back to look at the inspector. 'For a seasoned philanderer, I don't suppose it was hard for Maurice to read the signs in his wife's behaviour. Also, he was very much a ladies' man, and I think he would have realized quite quickly how bad things were for him from the way Laura must have started acting. It must have been clear to him that his wife was in love, with a capital 'L', and he'd know it wasn't with him.'

She sighed and rubbed the back of her neck absently. 'Naturally, he'd need to investigate further and, I imagine, it wasn't that hard to find out who the other man was, and realize at once that the competition was stiff indeed. Simon Jenks is handsome, unattached, in a reasonable profession, and not so young that Laura Raines would feel personally ridiculous, or suffer any serious social embarrassment, at taking up with him. Moreover, now that the children are grown and out of the marital home and away at university, what was to stop his wife getting a divorce?'

Trevor, who'd been listening closely, had no argument with her reasoning so far, but now he felt obliged to chip in.

'Yes, but why resort to killing? I mean, why not just *get* divorced? It's not as if it's anything to fuss about nowadays,' he pointed out. 'Murder seems rather drastic, surely? Especially when there's always the risk of getting caught and going to gaol.'

Jenny smiled grimly. 'To you and me, yes, divorce would be inevitable. But we're not Maurice Raines. We don't have his ego, or his sense of entitlement. And, don't forget, all the money in that marriage was Laura's,' Jenny reminded them. 'Suppose they did divorce—why would any judge in the land give him a big alimony settlement? His wife's money bought their house. His wife's money set him up in business. The children wouldn't need support. No, Maurice would probably have lost the house, and a large slice of the income that had him living the high life that he'd enjoyed for all his married life. Laura would almost certainly have let him keep his business I expect, but as we already know, that was suffering in these hard economic times. And all this doesn't even take into account the blow to his ego,' Jenny said. 'He was Maurice Raines, the great ladies' man, the man who had women eating out of his hand. Just think of the public humiliation if he got kicked out of his own house, and a newer, younger, better-looking man took his place.'

Jenny paused for breath. 'No, it didn't bear thinking about. He had to find another solution—but with his wife so enamoured, there really was only one way out, and that was to get rid of the competition. Since it was unlikely that Simon Jenks could be bought off, that meant murder,' Jenny mused sadly.

'And I wouldn't be at all surprised if Maurice hadn't felt quite indignant and self-pitying about it.'

'Come again?' Trevor said. In spite of himself, the cook's words, and the scenario they depicted, fascinated him.

'Well, it's just the way he was,' Jenny said, almost apologetically. 'I can just see him, stealing his mother's pills, having to set it all up, and all the time telling himself that it wasn't really his fault. That he was actually a decent man, but it was his cheating wife, and that wife-stealing lover of hers who were forcing him in to doing something so sordid.' Jenny shrugged. 'It was just the sort of hypocritical way that he would have seen it.'

Jenny looked back out of the window and gave a small sigh. 'Anyway, Maurice, whatever else he was, was a clever man. He had brains, and he had a certain amount of cunning. He knew that if Simon Jenks turned up obviously murdered in Yorkshire, then the police would be bound to get on to his affair with Laura. Which would mean that both she, and then by association *he*, would become the obvious prime suspects. Even if they couldn't bring Simon's murder home to him, it wouldn't take long for Laura to begin to suspect him, and then she'd divorce him, and he wouldn't have gained a thing.'

Trevor nodded. 'He needed to be cleverer than that,' he murmured.

'Exactly.' Jenny nodded emphatically. 'So, first, he

had to arrange to do it a long way from home. And then in such a way that he could hold up his hands and say, "What, me? How could it have been me, Officer? I was in Oxford at the time, with scores of witnesses." Also, he'd have claimed complete ignorance of their affair at all, which would have left him with no motive.'

'But surely his wife would suspect him anyway?' Peter Trent said. 'If your lover turns up dead, you'd almost have to suspect your husband, wouldn't you?'

'Oh yes. If he turned up murdered,' Jenny agreed. 'But what if he just didn't turn up at all? What if, on the day he was supposed to meet you, he just vanished? Well, then, Maurice would have some wriggle room. He could argue that perhaps Jenks had had a better offer. Or just changed his mind. Perhaps he met with some sort of freak accident. Perhaps he went abroad; perhaps he simply grew tired of being the plaything of an older woman and just made a new life for himself somewhere else.' Jenny held up her hands in the classic 'who knows' gesture.

'You're saying that Maurice intended to hide the body then?' Trevor clarified.

'Oh yes,' Jenny said. 'As soon as I realized the significance of the stuffed bear, that became absolutely clear.'

Again Trevor found himself exchanging a puzzled glance with his sergeant. 'OK, Miss Starling, let's just get back to making it plain and simple, shall we?' he said, his voice heavy with defeat. 'We've got Maurice realizing he has to get rid of his rival and planning his murder. Just how did he intend that to go, exactly?'

Jenny nodded. 'OK. Like I said, Maurice was clever. He needed a murder weapon, and that was the first obstacle to overcome. Maurice himself was middle-aged and slightly overweight and out of shape. Simon Jenks, in contrast, was younger and fitter. So, the direct approach was no good—the old blunt instrument, or knife, or what-have-you. The chances of Simon being able to defend himself and overcome any attacker made that far too risky. So Maurice must have looked around for a far simpler and safer method, and found an obvious solution in his mother's heart medication. A quick trawl on the internet would tell him how much was needed to be fatal, and a large enough dose would make it quick acting, and all without too much mess. So, poison it was.'

'That makes sense,' Trevor conceded. 'But just how did he expect to make Simon Jenks drink it?'

'Ah, well, again, he had to be clever,' Jenny agreed. 'He knew what Jenks wanted—which was to have Laura Raines free to marry himself, thus securing his own future, and he intended to play on that. That's why he stole his wife's mobile phone just before leaving for the conference. It wouldn't have been hard for a man like Raines, used to arranging clandestine love affairs himself, to find out about their plans to spend the week in Hayling Island. If he himself was going away on a conference, they were bound to want to spend the time together themselves anyway. So this presented him with the perfect opportunity to set up both his own alibi and separate the two of them long enough for the murder to take place. I don't know how, exactly, he came to know that they'd be travelling down separately, but he must have done, because he sent the text to Jenks using his wife's mobile, asking him to detour to the college.'

Trevor thought about that for a moment, and then nodded. 'OK. As I said before, Jenks would have recognized the number as being hers,' he agreed. 'Even if

Laura had told him that she'd lost her usual phone and had given him the number of her new pay-as-you-go, he might simply have assumed that she'd found it again.'

'Right.'

'But hang on,' Trevor said. 'Surely he must have known that Maurice was at a conference in Oxford? Getting a text from her asking him to go to a college there—surely alarm bells would have rung?'

Jenny smiled. 'Maybe. Or maybe he didn't know where the conference was. I don't suppose they made a habit of talking about her husband when they were alone together! You'll have to ask him,' Jenny said. 'It could be that he thought she was being spontaneous. Or maybe he did know, and thought that she'd arranged for them all to meet, and discuss a divorce. That, I think, was certainly what Maurice would have had him believe.'

'Sorry, you're losing me again,' Peter Trent complained.

'Well, let's go back to being Maurice then,' Jenny said patiently. 'You've got your victim away from your home territory, and you've set up your alibi. You've just lured your victim to you, and now you need to get him to drink a poisoned cup of coffee. How do you do that, except by either putting the man at ease—which may not be easy under the circumstances—or by putting him off his guard by giving him the one thing that he so desperately wants.'

Jenny smoothed her skirt down with her fingers and frowned thoughtfully. 'Of course, a lot of this is pure guesswork on my part, but I think Maurice intended to play it very cleverly indeed. I think he intended to greet his wife's lover with every sign of cordiality and sophistication. Play the man of the world. Dole out the old "let's be civilized about this" card. He'd have explained that he knew about their affair, and that divorce was probably the best way out, and that he wasn't going to make a fuss, and so on and so on. Then casually pour out two cups of coffee and hand one over, and glance at his watch and say how he had to get along to a lecture or something, but perhaps he could pass along his thoughts to Laura when he saw her, and all that; they'd have to get together and iron out the details. Jenks, who'd be only too relieved to find the embarrassing obstacle of the husband was being taken out of the picture in such an agreeable way, would be taken off guard. Why not have a friendly cup of coffee with the man—after all, he was in the middle of a busy college, in broad daylight, with an affable and reasonable-sounding man. Why would he suspect anything? He wasn't to know that Maurice had arranged the time and place very carefully indeed so that they wouldn't be disturbed.'

'Ah! All that stuff about arranging a lunch for the stallholders,' Peter Trent said, with a knowing nod. 'Yes, everyone said how such generosity and thoughtfulness on his part was out of place.'

'Yes, Vicki Voight and several of the others mentioned how unusual it was for him not to take the first lecture,' Trevor agreed. 'I see what you mean. He'd arranged for all the conference-goers to be elsewhere.'

'The time he'd given Jenks to meet him was also carefully arranged so that most of the college staff would either be in the kitchens or cleaning rooms,' Jenny pointed out. 'As soon as I heard all that, I knew that Maurice Raines was the only one who could have made all the arrangements to pan out so that he had the half hour alone in hall between eleven-thirty and twelve.'

'Because he was arranging that time in order to kill his rival,' Trevor said, with something like awe. 'The audacity of the man.'

'Yes. Well, to a certain extent,' Jenny agreed. 'But in reality, he wasn't running that much of a risk. Supposing someone had seen them together. What would they have seen? Two men, enjoying a cup of coffee. So what?'

'OK, but once Jenks collapsed after drinking said coffee, Maurice would be well and truly up the creek if someone had come across them,' Trevor pointed out.

'Ah, but that's where the stuffed bear comes in,' Jenny said, making the inspector grit his teeth in vexation.

'There you go with the stuffed bear again,' he snapped. 'Just what in hell has the stuffed bear got to do with it?'

Jenny blinked. 'Well, the actual bear, not a lot, really, I suppose,' she admitted candidly. 'But the crate it came in, well, that's another matter.' She shook her head with a wry smile. 'Suppose you saw Maurice Raines wheel in a large crate on a porter's trolley at the beginning of that day, and saw him take out the stuffed bear as part of his opening remarks. Then, a little later, saw the same Maurice Raines wheeling out the same crate on the same porter's trolley and take it back to his van in the car-park. What would you think?'

Trevor ran a weary hand over his face. 'That he was just getting it out of the way again. Yes, of course. In reality, he'd be getting rid of the body. All along that's been worrying me—how he intended to do that. After all, you can't just walk through the college with a dead man on your shoulder, can you?'

'Hardly,' Jenny agreed softly. 'So. You're Maurice Raines, you've just successfully poisoned your wife's lover, and now you need hide the evidence of that as fast as you can, but you're also stuck with a body, in the middle of a large hall, where you could be discovered at any minute. What can you possibly do?'

'You stuff the body as quick as winking into a handy crate, and Bob's your uncle,' Peter Trent agreed. 'Not only do you minimize the risk of being caught with a dead man, it's also a handy way of moving the corpse at the same time.' He shook his head. 'In a way, you can't help but admire the man, can you?'

'After that, all he needed to do was take the crate with the body in it to his van, and then, later that night probably, bury Simon Jenks's body somewhere,' Jenny sighed. 'I expect he'd already done his homework and had a place all picked out. Oxfordshire is a large and rural county, after all. Plenty of woods and out of the way fields to choose from. It wouldn't be beyond Maurice to find a good place to put the body where it wouldn't be found.'

'And hey presto,' Trevor agreed heavily. 'Exit one inconvenient rival. And if his wife, or the police, kicked up a fuss—yes, you were innocently elsewhere, with witnesses to prove it.'

'It should have worked, put like that,' Peter said. 'But it didn't, did it?' He looked at the inspector, who was obviously thinking the same thing.

'Jenks must have cottoned on to something not being right,' Trevor said heavily. 'Perhaps he got suspicious about the coffee. Laura Raines might have told him about Maurice's preference for tea, and he wondered why he was drinking coffee instead. Or perhaps some of the crushed up pills floated on the top, or it smelt funny or… I dunno. Something must have alerted him anyway. An instinct, perhaps.' The inspector got to his feet and began to pace. 'It makes sense. It explains why the killing itself had all the hallmarks of an unpremeditated crime, whilst all the other clues pointed towards a carefully laid out plan. With the careful murder Maurice had planned collapsing, he was forced to act on the spur of the moment. Jenks must have challenged Raines about what he was playing at, and Raines wasn't convincing enough in his denials. So Raines grabbed the fleshing tool in order to finish Jenks off that way, they grappled, and, like you said, Miss Starling,'—Trevor looked at her with a nod of approval—'Maurice Raines, being the less fit and older of the two, came off worst.'

'You could almost make out a case for self-defence on young Simon Jenks's part,' Peter Trent put in generously. 'After all, the man *had* tried to murder him.'

Jenny coughed gently. She really did hate to be a party-pooper, but really, she couldn't let them go on getting excited like this.

'I thought we'd already established that when Simon Jenks left the hall, he didn't have a bloodstain on him,' she pointed out. 'So just how did he fight with Maurice Raines and stab him without getting evidence all over him?'

The two policemen stared at her. It took a few seconds for it to sink in, and when it did, the inspector began to feel distinctly sick again. 'Are you saying…' Trevor Golder said faintly, then trailed off, unable to put it into words.

Jenny Starling smiled sadly. 'That Jenks isn't the killer of Maurice Raines? Yes, I'm afraid so. The evidence only points one way, doesn't it? Jenks followed what he thought were Laura Raines's instructions to meet her in the hall of the college, but found instead a man's dead body. He took one look and fled.' Jenny sighed in sympathy. 'His mind must have been a whirl of conflicting thoughts on that ride down to the south coast. On the one hand, it looked as if Laura had set him up for something; on the other hand, he wouldn't really believe it. He must have known she was in love with him. And when he got to the hotel and told her what had happened, Laura must have realized from his description and the name of the college, that it was her husband who was dead, and believed that Simon had killed him. What a rough twenty-four hours those pair must have had of it—each suspecting the other, but each with their own reasons for not wanting to believe it. And now they're both in the cells, wondering what's happening.'

'Forget about them!' Trevor snapped with a total lack of sympathy. 'Are you saying that knowing all this… knowing what Maurice planned to do, and about the poison, and the bloody stuffed bear, and all the rest of the shenanigans, we're still no closer to knowing who actually killed Maurice?'

'Oh no,' Jenny said, genuinely shocked. 'I've had an idea who must have killed Maurice for a day or so now, but,' she added, luckily not noticing how the inspector's hands clenched and unclenched into white-knuckled fists, 'I had no idea until about half an hour ago, *why* he was killed.'

Inspector Golder pushed to one side his fantasies of

fastening his hands around her neck and giving it a good shake, and said sweetly, 'And do you think you would be so kind as to share that with us too, Miss Starling?'

Whereupon Jenny Starling beamed a bright and lovely smile on him, and did just that.

THE AFTERNOON SUN was just beginning to cool when the Greater Ribble Valley and Jessop Taxidermy Society began to pack their collective bags and start to leave Oxford. Well, all but one of them, anyway.

Jenny was in the outer quadrangle, standing next to James Raye and thoroughly kissing him a fond goodbye. Eventually, she stepped back and gave a satisfied sigh.

James smiled down at her. 'I've left a present for you in your van. I hope you don't mind.'

'Of course I don't,' she said, stepping back as he opened the car door, and then bending down to kiss him again through the open window once he was settled behind the steering wheel. 'See you in three weeks' time.'

He did up his seat belt and blew her a kiss before driving away.

She was still waving to him when she saw Inspector Golder and Sergeant Trent pull up in the inspector's car and park in a space a little further down. Both men climbed out and beckoned her over, then watched as she approached.

She could tell from the satisfied look on the inspector's face that things had gone well.

'So she confessed?' Jenny said, before either one could greet her.

'Yes. Just as we hoped she would when confronted with it,' Trevor said. 'Although I'm still not sure how you came to the conclusion that Pippa Foxton was the killer.'

Jenny shrugged modestly. 'Well, really, when it came down to it, it was simple. Everyone else really did have a cast-iron alibi. Vicki couldn't possibly have got out of that lecture room without being seen, and poor Art obviously didn't climb out of his window or become invisible and get past his secretary. Once the married woman and her lover were out of the equation...well, that only left Ian and Pippa. Of the two of them, Ian couldn't possibly have done it. He was demonstrating a stuffing technique at the time, and was being closely watched by his students for every moment.'

'But we thought his alibi was Pippa's too,' Trevor said.

'I know. That stumped me at first,' Jenny agreed. 'Your own inquiries put them together all morning. It wasn't until I talked to Ian myself, and learned a bit more about the minutiae of that morning, that I realized what had actually happened. I have to say, he was very uncommunicative and suspicious of me at first, which is why I started talking about stuffed tigers to begin with,' she grinned, 'but once he was relaxed and talking freely, I slowly got around to getting him to describe that morning's class in more detail. It quickly became obvious that his small number of students were all clustered around the table and utterly intent on what they were doing. None of them would have noticed when Pippa, getting bored with being ignored, slipped out.'

'She was running a risk there though, wasn't she?' Peter Trent mused, and Jenny shot him a surprised look.

'Well, not really. I mean, she didn't leave the room intending to kill anyone, did she, so what did it matter, at the time, if anyone had noticed and commented on it?' Jenny said flatly. 'It was just sheer bad luck that she then ran into Maurice, on his own like that, in the hall.'

Peter smacked his own forehead. 'Of course. Sorry, I keep forgetting. It was a totally spur of the moment thing, wasn't it? She didn't make any plans at all.'

Jenny smiled her forgiveness at him. 'Did it go down as I thought?' she asked eagerly. She'd not have been human if she hadn't been curious to know just how accurate her prediction had been.

It was Trevor Golder, now in a benevolent mood, who nodded. 'It was almost exactly as you said, Miss Starling,' he confirmed.

A day had passed, and Pippa Foxton had been arrested, and her confession was down in black and white. The lawyers at the Crown Prosecution Service, not to mention his own bosses, were all looking on him favourably, so he was in a good mood, and willing to be magnanimous by filling her in.

'She'd just left her boyfriend to his acolytes, and was feeling bored, as you thought,' he confirmed, and was going back to her room when she spotted Maurice alone in the hall, and decided to have things out with him,' Trevor explained. 'She wasn't to know, poor girl, just what a bad time she'd chosen for it.'

Jenny heaved a massive sigh. 'No. Maurice would have been all worked up, waiting for Jenks to arrive, and wouldn't want to be bothered with Pippa just then.' She paused delicately. 'I take it Pippa has confirmed what she wanted from him?'

Again Trevor nodded. 'That she thought that he was her natural father? Yes. You were right about that too.'

Jenny sighed sadly. 'As soon as Ian said that Pippa had grown up in Wither Sedgewick, it clicked. Someone had told me earlier that Maurice had grown up there as well, and that he had a reputation for getting the local young women into the family way.'

'Pippa's mother apparently got drunk on her ruby wedding, and told her that her dad wasn't, well, her real dad,' Peter Trent took over. 'She started by tracking down Maurice Raines and getting close to him. We couldn't tell, from speaking to her whether she was fascinated or repelled by him.'

'No, I can imagine,' Jenny said with a small shudder. 'I suppose she cultivated Ian Glendower simply as a way to get an introduction to the society, and thus access to Maurice?'

'She admitted as much. And said that, almost instantly, Raines started coming on to her,' Trent confirmed, with a *moue* of distaste. 'That carries some nasty psychological baggage whichever way you cut it, and I reckon the shrinks are going to use it as a basis for a plea of diminished responsibility.'

Jenny sighed. 'Well, who's to say they're not right? She always struck me as being rather unstable anyway.'

'The way she tells it, she came upon Maurice in hall, and tried to talk to him about her mother,' Trevor Golder put in.

'She thought that in making the big dramatic statement that she was his long-lost daughter, it would be all hearts and flowers, or at any rate, have some sort of major impact on him,' Trent added. 'If you ask me, she watched too much daytime television. I think she saw herself as starring in her own soap opera, and expected Maurice to play the role of contrite father.'

'But he didn't?' Jenny asked sadly.

'No. Maurice only wanted to bundle her out of the

way, saying that they'd talk about it later. Of course,
we know why that was: he was desperate to get rid of
her before Simon Jenks showed up, and he only had
a little time to do it. By that time, he must have been
well worked up.'

'So I imagine he was rather brutal,' Jenny nodded.
'Yes, he would be.'

Again Trevor took over. 'According to Pippa, he said
he didn't even remember her mother, and couldn't care
tuppence if she was his flesh and blood or not. He just
dismissed her out of hand, and had even started to man-
handle her out of the room. That's when she lost it, according to her. She just grabbed the nearest thing to
her and stabbed him in the neck. She was almost blind
with hurt and rage by this point, to hear her tell it. Being
rejected by him and made to feel so insignificant and
unworthy was the last straw. I don't think, between
you and me, that once the shrinks have finished their
reports, that it won't come down to manslaughter, and
with diminished responsibility at that.'

Jenny sighed but made no comment. 'And you found
bloodstains on her shoes, like I thought you would,
right?' she added, almost as an afterthought.

Peter Trent smiled. 'Yes, we did. It was clever of
you to pick up on that, Miss Starling. You were quite
right, she *had* already got rid of the bloodstained clothes
she was wearing just after the murder, but she couldn't
throw out her shoes, it seems.'

'No, I thought not,' Jenny said. Then seeing the two
men look at her oddly, she shrugged. 'She was always
dressed so well, it was clear that clothes and fashion
meant everything to her. She'd be in a different outfit
every time I saw her. That's why I didn't think much

of it at the time, when she wore one outfit to breakfast, but another the next time I saw her—which was just after finding Maurice's body. Also, I was still in a bit of shock and not really paying that much attention,' she apologized. 'As it was, I just thought that she'd changed outfits. But when I heard her giving her statement to you later, and she didn't mention going back to her room to change, I realized what it could mean. But I still had no motive for her, so…' She shrugged.

'But you noticed she was always wearing the same shoes,' Trevor prodded.

'That's right. She might bring herself to get rid of the other clothes, but those Jimmy Choo shoes were easily the most expensive thing in her entire wardrobe, I'd guess, and certainly the most high status. When I saw her still wearing them, I knew that she must have just washed them thoroughly instead of dumping them. No doubt she thought she'd got all the evidence off them. But with modern forensics being like they are, I knew a lab would find traces of Maurice's blood on them.'

'As they did, in the stitches in the seams,' Trevor confirmed. 'It's what eventually got her to confess. And once she started, she couldn't stop. Like you said, she's not the most stable of people. Maurice couldn't have realized how much he was playing with fire when he refused to take her seriously, as he did.'

'Maurice had other things on his mind at the time,' Jenny reminded him darkly.

For a moment, all three were silent as they thought about this, and then Trevor stirred himself. 'Well, we have to be off,' he said, and held out his hand somewhat awkwardly. 'Miss Starling, it's been a pleasure,' he said.

If he was being somewhat just a shade untruthful,

she didn't hold it against him, for she smiled back and shook his hand heartily.

She watched the policemen depart, then turned and spotted her cherry-red van parked in the shady corner of the quad. Remembering that James had left a present for her inside, she walked towards it and looked through the open window.

Sitting on the passenger seat was a bright green chameleon.

'Norman?' Jenny said, exasperated.

Quickly she reached for her mobile phone to call James Raye, and ask him to come back for his niece's pet before he could travel too far down the road, then paused.

What if it wasn't Norman? After all, James was a taxidermist. Suppose her present was the gift of a stuffed lizard?

She'd rather have had flowers. Most definitely, she'd rather have had chocolates. But he was a man, and she knew enough never to trust a man's gift-giving sensibilities.

Cautiously, she squatted down a bit and surveyed the lizard more closely.

Was it Norman?

It was certainly the same size, colour and, to her untrained eye at least, the same species as Norman. But did that mean it *was* Norman? She squinted, trying to see if the creature was breathing, but she couldn't tell. Neither one of its eyes had moved. But then, chameleons were known for staying statue-still for long periods of time, weren't they?

She supposed she could give it a gentle poke, but

then, if she were a lizard, she wouldn't be any too happy to be prodded about by a big ape.

Jenny cast an increasingly desperate look around the interior of her van. Perhaps James had left a nicely wrapped gift in the glove box. A piece of jewellery maybe?

This could be just another example of Norman, the great escape artist, at work. But if it wasn't, just what the hell was she supposed to do with a stuffed lizard?

Jenny Starling once more peered down uncertainly at the reptile.

'Norman?' she said hopefully.

* * * * *